TO LIVE FOREVER:
AN AFTERLIFE JOURNEY OF MERIWETHER LEWIS

ANDRA WATKINS

To Live Forever: An Afterlife Journey of Meriwether Lewis is a work of historical fantasy. Apart from the well-known actual people, events and places that figure into the story, all names, characters, places and incidents are products of the author's imagination or are used fictitiously. Any resemblance to current events or locales, or to living persons, is entirely coincidental.

WORD HERMIT PRESS • USA

ISBN-13 978-0-615-93747-2
ISBN-10 0-615-93747-0

Library of Congress Catalog Number TXu 1-892-805

FOR MTM

Explorer Meriwether Lewis Dead at 35

The Natchez Trace, south of Nashville, Tennessee.

Meriwether Lewis, renowned co-captain of the Lewis and Clark expedition to the Pacific and territorial governor of Upper Louisiana, died Wednesday, October 11, 1809. He was thirty-five.

Accounts suggest his death was a suicide, though murder is still being investigated. He was found with gunshot wounds to the head and abdomen. No one witnessed the incident.

Meriwether Lewis was born on August 18, 1774 near Charlottesville, Virginia. After a successful military career, he served as personal secretary to Thomas Jefferson, third President of the United States. Jefferson selected him to lead the Corps of Discovery, an expedition to find the Northwest Passage to the Pacific. Along with William Clark, Lewis guided the thirty-three person team through thousands of miles of unexplored wilderness.

Upon his triumphant return in 1806, Lewis was appointed governor of the Upper Louisiana Territory, succeeding James Wilkinson. While he accepted the appointment with great promise, colleagues noted that he struggled in the position throughout his tenure. A source said he was more outdoorsman than administrator, more scientist than politician.

In September 1809, he embarked for Washington DC, both to explain his gubernatorial affairs to James Madison's administration and to publish his prized expedition journals. No one knows why he diverted from his planned water route through New Orleans to the notorious Natchez Trace in Tennessee, where he died.

Authorities are still evaluating the circumstances of his death. Lost in mystery, may his spirit rest in peace.

To Live Forever

EMMALINE

A New Orleans Courtroom
Thursday
March 24, 1977

A drop of sweat hung from the end of my nose. I watched it build, cross-eyed, before I shook my head and made it fall. It left wet circles on the front of my dress.

"Emmaline. Be still, Child." Aunt Bertie fanned her face and neck with a paper fan, the one with the popsicle stick handle.

A popsicle would be so good.

The waiting room of the court in New Orleans was full. People were everywhere I looked.

Reporters in stripey suits talked with some of Daddy's musician friends. I loved to watch their fingers play imaginary guitars or pound out chords on their legs. Once or twice, Daddy's band members came over to squeeze my arm or pat my head. "In spite of what they's saying in that courtroom, we all love your daddy, Kid."

Everybody loved Daddy. Well, everybody except Mommy.

My nose burned when I breathed, because the whole room stank like sweaty feet. My face was steamy when I touched it, and my lace tights scratched when I kicked my legs to push along the wooden bench. I left a puddle when I moved.

I snuggled closer to the dark folds and softness of Aunt Bertie. She turned her black eyes down at me and sighed before pushing me away with her dimpled hand. "Too hot, Child. When this is done, I'll hold you as long as you want."

I slid back to my wet spot on the bench. The wood made a hard pillow when I leaned my head against it and closed my eyes. Wishes still worked for nine-year-old girls, didn't they?

I thought and thought. If I wanted it enough, maybe I could shrink myself smaller. It was hard to be outside the courtroom, imagining what was going on inside. Behind the heavy doors, Mommy and Daddy probably shouted mean things at each other, like they used to at home. Both of them said they wanted me, if they had to fight until they were dead.

I watched Mommy's lady friends go into the courtroom: Miss Roberta in her drapey dress with flowers, Miss Chantelle all in white against the black of her skin, and Miss Emilie in a red skirt and coat that tied at her waist in a pretty bow. They all went in and came out, and they always looked at me. Miss Roberta even left a red lipstick kiss on my cheek, but I don't like her, so I rubbed it off.

Aunt Bertie took her turn inside the courtroom, leaving me to sit with a reporter. He watched me from behind thick black glasses, and he asked me all kinds of questions about Daddy and Mommy. I didn't understand much. I knew Daddy was famous, at least in New Orleans, but I didn't understand what the word "allegations" meant.

My daddy was Lee Cagney. People called him "The Virtuoso of Dixieland Jazz." He played the upright bass, and when he sang, his voice made women act silly in the middle of Bourbon Street. They cried and screamed. Some of them even tore their clothes.

I understood why women loved Daddy. I adored him, too. But some grown women sure did act dumb.

Anyway.

None of the lawyers asked me who I wanted to be with.

The Judge said I was too little to understand, and Mommy agreed. But if they asked me, I would shout it all the way to Heaven: I wanted to be with Daddy.

When he sang *Ragtime Lullaby*, the sound of his voice put me to sleep. He always splashed in the fountain with me in front of the Cathedral and gave me pennies to throw in the water. Thursday afternoons before his gigs, he sat with me at Café du Monde, sharing beignets with as much powdered sugar as I wanted. He didn't even mind my sticky fingers when he held my hand. He wasn't always there when I had nightmares, but he came to see me first thing in the morning.

People around me whispered about Daddy's "adulterous proclivities." I didn't understand what that meant, but it had something to do with his loving other women besides Mommy. No matter what they said, Daddy didn't do anything wrong. When he wasn't playing music, he was always with me.

Wasn't he?

A skinny reporter held the courtroom door open. "The Judge's ruling." He whispered, but his voice was loud enough for everyone waiting to hear. He kept the door open, and I saw my chance.

I struggled through all the legs to the door. Mommy's red lips curled in a smile as the Judge addressed Daddy. The Judge's face was loose, like the bulldog that lived in the house around the corner, and his voice boomed in my chest. When he stood and leaned over his desk, his hairy hands gripped the gavel.

"In the case of Cagney v. Cagney, I am charged with finding the best outcome for a little girl. For rendering a verdict that will shape the whole of her life. The welfare of the child is paramount, regardless of how it will impact the adults involved."

The Judge stopped and cleared his throat. I held my breath when his baggy eyes fell on me. I counted ten heartbeats before he talked again. "Mr. Cagney, I simply cannot ignore the fact that you had carnal relations with your then-wife's lady friends repeatedly, both under your shared roof and in broad daylight. The photographic evidence coupled with the testimonies of these poor women damns you, regardless of your expressed love for your daughter. From everything I've seen and heard in this courtroom, the evidence does not support your claim that you were set up. Justice demands that your nine-year-old daughter be delivered into the arms of the person who has demonstrated that she has the capability to be a responsible parent."

He looked around the room and sat up straight in his chair. "I am granting sole custody of Emmaline Cagney to her mother, Nadine Cagney, and I hereby approve her request to block Lee Cagney from any and all contact with his daughter until she reaches the age of eighteen. Mr. Cagney, should you violate this directive, you will be found in contempt of this court, an offense that may be punishable by imprisonment of up to 120 days and a fine of no more than $500 per occurrence. This court is adjourned."

He pounded a wooden stick on his desk, and everyone swarmed like bees. Daddy stood up and shook his fist. He shouted at the Judge over all the other noise. "Lies! Set out to ruin my reputation—my memory—in the eyes of my daughter! I'll appeal, if I have to spend every dime of my money. I'll—"

The Judge banged his stick again, lots of times, while my eyes met Daddy's. I ran from the doorway. The room was like the obstacle course on the playground, only with people who reached for me while the Judge boomed, "Order! Order! I will have order in my court!"

Daddy's lawyer held him and whispered something in his ear. It was my chance. I ran toward Daddy and his crying blue eyes. They matched mine, because I was crying, too.

Daddy elbowed his lawyer into the railing and reached out his hand. "Come to me, Baby."

I kicked at pants legs and stomped on shiny shoes. At the front, I stuck my hand through the bars and stretched as far as I could. My fingers almost reached his when my head jerked like I was snagged at the end of a fishing pole.

Mommy had the ties at the back of my white pinafore. Her glossy red lips fake-smiled. "I'm taking Emmaline now, Lee. Good luck to you."

She squeezed my hand. Her red fingernails dug into my skin.

"Ow, Mommy. You're hurting me."

Her high heels clack-clack-clacked as she dragged me through the chairs and down the aisle toward the waiting room. I planted my heels and tried to get one last look, my mind taking a picture of Daddy. Before we got through the door, I saw his shoulders shake. Three policemen held him back and kept him from following me. The world was blurry like the time I swam to the bottom of a pool and opened my eyes underwater.

Mommy picked me up and cradled me in her arms. Her blood-tipped fingers stroked my hair, but her lips whispered a different story, one the crowd couldn't hear. "Stop crying, Emmaline. You know this is for the best." She shifted me to the ground and adjusted the wide sash of her floor-length dress. Its sleeves fanned out as she pushed the bar on the door. I wished she'd take off and fly away.

Summer heat turned my tears to steam, and my eyes ached. Mommy struggled to pull me along through the reporters that blocked the path to the car. They shouted questions, but I didn't hear them. All I heard were Daddy's words. "Come to me, Baby."

Mommy smiled and pressed our bodies through the people. She kept her gaze glued on the car.

Aunt Bertie waited behind the wheel of Mommy's fancy red Cadillac Eldorado. Mommy always said the whole name with a funny accent. The engine was running. "There's Bertie. In you go, Emmaline. I'm ready to be done with this madness."

My legs squeaked across the hot back seat. Mommy ran her fingers under my eyes to wipe away my tears, but they kept coming. "Please. You're upsetting my daughter." She shouted over her shoulder.

The door slammed, and it was like a clock stopped. Like I would never be older than that moment. Everything would always be "Before Daddy" and "After Daddy."

Daddy.

His face appeared in the slice of back window. I put down the glass, trying to slip through, but Mommy ran around the car. She screamed and hit him, over and over. "You stay away from her, Lee! You heard what the Judge said!"

Her black hair fell out of its bun as she pounded him with her fists. He tried to move away from her. Toward me. He reached his hand through the window and touched my face. His mouth opened to speak to me, but a policeman came up behind him and dragged him away from the car.

"I'll write you, Emmaline! Every day. I promise," he shouted. "I'll prove these things aren't true! I'll give up everything to be with you!" The policeman pushed him through the courthouse door, and he was gone.

"I'll write you, too, Daddy." I whispered it, soft so nobody but God or my guardian angel could hear. "Somehow, I'll make us be together again."

THE JUDGE

I leaned my weight against an upstairs window, the ruckus of her daddy's court still unfolding on the other side of a bolted door. Breath ragged. White film on glass. Wet tracks trailed from my fingers, the record of my need.

My craving.

Had I waited too long to see her again? I used to watch her. How she played hopscotch on a broken slab of sidewalk. Colored chalk and creamy skin and sing-song. I stood in the shadows until I was sure. Until I knew it was her.

My little beauty. It was my name for her. Before. In another life.

She never saw me. All those times, I hid. I waited. I scribbled letters in cipher, that code we always used, but I never mailed them. Patience would yield to my desire. For as long as I could remember, all I had to do was wait for weakness to reveal the path.

That was before I saw her today.

Eye contact was electricity. It surged through my limbs and soared around my heart. She looked at me, and she knew me. I could see her there, behind those sea-like eyes. It was almost like telepathy when I heard her voice in my head.

What took you so long? She said.

To Live Forever

MERRY

Thursday. March 24, 1977. New Orleans, Louisiana.

I always came to in the same New Orleans drinking place, my journal adrift in a puddle of stale booze. I couldn't recall what happened on those pages. A record of another failed assignment, the words faded before I could capture them. Fleeting images on stained paper, encased in leather. I colored in a few words here and there, before they vanished. Became nothing. A palimpsest of another job already forgotten.

But I always remembered my life.

Two shots should have finished me.

One through the head. The other in my gut.

Some folks said I killed myself in the early morning hours of October 11, 1809. Others were sure I was murdered. I couldn't remember what happened. Someone tore out those pages. Erased those images. Took the final moments that might have given my soul peace.

But the sensational nature of my death did more than destroy my life. It took my chance to finish my journals, to spin my own story, to ensure that Americans remembered me the way I wished to be. Death blocked my view of how people thought of me.

If they thought of me. I didn't know.

I feared my reputation was buried with my remains. As far as I knew, my rotted carcass was shoved into an unmarked grave in Tennessee.

Death led me to Nowhere, a place for shattered souls to perform a good deed for the living, to erase the negative impact of the end of my life and its potential consequences on my immortal reputation.

Could one good deed help me be remembered the way I wished to be?

But my Nowhere was a continuation of my downward spiral, the misunderstandings that haunted the end of my life. I couldn't salvage my name, but failure didn't destroy the urge to try again.

And again.

Until I just wanted Nowhere to end. I craved Nothing.

I blinked. Centuries of embers caught in my nostrils, and fuzzy outlines shifted in the dark. Like every time before, he was waiting on me.

I couldn't recall where I'd been, but I always remembered the Bartender.

"Merry. Knew I'd see you again. What'll you have?"

He showed me his back before I could reply. Me, I rattled the exits, one by one. My sweaty hands slipped off the door handles. Perspiration burned in my eyes. That's what I told myself it was. Tough men, real leaders, we didn't cry.

Just outside, the crowd swayed beyond the cracks in the shutters. Random glimpses of life mingled with my reflection in the wavy glass. Voices drunk with booze and the promise of mayhem. I shouted, but my voice dissolved in the heavy air on my side of the divide.

The Bartender rattled his fingers on the counter. "You know them doors won't open, Merry."

I rested my forehead on blackened stucco. Why did I always fail? Time after time after time? What was next for me? A man with my skills ought to be able to see the way through Nowhere.

How I craved the end.

Resigned, I dragged my fingers across the fog on the window and stumbled back to my seat. It was always mine. Every time.

The Bartender, he stayed in his spot in the back corner. The muscles in his arms worked as he poured the dregs of others down the crusty sink. I squinted into the murk of the place, hoping for some company, some other lost spirit to let me know I wasn't the only one stuck here, the only fool who made this choice.

Glass clinked on glass. "You just missed my last guest. She drank up my top shelf Scotch. Hope you weren't thirsty for that."

"Give me a beer. Draft is fine."

He stopped dumping wet remainders down the drain. Set his amber eyes on me. "Sure you don't want something stronger?"

I scanned the glittering rows of glass bottles on the shelf behind the bar. What mixture might dull the edges of another failure? Whiskey was reckless. Vodka was for the drinker who wanted to disappear into his surroundings. Gin fellows possessed a snooty sophistication I found repellent. Wine-drinking boys were prissy. Draft beer was Every Man.

Every Man wanted to be remembered.

I closed my eyes and imagined myself as an Every Man, not a Nowhere Man.

"Beer's powerful enough."

He made casual work of pulling a foamy pint.

"You want food?" Bubbles frothed onto the sticky wood in front of me as he slid the beer my way. They turned liquid, puddled around the bottom of the glass. I studied my drink and made him wait. Weakness meant letting the Bartender guess what I was thinking.

I picked up the slick glass and downed it in one long draught. Foam sloshed in the bottom when I set it down in a sloppy ring. "I think I'll just get right to my next job. You know I can't abide it here."

Firelight flickered behind his eyes.

"Suit yourself. You got any money left this time?"

I rooted around in my damp jeans, my shirt pockets. In the front slot of my black leather jacket, I found a single note. Crisp. Clean.

I unfolded it slow. Tasted bile. Thomas Jefferson studied me from the face of a two dollar bill. I stared back into those familiar eyes while the Bartender laughed.

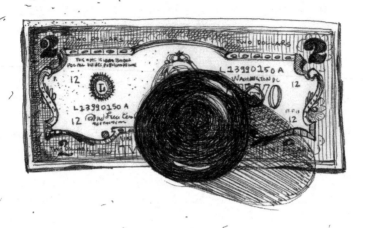

"I got new tricks, too. You ain't the only one can change things up."

Glasses crashed into the flagstone floor as I leaped over the bar. When I grabbed him, the front of his shirt was soft in my fingers. "Why is it always goddamn Jefferson? You know he abandoned me, right? At the end? He was happy to let everyone think I killed myself. Never even sent anyone to try and suss out the truth. I worshipped him like a father, and he let me go down in history as the ultimate prodigal son." My voice caught in my throat.

He shook free of me and stepped back, his boots crunching through shards of glass. "I don't make the rules here, Merry."

"Rules. I'll never figure out the rules in this place."

"Hey, don't blame me for your predicament."

My nostrils flared against the stench of spilled alcohol and smoke. Even as I balled up my fist to hit him, I knew he had me cornered. Boxed in. It wasn't his fault I couldn't get things right.

His eyes softened. "You seem to be in a hurry, and I didn't want you to run off without your two. That thing is supposed to be your good luck charm."

"These scraps of funny money haven't made any difference the last seven or eight assignments."

"A dozen, Merry. You're up to an even dozen."

I slumped onto my stool. Thumbed through the pages of my journal. A word here. A scrap of letters there. No hidden message to guide me past the obstacles of Nowhere. To help me avoid the same mistakes. Every Nowhere appearance was new. I couldn't remember them once I failed. Who I met. What I saw. No matter how I arranged what I managed to save from my other outings in Nowhere, I couldn't make sense of the remnants of twelve times tried.

Twelve times failed.

"So, this is number thirteen. Can I just go ahead and skip this one? Have another drink?"

"You been around long enough to know that ain't how it works."

"Goddammit. I know how Nowhere works. I just can't seem to make it work for me."

I closed my eyes and relived the moment Nowhere found me, when I looked into my own dead eyes being covered over with the dirt of a hole that was too shallow to hold me. It was a pauper's burial. An unmarked grave. I was barely cold.

That was when I saw it: a chunk of black leather. It stuck out of the ground at the head of my grave. I pulled it from the dirt, and when I opened it, I read these words:

Remembrance is immortality.
Make people remember your story your way.
Come to Nowhere.

My story was already in tatters. Newspapers trumpeted the supposed details of my apparent suicide. Two men who knew me best—William Clark and Thomas Jefferson—supported that tawdry version of events. Faced with a sensational story, no one cared about the truth.

With one muttered *yes*, I stepped through a portal. Woke up in a New Orleans bar.

The clink of ice teased me back. The Bartender stirred a sulfur-tinged cocktail and pushed it my way. "Seconds aren't allowed, but I'm feeling charitable today."

Liquid heat lit up my nostrils. "What is it?"

"A Thunderclapper. Of all my customers, I thought you might appreciate it."

An homage to the pills members of the Corps of Discovery took for every conceivable ailment. We called them 'thunderclappers' because they gave us the runs. Clark was always partial to them. I had to smile at the memory of him, running off to empty his bowels behind a rock. Afraid he wasn't going to make it.

I raised the glass and sucked the mixture down. Fire ripped through my gullet. Erupted behind my eyes.

The Bartender smirked while I coughed up smoke. "Think of it as a cleansing fire. Erases what's come before." He paused. Leaned his burly frame over the counter and touched my sleeve. "You know this is your last shot, right?"

"Thirteen is my last chance?"

"Yep. You fail this time, you get to be a bartender. Your life will be erased from human history. Nobody will remember you, and what's worse, you won't remember you, either. You get to live forever, though. Slinging booze you can't drink in a room you can never leave."

I looked at his weathered face and wondered who he'd been. What was his story?

How would it feel to forget oneself? To never again close my eyes and see the sun set over the Missouri? To fail to hear Clark's laugh whisper through the trees? To be Nobody?

I wiped my brow with the back of my hand. Whispered my plea. "Tell me. Tell me how to finish this. Please."

He pushed a button on the cash register, and the drawer popped open, a fat wad of bills on one end. He picked it up and tossed it from hand to hand. "I had my own failures, Merry. That don't mean I can remember them. I'm just here to do my good deed. To lubricate your ego a little and send you out again." He stopped and slid the cash across the bar. "This ought to be enough to see you to the end."

"Five hundred? That's too much."

He flicked his eyes to the door. A rattle crescendoed through wood and glass. "Not in 1977, it ain't." He swabbed the bar with a stained towel. "Look, Merry. I got another customer coming. Don't keep making the same damn mistake, all right?"

I grabbed his grimy t-shirt. "What mistake? Tell me."

But instead, he shook free of me. Leaned over and took something out from under the counter. "Here. You lost your hat, and you'll be needing another one."

I looked from it to the two dollars crumpled in my other hand. Jefferson's stare launched me into the streets, patrolling like a lunatic. Searching, seeking the unknown someone who could save me. Rewrite my story. Release me from Nowhere to find whatever was next for a broken soul like me.

And so it began.

Again.

EMMALINE

New Orleans

October 1977

Six Months Later

I knew Mommy would be mad when I tore my best dress at the zoo. She might even be mad enough to kill me. Aunt Bertie helped me sneak past her when we got home. It was hard to be invisible going up two flights of stairs in Mommy's house with her ladies everywhere.

Maybe the Wonder Twins could give me the power to be invisible to Mommy. Sometimes, I liked to pretend I was a Wonder Twin. One twin was the me that had to live with Mommy, the me everybody could see. But the real me was the other twin: the invisible one who lived with Daddy for the last six months, since the divorce. She didn't wear dresses and sit up straight and always be quiet and look pretty. She was the me I wished I could be.

Anyway.

We made it to my room without being seen. Aunt Bertie left me to take off my dress. She waited in her room for me to bring it to her to fix. The front hem was shredded, and part of the right sleeve pulled loose when I fell. Plus, all the dirt.

Bertie left me with a kiss on my nose. She told me she could sew the tears on my dress and wash it before Mommy saw. I made a real mess, though. I hoped Bertie kept some voodoo in her sewing kit with her needle and pink thread. Bertie could do anything, but I wondered if she could make this better.

Mommy didn't like mistakes. Especially mine.

I held my arms out straight at my side and fell backwards on the bed. The cool blow of the window fan felt good on my naked skin. I closed my eyes and remembered the freedom of running through the dirt underneath the branches of the oak trees. I didn't even care when I tripped over that root and fell. From the ground, the sky was so pretty through the twisty limbs. I wanted to stay there forever.

Instead, I had to put on another scratchy dress for Mommy.

I dragged myself to my closet and touched the fabric and lace that made up my dress collection. They were all selected by Mommy to "highlight my fair hair and clear complexion." Blech. I wished I was ugly. Mommy always wanted me to be perfect, especially in front of her men, but being perfect all the time wasn't any fun.

I liked looking at the colors, though. Pale pink. Easter egg purple. Grass green and tulip yellow. Lots of blues, like the picture of a coral reef I saw in geography class. Blue was a brave color, the color of adventure. When I wore it, I was powerful in spite of the stiff lining and tight elastic. Mommy liked frills and everything clean. I wanted to wear Levi corduroys and play in the dirt. But Mommy always had to be happy, or she made sure I was miserable.

I pulled out an especially flouncy one, the color of the late fall New Orleans sky. It reminded me of how good I felt when I fell at the zoo. I wrapped it around me. It had pearly buttons down the front and a Peter Pan collar edged with lace and pouffy sleeves with more itchy elastic.

I sat down at my dressing table and studied my ratty blonde curls. A few squirts of No More Tangles and some tugging with my Marie Osmond comb, and I made my hair go back to the tight rings Mommy liked, the ones that framed my face like Cindy in those Brady Bunch re-runs.

I licked some spit on my fingers and scrubbed a spot of dirt on my cheek 'til it was clean and red. Mommy said she could zero in on dirt like a spotlight followed a true performer. She was proud of it, too, especially when she shined her light on me.

Three knocks rattled my door just as I finished. Bertie stuck her brillo pad hair through the crack, her lips already glowing their usual evening red. "Miss Nadine is chomping at the bit, Child. I stalled her as long as I can do. You need to hurry up."

"You didn't tell her about my dress, did you?"

"You think I want to see you beaten into next week? I told her some awful boy spilled his Coca-Cola all over you on the streetcar, and I ordered you to go straight up to your room and change to spare her tender eyes the sight."

My Sunday shoes echoed all through the house as we walked down two flights of stairs, clunk-clunk on wood and tap-tap-tap on marble. All six doors were closed on the second floor. Most of Mommy's ladies rested during the afternoon, because they were up most of the night. Entertaining, Mommy called it.

My stomach tied itself in a knot when I saw the black-and-white checkerboard floor at the bottom of the stairs. It was the only path to Mommy's office, past pictures of almost-naked ladies from a long time ago. My face always turned red when I had to go that way. When I was littler, I got a chair from the dining room and drew more clothes on them, but Mommy got real mad. She made me stay in my room for most of a whole week that time.

The door to Mommy's office was open. Bertie took my hand. "Just let me make sure she's ready for you." Her dark skin jiggled as she went to the doorway and looked around the room. With a smile of relief, she turned back to me. "She ain't here. Why don't you wait for her? Sit there, and be real pretty when she comes back?"

Bertie blew me a kiss and left me in Mommy's office. I crawled into her cushiony chair and made it spin like the merry-go-round at school by pushing off the front of the desk with my hands. If I spun fast enough, maybe I could disappear.

When I started getting dizzy, I sat still and looked at the things spread out on top of her desk. It was a roll top, almost always closed when I came in there. I picked up a black book with "Appointments" on the front and slipped Mommy's big silver ring with the blue Indian stone on my finger.

And that was when I saw Mommy's special cards.

My mommy liked to play rounds of cards with some of her men. Two nights a week, she'd set up tables in her parlor, get several of her ladies, and play her games. Aunt Bertie always put me to bed early, those nights. She had to play, too. Mommy's rules.

Mommy had different rules for me. Sometimes, Mommy or Aunt Bertie played Go Fish with me, or Old Maid. Mommy even let me yell when I told her to go fish. I got so excited when I was winning. Like it was my one-and-only way to beat her. She'd smile and draw her card and tell me to never forget what it felt like to be the underdog. Acting like the underdog would get me far in life.

I didn't understand, but this was Mommy; she didn't explain.

One time, I snuck down to her office. Late. I knew she played cards with grown men different from the way she played with me. But everybody was shut up in the bedrooms by then, playing cards of a different kind, I guess.

Anyway.

That night, I was looking for a deck of cards to play solitaire. I played for hours sometimes, but Mommy didn't let me keep cards in my bedroom.

I opened her desk drawer, and I found a deck in a pretty ceramic box with jewels glued on top. When I turned them over, every card had pictures of me on one side with scribblings and notes on the number sides. I was younger in the picture, but I remembered posing for it. Mommy made a big deal out of how I looked that day. I stacked the cards and hid them under my pillow in my room.

The next morning, I found Aunt Bertie in the kitchen. I spread the cards out on the table and asked her why she and Mommy played with cards that had pictures of me.

She scooped them up and stacked them back together, really neat, even though her hands shook. "Child, don't ask me about these cards again. Ever. I mean what I'm saying. Lawsy mercy. I need a cocktail to go." She wobbled when she left me to take them back to Mommy's desk and put them back just like I found them.

I never saw those cards again until the day I tore my dress at the zoo. They were magnets I had to pick up and shuffle, more worn around the edges than last time. One by one, I turned them over and read the numbers and words on the backs. Mr. Devereaux $100K. Mr. Carnell $475K. The Sugar Daddy $500K. The last one had red stars around my face and the words "the winner" written in cursive. When I tilted the chair closer, I almost fell on the floor at the bark of Mommy's voice.

"Emmaline Cagney. Whatever are you doing, pilfering through my private things?"

Mommy's nasally voice filled the room from the open door. I dropped the card on the floor and rolled the chair on top of it. Maybe she didn't see.

She sashayed into the room, her shiny white robe flying around her. Aunt Bertie came in and planted herself next to the door, her black eyes not meeting mine. Mommy walked up to me and squeezed my arm hard enough to leave a mark on the skin under my sleeve.

"Get out of my chair."

I slid to the floor, and she sat where I'd been. She ran her red-tipped hands around the desk, touching each object. When she was satisfied that everything was where it should be, she turned back to me. Her face wore that smile. The fake one.

"Come closer, Emmaline. Stand under the light here." She took my chin in her hand, and her brown eyes drilled into me. I fought to stand still, to not squirm, because Mommy hated it when I got all "ants-in-my-pants." She said it wasn't ladylike.

"Is that dirt on your face, young lady?" Mommy squinted at my clean face for what felt like a solid minute before releasing me. "No. I must be imagining the hideous grime that was there earlier."

My stomach jumped into my throat. "Earlier?"

"Emmaline Cagney. Your mother is not stupid. I saw you and Bertie, you in that pretty pink dress that cost me fifty hard-earned dollars. It was ruined." She turned her glare to Bertie. "And not by a mishap with an obnoxious boy and a spilled Coca-Cola on the streetcar."

Bertie shriveled like her roses in the summer heat. I wanted to run to her.

"But Mommy. Bertie saved me. I fell and—"

"Emmaline, I am NOT in the mood for products of your hyperactive imagination this afternoon. I will deduct the cost of the ruined dress from Bertie's nightly fees until I am repaid."

Bertie's jaw clenched. I tried another Wonder Twin power, the one where people talked with their minds. I looked at Bertie and thought really hard. *Please be quiet please be quiet.*

It must have worked, because she didn't say anything. She just stood there and looked at the floor. I smiled a little and wondered how I did it.

Mommy rotated back to me. "At least, you are presentable enough. A man is coming around in five minutes for a nice tea and a visit with you, Emmaline. Bertie, you may leave."

"But—"

"Your fees for the week, Bertie. I'll have them all if you do not vacate the room this instant. Leave *my* child with *me*."

The door clicked shut, making the room even darker. Mommy liked "mood" lighting." Whatever that meant.

Anyway.

Mommy's makeup glowed under the lamp on her desk. She pulled me to her and hugged me close in her arms. I closed my eyes and breathed in her flowery perfume. I wished Mommy's embrace could protect me from everything bad, even from the bad things she did. When she held me, I always believed she was a good mommy who loved me back. If I thought it enough, maybe I could make it true.

She squeezed me, and her voice tickled my ear. "I'm going to have to stop letting you spend so much time with Bertie. Her example doesn't aid in your proper development, I'm afraid."

"But I love her, Mommy. She's so much fun."

"Ah, yes. Fun." She turned me to face her. One red fingernail stroked the side of my face.

Mommy's love. It went on and off like the sign that blinked in the window of the bar on Bourbon Street, the one closest to our house. When she loved me, it was like someone turned on the sun. I tried to get warm in its glow without getting a sunburn.

"Emmaline, some little girls are not meant to have fun. It gets in the way of their great beauty."

"But I'm not a great beauty, Mommy."

"Yes, you are. You have glorious blonde hair, blue eyes to get lost in, perfect fair skin and a tempting smile. People appreciate beautiful things. Some people love them so much they will pay a huge sum of money to possess them."

Mommy's fingers moved from my cheek to my dress. She undid half of the pearl buttons on the front, starting at the lace collar. My face turned red when I saw my naked chest and my pink nipples. It was more than Mommy had ever forced me to show any of her men.

I grabbed the loose ends, trying to hold them shut, but Mommy took my hands away and held my arms by my sides.

"Now. Stand up straight. Plant yourself right in front of this nice man when you pour his tea. Let him see you. Tempt him with that smile but don't let him touch. Today, I'm giving him a little tease. You play along like you always do, like a good girl. Mommy's very good girl."

"What do these men want with me, Mommy? Why do you make me see them?"

"I am your mother, Emmaline. The horrors I endured to have you give me the right to make the rules."

"But I don't know how to play the game if I can't understand the rules."

Mommy sighed and ran her fingers through my hair. Loving Mommy once more. "My smart, smart girl. It will be your undoing, but I will humor you. One of these nice men would like to be your new Daddy. They just need a chance to get to know you."

"Are you in love with any of them, Mommy?"

"In a manner of speaking. Sometimes it's best to be in love with what love can give a girl, especially when a man offers exactly what a girl loves in the bargain."

I bit my lip. What could be worth more than being loved?

The doorbell echoed through the house. My heart beat twice as fast. I hated meeting Mommy's men. Being ladylike when my clothes hung open was too much for me, and when things were too much, I made mistakes.

I took my place next to the tea things, my dead Mamou's white china pot and cups with pink roses. In my mind, I imagined my Wonder Twin running through the park, in pants, with knots in her hair. If I closed my eyes, I was almost there.

Mommy beamed at me before opening the door. "Now, be charming. Make this man love you more than any of the rest of them do."

EMMALINE

After it was over, I ran away as fast as I could. It was easy to slip out the back door and into the garden. Aunt Bertie's roses got up my nose as I ran down the alley and crossed the street to my school. I liked to go to the playground after meeting one of Mommy's men, because I could run and swing. I could forget.

When I climbed the slide, I saw Sister Mary Catherine's face in a window of the school building. She waved, and I waved back before flipping over the bar at the top of the slide. I always went down the slide faster when I started with a flip.

My feet stopped me at the bottom, and I sat there thinking. About Daddy. The metal was warm. If I stretched out on it, I imagined it was the heat from Daddy's embrace. He always hugged me best. When I was with him, nothing bad could ever happen to me.

A bird flew against the wide-open sky, all red.

"That would be a cardinal, Miss Cagney."

Sister Mary Catherine made a long shadow squatting next to me. I sat up and smoothed my skirt. When I looked down, my buttons were fixed wrong, and I crossed my arms in front of my chest to hide the mess. "A cardinal like the ones in Rome?"

"Not quite the same, but yes, there are cardinals in Rome."

"How far is Rome? Can a person fly there?" I ran around to the ladder and went up the slide again. At the top, I bounced against the bar, getting ready to do another flip. Adults answered questions better when kids kept moving.

"Well. You know that Rome is in Italy. Which continent is Italy part of?"

"Europe. Right?" Flipped. I held the bar to keep from sliding to the bottom.

"Very good, Dear. I suppose one can fly there in a day, provided the airplane is fast enough."

"Do they let little girls on airplanes?" Let go. Hit the bottom and got up to do it again.

"Why, I'm sure they do, if an adult goes, too."

"But what if an adult can't go? Then what happens?" Climbed the ladder. Flipped and held.

She squinted up at me. "That child would have to buy a ticket, and tickets to Rome are very expensive."

"How much?"

"Hundreds of dollars, at least."

Pushed off with my hands and went as fast as I could to the bottom. "But if the child had hundreds of dollars to buy a ticket, could she get to Rome on an airplane? Or, somewhere else? Maybe closer?" My feet hit the ground. I waited.

Sister Mary Catherine stared at me with her head cocked to one side before she stood to brush off the front of her black outfit. "Emmaline Cagney, why are you asking these questions?"

"Because, someday, I want to be a stewardess and fly all over the world."

"You are such a bright girl, always thinking ahead. I'm certain you'll figure everything out when the time comes." She slapped her hands together to get rid of the rest of the playground dust and patted me on the head. I looked around the drape of her sleeve and found her eyes.

"I hope so."

She opened her mouth and closed it. Opened it again, almost like a fish. "Well, if you need me, I'll be in my office."

I watched her pull the rusty doors and go into the school building.

Would I go to hell for lying to a nun? Sometimes, I didn't think the Devil could be much worse than Mommy on a bad day.

If I called a telephone number, put a cloth over the phone and talked really low, would anyone on the other end mistake me for an adult when I tried to buy a plane ticket? My voice sounded high and baby-fied when I talked out loud. I walked into the parking lot and stood next to a car to hide from Sister Mary Catherine. I practiced my grown-up voice, but nothing gave me that Aunt Bertie sound. After closing my eyes to focus every drop of my Wonder Twin powers, I cleared my throat and tried again.

"Child, I just want to buy one ticket. To Nashville, Tennessee. For my daughter. She's flying all by herself to meet her daddy. She's going to live with him forever."

When I looked up, a man was watching me from the other side of the parking lot. He made a big shadow, and his navy blue suit did not smooth out curves like Mommy said dark colors could do. Loose skin hung from his jaws and down his neck.

Like a bulldog.

I walked around a car to get to the alley and go home, but he blocked the way. A cigar burned between his lips. He took it out and blew smoke that made me cough. Sometimes, that stink was in Mommy's office after one of her men left. Almost all Mommy's men smoked. Boys were dirty.

I scooted behind another car to get around him, but it was too close to the wall. When I tried to squeeze along the back, I didn't fit. I couldn't get around the car parked on the other side, either. The man stood at the opening of the path between the two cars and smiled, the cigar still smoking in his mouth.

"I won't hurt you, little beauty. Come on out." He held out his hand. "I walked all the way over here to talk. Just talk. That's all."

I held my breath and waited, until my face got hot. The space underneath the cars was too small for me to crawl under, even if I could shrink myself with my Wonder Twin power. Besides, he would just be waiting for me on the other side. He blocked the way, watching my mind work and breathing his cigar.

Looking at me funny.

"What are you doing out here, little beauty?"

Why did he keep calling me "little beauty?" Still, he was smiling and being nice. I took a couple of steps toward him.

"Playing." I sized up the number of steps to the alley. How I could try to hurt him and run. But he was so much bigger than me. If I stepped on his foot, he probably wouldn't feel it, and he had so much fat to bite through.

"Motor vehicles are dangerous places for pretty little girls to play." He leaned on the hood of a car. It crunched a little. "Perhaps you'd let me take you home."

"I don't need a ride. I live close by."

"I know where you live."

The bricks scratched my elbows when I backed into the wall. "How do you know that?"

"Why, because I'm Wilkinson. Judge Wilkinson." He took another step toward me. "I remember you. You're Nadine Cagney's little girl."

I shrank into the corner. The dangling chin. And the voice. It was the one behind the wooden stick in the courtroom. This was the man who took my daddy from me.

His jangley mouth kept talking, closer to me, and he breathed fast. He still smiled, but smiles can be nice or not nice, and his was not nice. "I'd like to spend some time with you. Maybe take you to Café du Monde for some beignets." He felt the buttons on the shirt that strained against his belly. "As you can see, I'm partial to sweets, too. We have a lot in common, you and me."

He reached his fingers out to touch my face, and I blurted out the first thing I could think. "Are you one of Mommy's men?"

His eyes narrowed. His breath breezed along my face. "Your mother is a skilled entertainer of men. That I know."

"Lots and lots of men come to see her."

"How do you know that? Do they see you, too?" He ground his cigar under his foot and took out another one. His big hands shook when he chopped off one end with a blade thing, stuck it in his mouth and lit it. He spoke through clenched teeth. "I said, do they see you? These men?"

"Sometimes. Mommy makes me dress up and serve them tea."

The cigar fell out of his mouth and rolled toward me. He pounded his fist into one of the car windows and yelled. When the glass cracked and cut into his hand, I ran. Through the alley. Across the street. His shouts followed me through the middle of the next block and to the back door of Mommy's house. I didn't stop running until I was upstairs, locked in my attic bedroom. I turned on the window fan to block out the memory of the sound of his voice, still shouting in my head.

"You're mine! You're mine! You're mine!"

To Live Forever

THE JUDGE

Her voice. It rang inside my skull. A warning that died against the echo of my screams.

Our plan was in jeopardy. She wanted me to know. Even as she was swallowed up by the alley, she turned her head, and I heard what she said.

Nadine was trying to keep us apart.

I wound a handkerchief around my hand and sliced the head off another cigar. Cuban, rich and raw. Flame lit up the tip and sizzled toward my mouth. Even the finest things could be consumed. Enjoyed. Destroyed.

Smoke haloed around my head. I shook it off when I turned toward the tap on my shoulder.

A nun, the old fashioned kind. She could've worn the same black robe two hundred years ago. A phantom from another time.

Can I help you? She said. Brisk. Efficient. Already done with me.

My fingers tingled. Her sort never did much for me, but I kept my eyes trained on hers. Bland ones, still young. Not used up.

Her neck hovered in the periphery. A tease of impossible length shrouded in coarse material.

I shifted my jacket to hide the bulge. She would have to do. For now.

When I cleared my throat, my voice was angelic.
Why yes, Sister. I'm here to make my confession.
Follow me, she said.

EMMALINE

A door slammed. I sat up on my bed, still wearing my blue dress. It was night. I crawled out of bed and opened my door to a crack. A man yelled that he was coming up the stairs, causing all kinds of commotion on the second floor. I heard somebody whisper that they would climb down the back balcony. A shoe hit the floor, and doors opened and closed. Several ladies talked in high, tight voices.

Feet thud-thud-thudded up the stairs, and a beam of light blinded me before a shadow got in the way. I closed my door and looked for the best place to hide. What had my mother gone and done now? I could no longer think of her as Mommy. Not after seeing the Judge in the parking lot.

Aunt Bertie pushed through my door as I scooted under the bed. She slammed and locked it behind her. Her voice came out breathy. "Let me see you, Emmaline Child." Dust tickled my nostrils when I backed out from under my bed and sat on the floor, Indian-style.

She leaned against the door. Her whole black chest showed through the front of her rainbow robe. She looked down and pulled it closed. Her fingers shook when she took my face in her hands.

"What're we gonna do with you?"

"What's going on, Aunt Bertie?"

"Your fool momma. She done crossed the wrong man."

I inched closer to her. "Who? Which man?"

"Doesn't matter now. We'll all go to jail tonight. All except you."

"Then I'm going to jail, too. I have to stay with you."

Bertie's fingers brushed a tear along my cheek. "No. NO. You listen to me, Child, and listen good. That Judge, he's behind this business."

I swallowed. Was this whole thing my fault? Because of what I said on the playground earlier? "I—"

"Listen to me. That man's got pure evil where his heart should be. Whatever happens, don't let him get you."

Steps hit my landing. Bertie gasped over Roberta's muffled screams that floated from the room across from mine.

Bertie smoothed my hair with her hands. "Cop'll be busy with her for a minute." She chewed her lip and studied me, almost like she thought she could make me disappear. A dab of blood shone on her front tooth when she spoke. "I want you to sneak downstairs. The first door you see to the outside, you run, you hear me? Run away from here, Child. Fast as you can."

"But—"

She hugged me into her lumpy chest, and I breathed her scent of cinnamon and sweat. The smell of love. Of safety. Of home. I tried to pull my face away, but she kept it buried. "There's no time to argue. You have got to get away from the Judge. What he wants with you—it isn't right. That man'll hurt you worse than anybody can."

The policeman banged on the door across the hall. Wood broke apart, and he shouted, "Come out. I know I've got at least one whore and her man hiding in here."

Bertie put her hands over my ears. She unsnapped the front of her robe and held it open. Her rolls of fat sparkled. "Quick. Pick up those shoes there."

I grabbed my Sunday mary janes and pulled them on, my fingers clumsy with the buckles. I never could get them on when I had to hurry.

Before I was done, she beckoned me to her. "Good, Child. Good. Now, I want you to stay right behind me under this robe. You bury yourself as deep as you can into my back. When I walk, you step with the same foot as I do. Don't make a peep, you hear me?"

"I won't, Aunt Bertie."

I tried to memorize her face. Her round cheeks and frizz of hair. After tonight, would I ever see her again? If my mother went to jail, would Bertie go with her? I could imagine life without my mother, but since Daddy was taken from me, my whole world was Bertie.

Before I could tell her that, she grabbed my hand and pulled me to my feet. "You better not, or the Judge'll take you, and he'll hurt you for the rest of your life. As soon as your feet hit the floor downstairs, you pop out from under there, and you run. You run like hell-fire is chomping at your heels. Don't stop. Don't look behind you. Promise me you won't ever come back here."

The crash of furniture shook the floor, and a man's voice whined like a baby, littler than me. "Please, Officer. Don't tell my wife where you found me."

"Fat chance, you horny bastard. Now, get on out of that trunk. How did you fold that gut of yours up in there, anyhow?"

Bertie rubbed my back and smiled at me through her tears. She shoved a stack of envelopes into my hand, tied with a red string. "Promise me you'll find your daddy. He's in Nashville these days, remember? Here's a bunch of his letters to you. Your momma would've burned them, but I hid them from her."

I ran my thumb along the uneven paper. "You mean, Daddy wrote me all these times?"

"Uh-huh. Almost every day. I saved all the ones I could. Addresses are all over the place, but this last one's in Nashville. I told you. Remember?"

I could just make out the word 'nash' in the smeared postmark.

"You get somebody to take you to him. He's the only person you got in the world now. Nobody left here for you to go to."

Footsteps stopped at my locked door, followed by a knock. I stuffed

Daddy's letters down the front of my dress. After a beat, a man shouted, "Don't make me break one more door tonight, and I might be in a good mood when you open it."

"Just a minute, Officer." Bertie pushed me under her robe and clicked the snaps closed in front. "I just need to make myself presentable."

"I seen it already. Open this door. Now."

She whispered it one more time. "Stay behind me and run."

The lock squeaked, and the door opened. My nose itched from the dirty cigarette smell. I pinched my nose together to keep from sneezing.

"Well. Now, ain't you a whole lotta woman. You head on downstairs. I think I've rounded up everybody else here."

Bertie's back went stiff. When she shifted her weight to one leg, I followed her with my body and copied her stance, the one she got when she flirted with my mother's men. "Oh, Officer. I'll come on down right behind you. Make it easy and all."

Silence.

I held my breath and waited for the man to answer. My mother screamed at someone in the distance. Something about injustice being the highlight of her life, about being double-crossed. Her voice shook me into Bertie, causing her to lean toward me a little. I buried my head in her back and tried to be still, but it was hard.

"Well now. You know your place. I like that." His toe tapped on the wood floor. Five taps. Ten taps. Fifteen—"All right. Come on down behind me."

Bertie moved backward as he came further into my room, and I made my feet follow her. He slammed doors and rustled my dresses, and his knees popped when he knelt to look under something. "Some of your clientele into having you dress up like little girls?"

Aunt Bertie sniffed and turned her head.

He snickered. "Just follow me and let's get this loaded train of crazy on down to the station."

His feet bounced down the stairway ahead of us. Bertie didn't change her normal hip-swinging walk when she followed. I had to fight to keep up with her. In my head, I counted the stairs to the second floor landing, turned, and counted the steps to the bottom.

A wet breeze moved through the folds of Bertie's robe. The front door was open, and from the smell of the rain mixed with oil, I could tell that the door was close. Bertie reached around and pinched me, my signal to slip out and run. I crawled out from under the wispy material, hot and confused, looking for the open door.

The officer was shorter than Bertie. His dark suit swallowed his skinny body. His eyes almost popped out of his face. "Hey!"

My mother's voice called from her office. "Emmaline! There you are. I never meant for this to happen. You have to believe me. Your mommy loves you."

Hot tears stung my eyes, and I started to run to her, but another man stepped out of the shadows. All fat over muscle, with one hand wrapped in bandages. The Judge. He wore the same ink blue suit, and the tips of his fingers shook.

His face softened when he saw me. He almost smiled.

"Judge, what do you want me to do?" The policeman's hands came at me like pinchers on a crab.

The Judge was lost in me. He took a step toward me and held out his bloody hand. "Wouldn't you like to live a better life, little beauty? In my house? With me?"

His bulldog head nodded toward me, and the officer pounced. He reached around Bertie and tried to grab me, but I slipped through his fingers and ran. Out the front door. Into the rain. Away. My mother's screams were sucked into the wet wind. I ducked my head to keep the water out of my eyes and ran around the side of the house. Shouts echoed through the courtyard, and feet galloped after me.

I crawled on my hands and knees to get under a house. It was all open underneath, and I could squeeze out the other side. As I worked my way along the dirt, I kept my eyes on the alley at the far end, the one that led to my school. If I waited until the footsteps ran away, I could sneak through the alley and run across the street. Maybe one of the nuns would open the door and let me in.

I put my head between my knees and counted. Ten. Fifty. One hundred. Five hundred. When I listened for the officer, all I heard were the sounds of people laughing and singing on Bourbon Street. I smelled the air, but it was all dirt and Bertie's roses. No cigarettes or sweaty men.

I slipped out from under the house and ran down the alley as fast as I could. When I came to the street, I hurried toward the light in the window at school. One light.

It was my only hope.

MERRY

Tuesday. October 4, 1977. New Orleans, Louisiana

Rain. It tumbled down the end of my nose and slid into the street outside the bar. The French Quarter. I don't know how I knew it. Even if I didn't recall my other assignments, New Orleans was a strange familiar.

I let go of the door knob and slipped into a different day, months from where I started. A visit to the bar erased all sense of time, just like it obliterated the words in my journal. A few hours with the Bartender could be six months, six years in the living world.

Along Bourbon Street, people ebbed and flowed in a sea of stale alcohol and human piss. I stopped long enough to wipe my face and secure my hat before I pushed into the party, fighting to stay upright in the midst of them, when an old woman bumped smack into me and stopped. Blocked my way.

She wobbled a little when she winked a fish eye at me. "Would you like to buy a lucky bead?" Her voice rang with an accent. Germanic, maybe. I had more experience with Spanish and French. She was one of those New Orleans eccentrics, indigenous to the place. Her gold football helmet was streaked with rain, and her dress was a black shroud that stuck to her sparse frame.

She opened her shriveled hand and flashed it. A single purple bead. Glass, it was, with a ring of smoke through its center.

My pocket burned next to my groin. The two dollar bill. The closer I got to finding my next charge, the hotter it got, until I would have to release it into the air. It would lead me to the person I sought. Now that I was out of the bar, my need to find my charge consumed me, like an alcoholic to the next drink.

I swallowed and pushed past the Bead Lady. She would find a buyer. Part of experiencing the Quarter was a little give-and-take between drunks and eccentrics. It made everyone on the street the same.

Someone swerved into me from behind, knocked me off-kilter. I hung there, suspended above a river of Bourbon Street pollution. My eyes registered a blue dress and tangled blonde hair. When she looked over her shoulder, her eyes branded a place in my heart.

Pain tore through my right kneecap as it struck the concrete, the momentum hurtling me face forward into the thick, coursing muck. I reached out to stop my fall, but at the same moment, a pair of strong hands gripped my shoulders. Jerked me to a halt. I turned away from the stinking bilge to meet my savior.

The football helmet and fish eyes. The Bead Lady helped me to my feet. She did not blink. "You see what happens to those who do not buy the lucky bead."

"Come on, Bead Lady. Someone just plowed into me, and you're still trying to sell me beads?"

"The lucky bead wards off all bad luck."

I gripped her arms and put weight on my leg, gritting my teeth against the hot waves of pain. I thought back to the expedition, to the time I fell over the side of a sandstone cliff along the Missouri. Had to dig my knife into the soft dirt to catch myself. My arms were sore for days, but I ignored them. It usually helped to push through the pain. I ground my teeth and shifted my weight.

The Bead Lady's stale breath blew into the space next to me. "The lucky bead will help you find what you seek."

"Who says I'm seeking anything?" I looked around for the little girl, but she was replaced by a couple of men. Plainclothes. They worked their way through the crowd. Shook their badges and showed a picture. When they got close, my gut lurched at the blonde hair and longing eyes.

I turned back to the Bead Lady. "Tell you what. I'll buy your lucky bead if you can tell me something about my future."

"Lucky bead make lucky future. You buy." She waved it, hypnotic-like, in front of her pit eyes.

Of all people, I should've been superstitious enough to believe in the luck of a spell. The natives cast plenty of spells on my travels with Clark: for rain, for safety for our team, for clear passes and a herd of buffalo at the right time. We were lucky, more times than I could count.

But, as I wiped rain out of my eyes, I remembered: my luck ran out on a moonless October night. It couldn't be resurrected by a gaudy purple bead.

Ignoring the voice in my head, I reached into my pocket for my wad of cash. "Here's a dollar. Give me the lucky bead."

She took my money and put the bead in my palm without touching me. I closed my hand around it and followed the path of the little girl. I blinked more rain out of my eyes and scanned the street. Where was she?

In a crack of thunder, the wind blew that two dollars out of my hand. It fluttered over people's heads, but I could see it, lit up like a lantern in front of an alley, right before it disappeared. Sucked into a crack in the wall.

Panicked, I shoved the drunks that stood between me and the two dollars. If I lost sight of it, I might miss my last chance. Doomed to the back side of a bar, one of the most forgotten men in history. A Nowhere man.

It was time to rewrite that story.

I reached an uneven wall of coral stucco and followed it, until I found a door that opened into the alley. As I swung it back, a tease of cool air hit my face. Inside, the rain pinged on the metal roof like a classical music piece I'd heard long ago. Teased from a fiddle under a stardusted Western sky.

The two dollars strobed on the rock pavement beyond the entrance. I slid into the dark, feeling along the wall with one hand while reaching toward my money with the other. As my skin touched it, I heard a whisper, or a sigh. Further off in the darkness. Caused my heart to lurch.

The money singed my fingerprints, but I held onto it. Soles clattered on wet stone and mingled with the sound of my breathing. I took another step, and a shuffle scraped in the dark.

"Who's there?"

I stopped breathing and waited for an answer. My ears strained to hear through the barrage of Quarter sounds.

A sob.

It ripped through me, followed by a crash. Steps ran through the dark, and a ghost brushed past me. I fished the air with my hand and caught the body of a child.

The little girl.

I dragged her around a corner, to a shaft of weak light from a high window. Knotted blonde hair and eyes rimmed in red. I gazed into them and knew she was the person I sought. She kicked my shins with her Sunday shoes, powerful in her fury. Her fear.

When she tried to bite through the leather of my coat, I grabbed her other arm and turned her to face me. Still, she thrashed against the grip of my hands. The two dollars, it burned like a bonfire, lodged between her left arm and my palm. I let it float to the ground. It twisted through the light and landed at her feet. Instead of following its slow trajectory, she turned her dirt-streaked face up to me.

I kneeled in front of her to get myself eye-to-eye. "Let me help you."

"Did the bad m-man send you to find me, Mister?"

"Who?" I thought back to the men on the street, the ones brandishing a badge and a picture. "I may be many things, but I'm no bad man. I promise you that."

Her face was red with crying, and her chest heaved with the kind of helpless kid noise that hacked into my heart. "H-how do I k-know that? I just ran from a b-bad man, and he's got people that look like police chasing me."

"Did you see these men who were chasing you?"

"Y-yes."

"Were any of them dressed like me?" I looked down at my stained denims, emphasis of a point.

"I don't r-remember. Everything happened so fast."

She studied my face through her tears, recording every detail of my dress, from the crumpled brim of my hat to my wet leather jacket and jeans. When she got to the ground, she stopped, transfixed. Her voice was quiet when she spoke.

"Two dollars? I don't think I've ever seen a two dollar bill before."

"Merry. Call me Merry."

"That's a funny name for a man. Especially one big and scary like you."

"I use it so I'm not so big and scary."

A smile played at the edges of her mouth, and she swiped at her cheeks. "Isn't Merry a girl's name?"

"Nah. That's Mary. Like the Virgin. My name's Merry, like Merry Christmas. Only I'm not very happy most of the time."

"Me, either. It's been years since I've been happy."

I had to smile at her measure of time.

"Mister Merry. I like that name."

"What's yours?"

"Emmaline, like 'Emma, hang the clothes on the line.' People always get it wrong. Emmaline Cagney. I'm nine."

She stuck out her hand, and I shook it. Old-time gravity and a deep bow worked wonders on ladies of any age. "A pleasure to make your acquaintance, Miss Emmaline Cagney. About this running away from bad men business—"

She jerked her hand away. "Please, PLEASE don't make me go home. I can't go back there. Ever. My mommy—mother—does business with bad men. The worst of them is after me. The Judge. Pure evil where his heart should be. That's what Aunt Bertie says. I know if I go back—"

"Wait, Emmaline. Slow down." I looked at the two dollars. It pulsed in time with her beating heart. I closed my eyes, and I knew I had to help this little girl. Save her from a tragic end no one would remember. Rewrite her story before it ruined her life. When I opened my eyes, they met hers. "You don't have to worry. I won't take you back there."

"You won't?"

I was surprised to hear my voice shake when I replied. Did my reactions always get clogged up with emotion when I found my charge? I closed my eyes and tried to recall one image—anything—from a Nowhere time before. Blackness. Quiet. Nothing was all I saw. "Emmaline. I'm going to take you away from here."

Her liquid eyes widened. "To Daddy? All the way in Nashville?"

"Yes. I'm taking you to your father in Nashville."

My quiet heart twisted in my chest when I said the words, because I knew the way I would take her.

The Natchez Trace.

I remembered the last time I stood on that forgotten ribbon of earth, a path worn down by thousands of years of listless feet. Air that mingled with the ghosts of buffalo and red men, of thieves and bankrupt souls. I shuddered. Phantoms. They would be everywhere, especially after what happened to me the last time I rode through its tunnel of hardwood trees.

It was the second gunshot that snuffed out my life. That robbed me of death. I was convinced it took away the full measure of my name, my immortal mark on the timeline of the earth. That propelled me into Nowhere.

EMMALINE

"What's the matter, Mister Merry?"

Her voice pulled me back from the shadowed haunts of an ancient trail. To the present. To my last chance at redemption. To a rainy New Orleans night and a lost girl named Emmaline.

I sat back to take the weight off my knees. "Nothing. Nothing's the matter. Tell me about your daddy."

Her smile was like sunlight. "I write my daddy most days. Letters. I write the best letters. Decorated with hearts and flowers. And music notes just for him. That's what he does for a job. Plays music and sings. I mean, he used to, anyway."

"You don't know what he's doing now?"

She reached down the front of her dress and pulled out a wad of wet paper, bound with a red string, and held it out to me. "I have these letters from him. Aunt Bertie gave them to me right before I ran." She rubbed her fingers over frayed edges, like her mind could consume the words by touch. "He wrote me all the time, see? But my mother wouldn't let me have his letters. Aunt Bertie saved a few of them, though. Maybe we can find him that way."

I tried to touch a smeared postmark. Indiscriminate. Illegible. She pulled them back and cradled them in her arms, her eyes clouded with suspicion. "Why should I trust you with Daddy's letters? How do I know you're not just another bad man?"

I kept myself neutral. No big movements. Nothing to give her cause to flee. "You can't know my intentions, Emmaline. I wish I could do something to make you trust me, but I can't. All I know is that's quite a stack of letters. Your father must love you very much to pen such a volume of words."

"It's six whole months' worth." Her eyes remained shuttered, and she gripped the letters to her heart. "It feels like forever since my mother divorced Daddy. I haven't seen him since then. Not one time. My mother fixed it with the Judge so that he couldn't see me. Not ever."

"How did she do that?"

"She did her mothery things, I guess." Her eyes grazed wet stucco and glass, humid air and sky. "When she does those things, she gets whatever she wants. Anyway. Daddy told me not to worry. He said he'd write to me every day, but my mother must have hidden his letters, because I only got a few. Until tonight, when Aunt Bertie gave me these." She stopped for breath and studied me. Took a step back. "How did you know about my daddy? Who told you?"

A smart little firecracker. Just what I needed. My knees groaned when I crawled up on them again. I'd been around too damn long.

"Emmaline, I know what it feels like to lose a father. I guess that longing—that hole in the soul—well, I recognize it in other people."

"You mean, your daddy was taken away from you, too?"

"Not the same way, but yes. When I was younger than you. That's why I want to help you find your dad. To help you avoid growing up with that empty place I had. It's a job I can be proud of.

She took a step toward me. "But how did you *know* it was your job? Who gave it to you?"

Even when she scowled, she radiated fragile beauty. I leaned forward and put myself on eye level with her, like convincing her that I was the man to help her find her father was the only thing that mattered in my life. Failure was easy to face again, because I couldn't remember what it felt like. Except for the failure of my life, the ending that drove me into this timeless place, this Nowhere.

I gave her my best smile. "My intuition told me. Do you understand?"

"No. Not really."

I wobbled on my knees. Winced. "Do you have any imaginary friends?"

"Yes!" She hopped from foot to foot. "The Wonder Twins. One is the real me, and the other is the pretend me. The girl I'd be if my mother would let me. I'd wear pants and get dirty and have all kinds of adventures."

All kinds of adventures. I thought back to my time with Clark. Our trek out west. Where every stop presented new people. Otherworldly languages. Bizarre food and interesting rituals. I could give her adventure, but could a sheltered girl handle it?

I pressed her. "Okay. When you're playing with the Wonder Twins, and you know you're supposed to make them do a certain thing, but you don't know how you know. That's intuition."

"My mother says that's my hyperactive imagination and that I shouldn't listen to it."

"Emmaline, your imagination is the most valuable thing you have. It can take you anywhere. Make you anyone. Give you anything you want. Don't ever, ever stop heeding it."

She backed away from me and paced the cobbled alley. Her small face worked to comprehend the finer points. My inner voice warned me to let her have her space to ponder her misgivings. I couldn't blame her, really. She was no pushover, even at the age of nine.

"Will you get money if you take me to my daddy?"

"There's no money. It's not that kind of job."

She stood, aloof. Straight. Nervous hands pressed on her stack of sodden words. I inched toward her.

"You're a smart girl to be wary of me. But I promise, I won't hurt you."

She stopped pacing and watched a spider weave a web between two blooms that sprouted from a potted geranium. The damp soaked through my blue jeans while I tried to read her mind. Her voice was a whisper when she spoke again.

"My mother let me watch television to keep me busy, Mister Merry. I've seen what bad men do to children like me. Make them disappear and stuff."

I creaked to my feet and gritted my teeth against the fire in my knees. "Okay. You tell me. How do you think I knew about your dad?"

"I don't know. You're a good guesser? You've been watching me?" Her mind whirred. "Wait. I know. You're one of the men who visits my mother and her ladies. That's how you knew. It has to be."

I watched her face and cogitated the meaning behind her words. Imagined who—or what—her mother was, right before she told me. Not in so many words. A nine-year-old girl should never have to say her mother is a prostitute. But, she colored in the picture for me with broken crayons in damaged hues.

In some respects, she was an older soul than me. On the run from police, the very people who were supposed to protect her. No wonder she had trouble trusting me. I watched in dismay as her face crumpled under the weight of her tears. Pavers stabbed my knees when I knelt and folded her into my arms. She clung to me and sobbed a fresh rainstorm on the front of my jacket.

"I don't want to go back there. Ever. I don't know what I'll do, but please don't make me go back. I'm scared of my mother. That house. Her men." She shuddered. "I want my daddy. I just want my daddy."

My eyes burned with tears of my own. I stroked her tangle of hair. "Emmaline. I can't prove to you that I'm not a bad man. But, I will get you to your father if it costs me my life." I tilted her chin up to face me. "Let's make a pact. See that two dollars on the ground over there?"

She nodded, then tiptoed to it. When she picked it up, she held it out to me.

"No, you keep it. Look at the front." She squinted at the paper. "That man. Do you know who he is?"

"Thomas Jefferson? Wasn't he our President once?"

"Smart girl. You know your United States history. He used to be one of my heroes. He once said that honesty is the first chapter in the book of wisdom, and I still hope he believed that."

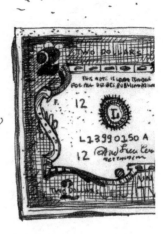

She stroked the note with her fingers. "What does that mean?"

"It means that wise people don't lie, because it's wisest to be honest. You can't know this about me, but it's how I try to live."

She flung one hand to her hip. Defiant. "Unless you're lying about telling the truth."

"I want you to keep that two dollars, Emmaline, as a token of my promise that you'll see your daddy again. I'll take you to Nashville, and I won't let anyone hurt you."

Exhausted, I fell back on my ass. It felt good to stretch my legs out in front of me, to start up the circulation again. I focused on movement to give her some space to make her decision. Choose her path to navigate. The drum of the rain on the roof filled the silence. A watery clock that punctuated minutes. Dripped seconds.

Tentative, she approached and offered me her right hand. I made my most solemn face and shook it, businesslike. "Mister Merry, I will go with you. I can't go back where I came from, so it's time to go on."

"I only have one condition." Her warmth ran along the nerves of my arm. Through my shoulder. To my heart.

"What is it?"

"Stop calling me Mister. It's Merry. Just Merry." I groaned to my feet. "Now, let's get going."

When I took her hand and walked her back toward Bourbon Street, she braked her heels at the doorway and gasped. Transfixed. I followed her gaze through the alley's opening.

Two men blocked our way. I pushed Emmaline behind me. With the scrawny build on the first one, I knew I could take him. It was the eyes on the second man that stopped me.

I knew those eyes, the empty Nowhere pits within them.

His eyes were just like mine.

The eyes were markers for other Nowhere Men. Where most people's eyes contained sparklers of life, ours were flat. Dead. Mostly black where color should be.

I'd run into a couple of Nowhere Men. Usually in the bar. Never anyone I knew.

But, I knew him. He was a shade that haunted the trajectory of my life.

His lips stretched out in a smile I well remembered. Almost two hundred years, and even the drawl of his voice was the same. "Well, Merry."

"Wilkinson? James Wilkinson?"

His chin wagged when he laughed. "Good take on your name. Ironic. But, irony always suited you."

My thoughts raced back. St. Louis. The last time I saw Wilkinson, he slammed the door of his office—my office—after being replaced as governor of the Upper Louisiana Territory. By me. I took his job.

Or, President Jefferson gave me his job. Didn't trust Wilkinson. He said he needed someone loyal, someone upstanding, in the position. Someone who'd proven he could deliver results instead of strutting around in service of self.

Wilkinson didn't take the news well. He had months to sow enmity and destroy my credibility before I got there. While I floundered in my first attempt to publish my expedition journals back east, he excelled at wrecking my chances in the life I was about to enter.

He rewrote my last chapter. Hijacked my reputation. I think he had a hand in killing me.

I always hated him.

He took a step forward. I could smell the stench of cigar on his breath. It crawled along the skin of my face, just like it did the last time I saw him. His finger shook when he pointed at me. "Revenge, Lewis. You killed my wife. Now, I will finally finish you."

My thoughts reeled with his outlandish accusation, when Emmaline popped from behind me. Yanked at my hand. "Merry, it's the Judge! He's the bad man! Run!"

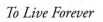

To Live Forever

THE JUDGE

Meriwether Lewis. I always knew he was here.

A Nowhere Man.

Like me.

Still the self-righteous bastard. Always followed the rules.

The opposite of me.

I'd been in Nowhere for almost two hundred years. Several stints. That whole business about recovering my good name, ensuring my immortal place in history? Bullshit. I skipped out on my last assignment and built the life I always wanted. Right here. In between the margins. Where power could be my heavenly reward.

I constructed my empire and looked for the spirit of my wife. My Ann. I always knew she was here somewhere. That she was housed in the body of a little girl was something I couldn't help.

'Find me again.'

She whispered it through bloody teeth, her lungs rotted by tuberculosis. It got worse after we were forced out of St. Louis. She couldn't last in the Natchez heat.

All because of that damn Lewis.

In a way, I was glad he had her. Obliterating him would give my reunion with Ann another edge. It was like a bonus.

I thought back to the blue tinge on that nun's face. Her thick tongue and bloodshot eyes. That croaking sound she made when her soul gave up and floated away.

Violence always made sex a shivering rhapsody of desire.

MERRY

"Get them. Don't shoot the girl." I looked back to see the Judge duck into the street and evaporate into the swirl of humanity, while his sidekick started after us.

Emmaline bolted down a tunnel that led from the back of the court-yard, dragging me behind her. The crash of a wooden door rang through the footfalls of pursuit. She turned left at a T junction that led us into cavelike dark, morbid and damp. I breathed through the sensation of being suffocated by the intense weight of it. My knee grazed a sharp corner. A chain reaction of toppled yard furniture or ironwork.

Blind, I reached through the nothing in front of me and felt Emmaline's snarled hair.

"Know where we're going?"

Her voice bounced back to me. "Dead end. Up ahead. Almost there."

"Dead end? How's that going to get us out of here?"

"We can climb the wall. I've done it before."

A crash of metal and a cry of pain echoed through the alley. Whatever I knocked over, it was a only temporary roadblock for the Judge's henchman.

Wilkinson, of all people.

His shadow haunted every hour of my tenure in office. He used his connections in Washington to lobby for shifting trade rules. Less money for the territory. Spread rumors that I was a drunk. He even made mortifying insinuations about my friendship with Clark. He hounded me until the night I died, with one of his men just outside.

Or was he? I couldn't remember.

Steel scraped on stone, and the beat of footsteps resumed. The weak beam of a flashlight snaked around a corner.

"Hurry, Emmaline. We almost there?"

In answer, she dragged me through a narrow opening, a break between two buildings. Light streamed like whitewater falling through a crack. Emmaline wrapped her hands around the gutter and scaled the brick-and-stucco corner to the top of a wooden fence. She mouthed the words *follow me* before dropping over the side.

I had one shot to get over the fence before they'd be on me. Maybe. Easier said than done, with my sore legs and banged-up knee. I grabbed the drainpipe and hoisted myself along the wet wall. My shoes slipped. No traction. I used all the strength in my arms to pull myself up, but the opening where Emmaline disappeared was a tight squeeze. I leaned forward and put my chest flat, ready to push off the wall with my legs and dive head first into the other side of the unknown.

"Stop right there."

Eyes squinted up at me through the line of light in his hand. The beam shuddered as he panted. In his other fist, the round silencer at the end of a pistol was trained up at me. I hung there, suspended, a human bulls-eye.

"Reach over that wall. Pull the girl back over." The man jerked his gun hand through the beam of light to make sure I saw it. Static blared from a box. He pulled it in front of his mouth. "Yeah. I got 'em. You can go on back to your house and wait. Over."

I glanced over the wall. Emmaline looked up at me, her dress torn at the hem. Her right knee was slick with blood. Details I wished to remember in case I woke up in the bar, a publican for all time.

I could wish, but I knew I would never remember.

She motioned to me. "Just fall, Merry. It's not far."

I closed my eyes and inched my body over the divide. Steel ground on steel. A silenced click tore through me. Sent me over the wall in a free fall. The impact knocked the wind out of me. I realized I was still breathing when I bounced on asphalt.

Emmaline ran over and tugged on my jacket, trying to pull me to my feet. "Get up. Hurry."

I fought to breathe and ran my fingers over my chest, before shoving them inside my denim shirt. I felt a clear sheen on my skin. Sweat. Nothing more.

Head pounding, I pulled myself to my knees and crawled for cover along the back of one of the buildings, her in tow. The crooked cop was still in the alley, cursing and scratching at the barrier. When he fired a couple of bullets, they broke through and whizzed into empty space. Rounds of light and a rush of breath.

"I'm not hit, Emmaline. Bastard missed."

"He's trying to climb the fence."

"That sack of skin-and-bones can't climb a fence."

"Are you sure?"

I nudged her back. "Come on. The Judge might have other people out here looking for you."

Wide-eyed, Emmaline scanned the parking lot where three cars sat cold under a single floodlight. "Can you get one of those cars started, Merry?"

I eyed the machines. Mystical devices that replaced the grit of human effort. I might've learned to drive on a different assignment, but every Nowhere experience was new. I started every job with the tools I had in life.

They didn't include driving.

"I'm not so great with cars." I studied the rest of the space. Uneven brick. An iron porch or two. A blank hole, recessed into a wall. "What about that opening there? Other side of the lot. Where does that go?"

Her lips moved along her mental city map. "It comes out at the end. Close to the Cathedral."

"Can we get to the river from there?"

Scratches drifted over the fence, and a thud rattled the wooden slats. The man shouted orders through the static on the handheld radio. I couldn't hear who answered.

"We don't have much time. Can we get to the river? Think, Emmaline."

She chewed her lip. Nodded. "We can run along the side of the big square. It comes out at Café du Monde. Daddy used to take me there."

I nudged her in the direction of the arched doorway, dragging myself to a run behind her. "Get us out of here."

When I made to follow her, I was blinded by brick shrapnel. Tasted blood. Another shot, followed by more staccato footsteps and another voice.

"Quit shooting! The Judge wants the girl alive."

I ignored the rest and kept moving, forced my body between the possibility of more gunfire and Emmaline's bouncing curls. Kept my eye on an arch of light at the far end of the alley. Emmaline tugged at an iron gate, and we pushed into a circle of party girls on the sidewalk. Sequins every place. Their sparkle blocked my view of Emmaline. "Watch the dress, jerk!" One of them slurred.

I forged ahead, fighting to keep Emmaline's head in my sights. She weaved through the people on the sidewalk with the advantage of size and a low center of gravity while I bumped and shoved, clumsy.

"Stop that man!" A gravelly voice shouted. From a side street, another uniform sprang into the sidewalk, eyes locked on me.

I pushed around a teenage boy and sprinted along the iron fence at Jackson Square, lungs burning. The awning at Café du Monde glowed green and white up ahead, people swarming underneath. Vultures, hungry for white powder and fried dough.

Where the iron fence gave out, Emmaline hung a sharp right and disappeared. I closed the few steps and rounded the fence just in time to see Emmaline tear through traffic to a wall on the other side of the street.

The levee. It had to be.

Car horns blared as I plowed through headlights to the other side of the road and crawled up the grade to the top of the levee. Emmaline waited there, bent over with her hands on her knees, panting hard. Across the street, our two pursuers dove into traffic. I nudged her. "Move it. Now."

I forced my agonized legs into another run, pulling Emmaline with me.

The levee was a series of barriers that held back the river. Dark warehouses. Smokestacks. Railroad tracks. The Mississippi slipped into nothing around a sharp bend. I stopped and scanned the docks, seeking any kind of boat to steal. Empty water lapped against the levee, holding nothing that would float.

"Last call for the Cotton Blossom! See New Orleans at night!" A voice cracked over a loudspeaker. Close. I pushed toward the sound, through industrial canyons and the stink of engine oil, my heartbeat a thud in my ears.

Lights along the levee lit up whirlpools of muddy water. A horn sounded, low and long. In front of us, a steamboat was anchored. Its red wheel turned, ready to depart. I took Emmaline's hand and ran toward it.

The Cotton Blossom. A ticket taker was closing his window underneath that sign. I stopped in front and knocked on the glass. The man ignored me, intent on shuttering his space.

I looked over my shoulder. The uniformed goons advanced down the embankment. In less than a minute, they'd be upon us. I pushed my desperation aside and mustered a weary smile. Tried to catch the man's eye. "Bend the rules a little? I promised my daughter we'd have a ride tonight. She's got her heart set on it, but her fool mother didn't bring her over to my place on time."

He looked me over through the glass, hard-like. Emmaline shook her dripping head and flashed a shy smile. He leaned on the counter and sighed. Softened. He pulled out two tickets and pushed them toward us. "Ride's on me. Hurry. It's leaving any second now."

"Thanks, Mister!" Emmaline called. We ran up the metal ramp to the entrance of the boat. Somebody shouted over the jazz band tuning up on deck. A steward moved a bar aside to let us on board.

"Welcome to the Cotton Blossom. May I punch your ticket?"

I handed the man two tickets and scooted us into the jeweled crowd on deck. One last look at land, and I spotted Wilkinson's men following us up the ramp. They leapt over the gap the boat left when it pulled away.

Emmaline swallowed a scream. I slipped us around to the other side of the boat and draped a protective arm around her shoulder. "Let's mingle, Miss Emmaline. Stay close to me. You're in my territory now."

EMMALINE

I glued my hand to Merry's and followed him into the crowd of dancers on deck. A jazz band played "Am I Blue" with a not-fast beat, and I thought of Daddy. I imagined him among those white suits, strumming his upright bass and singing. The song was one of Daddy's favorites. A jam, he called it, even though it was about sad things.

Merry lifted me into his arms and twirled us around the dance floor. My feet spun above the ground, my own merry-go-round. The Judge's men were out there, watching us. I threw my head back. Powdery clouds spun with stars as Merry twirled me.

All the time I'd been longing for Daddy. I couldn't believe I was on my way, if the Judge's men didn't stop us. I peeked around Merry's head, but I only saw ladies in fancy dresses dancing with men in suits.

At the far end of the deck, Merry pulled my head close to him and whispered in my ear.

"Those two are along the railing on the right-hand side. They can't do anything to us right now."

He dipped me close to the floor, and the wind whipped my hair. A dance with Merry was the best playground ever, but his eyes were serious when I popped up.

"Don't look, but there's a life boat hanging along the railing, about half-way down the upper deck. Head that way."

"But what if I can't follow you?"

"I won't let go of your hand, Emmaline. I promise." He dipped me again, and I almost smiled. When I came close to his face, he kept talking. "Those cretins haven't figured out where the boat is yet, but they will. I'm sure they'll block our approach."

"How will we trick them?"

"We've got to make a run for it now, Emmaline. Climb in, crouch low and hang on. It'll take a few seconds for the boat to fall into the river. Brace for it."

I wanted to turn my head to see where the boat was. Merry was being so good to me. I needed to get my part right. But all I could think of was Daddy.

I closed my eyes and nodded along with the beat of "Blue." It made him closer to me.

"I'm coming to you, Daddy."

My mumbled words were lost as the red wheel of the boat turned faster. The steamboat drifted into the night. I held on to Merry as he worked us to the edge of the dancers and sang with the last chorus of "Am I Blue." Merry dipped me again. Once and up. Twice and up.

The third time, he put my head close to the deck and gripped me in the basket of his arms. With the dancers as a shield, he kept our bodies hidden and moved toward the escape boat. In three steps, he had us in the side walkway and set me on my feet.

A white boat hung from a bar close to the ceiling. Merry climbed the railing and rustled the cover. Without explaining, he picked me up and pushed me over the wooden side. I flew over the Mississippi, before the world went dark, and my knees hit the bottom of the boat. When I peeked over the edge, Merry stood on top of the railing, ready to throw one leg up and climb in with me.

"Stop!" A deep voice called from the front of the steamboat. "A thief on the lifeboat! Stop the music! He's stealing the lifeboat!"

"Em, hang on tight." Merry had one leg over the side, the boat tilting like a scary carnival ride as he slid his other foot off the railing. I kept my head down while the boat swung back and forth. The cover lifted away and Merry pulled himself into the boat with me. People raced along the deck while we tick-tocked over the dark river. I held onto the side as hard as I could.

"Stay down!" Merry shouted. He worked a lever with one hand, but one of the men jumped up and grabbed the side of the boat. The motion caused Merry to stumble, and his hand slipped off the lever as he fell. When he came up, Merry balled up his fist and popped the man in the face. His nose crunched and started to bleed, but he threw one arm over the side of the boat and tried to pull his legs inside. With his other arm, he reached for me, but I slid along the bottom of the boat to get behind Merry. I felt the man's fingers brush against my leg as he swiped at me again, and I kicked at his hands.

He yelped and shouted, but his hands kept grabbing for me.

I crawled into the back corner, but the man spat mean words as he gripped the side of our boat. With the toe of his boot, Merry kicked the man's hands until they were sticky with blood, over and over. I ducked my head between my legs to hide my eyes and ears. Finally, the man cursed and let go, and the boat lurched again. I sat up and looked over the side, my fingers running along the bloody bits he left. His body fell away, knocking over some of the people who were watching from the deck.

"And stay out!" I shouted. We rocked harder as Merry lowered our boat to the water, ping-ping-pinging against the side of the steamboat.

A man in a different uniform shouted through the microphone from the front of the dancers and the quiet band. "I am the captain of this vessel, and I command you to stop!"

Another hand sailed over the railing and grabbed my shoulder. Angry brown eyes locked onto mine a split second before my whole world fell. Sound roared in my ears. I screamed as the boat twisted into the black night and braced myself for whatever came next.

I was scared, but being with Merry was more fun than I could ever remember. At least, since Daddy. It was like I was alive again. Life was an adventure. As the wind beat against me, I squeezed Merry's leg to keep from falling out of the boat.

"Hang on, Emmaline! Hang on!" Merry shouted. As we spun into space, my arms hurt, but I didn't break my grip. I was too young to die, and I couldn't die until I saw Daddy again.

It wouldn't be right.

MERRY

Emmaline screamed, and I steeled myself for the consequences of doing a belly flop into the Mississippi in a wooden rowboat. The impact knocked me sideways, and I launched over the side, force-fed river water. Like the time I surfed the falls of the Columbia River in a single canoe. My men stood on the shore and watched me. Ready to pull my drowned body from a watery tomb.

I showed them.

Me and my daredevil life.

When I breached the surface, I was turned around, disoriented. I kept my head low, only my eyes above the water, spinning my body with my legs and feet. Lights from the boat combed the river, but I dove when they shone close to me.

"Merry!"

Emmaline's call ricocheted off the water. I ignored the voices yelling from the boat and pumped my arms through the current. Always was a good swimmer, but the Mississippi was fast-moving. My chest groaned by the time my hand knocked into the side of our boat. I dragged myself over the side and flopped onto a middle seat.

In back, Emmaline was hunched on the floor, trembling. With all the energy I could muster, I reached out and pulled her closer to me. A spotlight blinded me as I groped for the oars along the bottom, my fingers finally encountering a smooth piece of wood sticking out. Energized, I grabbed it.

People shouted for us to stop from the deck of the steamboat. One female voice pleaded for me to turn myself in, like I was the one who'd been shooting up the Quarter. Chasing innocent little girls. People were hypocrites. No justice to be had in New Orleans for either of us.

I rowed our boat as fast as I could through the wake of the steamboat in our creep downriver. Lights flashed behind us, scouring our wake. If I applied myself, I might out-maneuver a steamboat, especially going with the current.

"Emmaline, stay close. Sit in front of me and hold on, okay?"

Without a word, she obeyed. Her wet hands gripped the edge of the bench, and her jaw was firm. Stubborn. She turned her face downriver and closed her eyes.

I jerked the oars and our craft picked up speed, drifting away from the crowded steamboat. In another lifetime, I'd run a boat in the dark. Clark and me, we'd help the men pole up the Missouri after sunset when we ran behind. I could still feel the water grab at the muscles of my back through the end of my pole. I thought I could do anything.

Lack of opportunity robs us of every skill eventually. I gritted my teeth and hoped I hadn't been away too long.

I dug into the water and tried to recall that place. Montana. Deserted. Unpredictable. The mournful cry of a coyote, off in the distant dark. I pushed New Orleans out of my mind and relaxed into my body's memory, the graceful motion of back and forth.

Adrenaline. It was always a good drug in a tight place. It made my hands sure as I yanked the oars. The noise of the party boat faded, replaced by the click of paddles and spray of water. The lights dimmed behind us. When I looked back, no Wilkinson stooges were on our tail. I stopped rowing and pumped one hand over my head.

"Woo-hoo! We lost them, Em! I haven't had this much fun in...well, a long time."

I waited for her smile but instead Emmaline tugged my sleeve and pointed upriver, her face lit by a faint blue glow. "Lights, Merry. Behind us." I studied them with her. "Police."

"It's one boat, looks like."

"Do you think they're looking for us?"

"Don't know."

Emmaline hugged herself, her eyes wide. "It's the Judge. I know it. He's going to catch us."

I turned the boat a sharp left, shifting our path toward the northern shoreline. Light poured into the river from concrete piers and docks, but I kept us just beyond its reach. We scrolled by ocean-going vessels and the metallic snarl of industry. Everywhere, a mechanical hum.

I needed a dark place, somewhere I could ditch the boat. Maybe tie it up or sink it to keep it from being found for a little while. Long enough for us to identify another means of getting up the Mississippi.

The police lights loomed larger. Commotion. Shouted commands. Static.

I turned my attention back to shore. An abandoned factory site floated into view, at least one warehouse behind a rusted chain link fence.

I worked the boat behind a ruin of a dock, weaving through its broken piers until we were close enough to shore for me to pull in the oars. I turned Em to face me, motioning with my free hand. "You see that concrete platform?"

"I see it." She fingered her stack of letters and chewed her lip.

"Good. That's where we're headed. If we get separated, can you swim?"

Emmaline nodded. Hesitant. Fearful, but willing. In my experience, willingness is usually the best part of bravery.

"Okay. You jump in ahead of me. Swim to that platform. Straight to it. I'll be right beside you. We're both going to make it in one piece."

She held out her father's letters. "What about these, Merry? They can't get wet."

I grabbed them from her and put them under my leather hat. Best I could do.

Emmaline took one deep breath and splashed into the river. I dove in after her. When I came up for air, she bobbed beside me. Arms like propellers, we cut through the current. She gasped and sputtered, but never sank. That little wisp of a girl fought her way to the concrete edge without any help from me.

My hand grazed slime. I grabbed the back of Em's dress and flung her, coughing, onto the platform. I lifted myself out of the river and stretched my shaky limbs out beside her. Numb, I vomited water from my lungs and listened to the night. Our abandoned craft nodded, still sheltered behind the broken pier. A scold. I should've tied it up to keep the current from dragging it to open water.

We wasted get-away time, lying there.

I rolled over and shook Emmaline's shoulder. She spewed a little of the river and lay on her back, staring up at the sky. Her pale face glowed in the waning moonlight. She shifted her eyes to me.

"When I was little, I used to crawl out on the roof with Daddy and look at the stars. These stars. Do you think he sees the same sky in Nashville, Merry?"

"I'm sure he does. It isn't that far."

A whisper. "Do you really think we'll find him?"

I sat up to block the sky, to make her look at me. Like the power behind her eyes could make me succeed. Could a scrap of girl redeem me? I touched her hand. "Em, we'll find him. I know it."

She scrabbled at my hat. "At least, we have his letters. They can tell us where he— aaaahhhh!" She keened. Shrill. Piercing.

The river wreaked watery havoc with the stack of paper. Bits of it had already torn away, and when she tugged at the red string, the ink bled in her hands. Stuck to her fingers, stained black with globs of ink where her father's words once were. Her face crumpled in disbelief as she covered it with her papery hands and sobbed. "You ruined Daddy's letters. You ruined them."

Sodden bits of paper swirled through my hands. The few scraps that stuck to my skin were blank. Erased. Just like my journal in this infernal place. How would we find her father now?

I dragged a hand over my face. Tried to think. What could I ever say to make her glad she ran?

"Em, I'm sorry. Look at me. I did the best I could, but we didn't have anything to keep them dry. My hat was our best shot."

"Now, we'll never be able to find him. We don't even know his address. You messed up everything." Her slender body heaved.

"Em, stop crying and look at me. Please."

She dragged her hands away from her face. Her eyes were almost swollen shut.

"I promise you, Em. We will find your daddy. Even without the letters, we'll find him. We know he's in Nashville, and we'll figure out the rest when we get there. Everything will be all right. Don't you worry."

"Maybe I shouldn't have run away from home, especially with somebody who can't even keep Daddy's letters safe. I—"

Blue lights strobed closer. Lit up the edge of our perch. "Em, we can't stay here any longer. I know you're tired and upset. I'm walloped, too. But we have to keep moving. That means getting out of New Orleans."

"But where can we hide?" She picked flecks of paper from her fingers. Squinted at their blankness and swatted them away.

"We have to get out of here. Now. If those guys are looking for us, they're going to realize we jumped ship. They'll swarm both sides of the river. We've got to get out of the open." I sat back to study our surroundings. "If we push upriver on land, we can get further, maybe in a way they won't expect. Find another boat to swipe."

Emmaline closed her eyes. A tear slid into her mouth. "I'm so tired, Merry. The Judge is never going to give up, and I think my mother will help him. He isn't used to not having his way. He will chase me until he finds me. Maybe even until I die.

"The Judge is not going to get you. Not as long as I'm around." I hugged her to me and willed her to believe.

In me.

"Now, stop all this claptrap and get a move on. There's an opening in the fence. Just there. We can both slip through and find another way out before they realize we've been here."

With one last glance at our boat, I pushed myself to stand and dragged Emmaline up beside me. The concrete platform gave way to an uneven shoreline strung with a ribbon of fence. Beyond a tear in chain link, an asphalt parking lot yawned toward four warehouse buildings. Their bulk sprawled all the way to the water.

I pushed Emmaline up the slick surface ahead of me and made sure she had a firm foothold before advancing another step. We shimmied through the fence and gained the parking lot inside the barrier. I pointed to the last warehouse. "There. See? A door. Looks like it's open. We need to make for it, Em."

"How?"

"Run across the lot. We'll be exposed, but it's dark here."

A voice crackled through a bull horn. It was distorted by distance and lapping water, but it meant one thing: the police found our boat. I nudged Emmaline. "Hurry, Em."

"But what if we can't find a boat with a motor? You can't row a boat all the way upriver. I may be a girl, but even I know the current is too strong."

Exasperated, I tugged her arm and started across the macadam. "Why does that matter?"

"Well, you said couldn't drive a car, so does that mean you can't drive a motorboat?"

Smart girl.

"Let's just say I'm better with boats. I understand them. I—"

"Sure. Right."

"You just leave that to me to figure out when we get there."

We huffed to the shadow of the warehouse in a couple of minutes. Light guided us to a door open just enough for us to slip through. I dragged it shut as another horn blew. Police lights floated into my sight lines, out on the water. A whoop split the air.

The door thudded like a marble slab on top of a tomb. Encased in gloom, I whispered, "They found our boat. We've got no time, Em. Let's move."

EMMALINE

When Merry pushed me into the warehouse, my lungs burned, and my eyes blurred. I slid through the crack in the sliding door and waited for my eyes to adjust to the darkness. The warehouse was one ginormous room. My voice talked back to me even when I whispered.

Merry shut the door, but I still saw blue lights in my mind. They were close, so close I could almost see that bulldog chin and smell cigar smoke. The Judge. He was out there, and I was trapped here with a man who destroyed my only connection to Daddy. How could he get me all the way to Nashville when he couldn't even keep Daddy's letters safe?

I felt with my hand for a place to hide. Sheets hovered over everything. I tugged a corner, and a whole piece pulled away in my hands.

A tall clown head with a pointy hat smiled down at me. Purple and green and gold sparkled everywhere. Bells tinkled from the ends of the clown's hat. Mardi Gras floats. I wanted to jump up on the platform and bat them with my hands. When I heard Merry's voice, I realized I had.

"Em, get down from there."

"But I remember this one. I saw it last year with Aunt Bertie. Ladies danced on it, and they threw candy and plastic beads but mostly candy, chocolate bars that were gooey inside, and I crawled in the street to get as many of them as I could, and—"

Merry's hands were firm under my arms when he lifted me off the float and set me on the ground. "I'm not negotiating with you, Em. Let's move."

A siren ripped the air outside. It made me jump, but Merry steadied me with his hand and steered me along a sheet-covered row. The warehouse was lit by two overhead lights, high up on the ceiling, making Mardi Gras float shadows on the floor and up the walls. I ran my fingers along the row, feeling plastic flowers and shiny streamers and round beads up close.

We wandered down an open path through more tall, sheet-covered blobs. The whole room smelled like the white stuff Aunt Bertie threw around the bottom of her roses and hand-mixed into the dirt. It cracked on her dark hands in rings.

Less than a night, and I missed Bertie so much. I closed my eyes. Would she hear me if I used my Wonder Twin power to tell her I loved her?

A shadow moved in front of us and planted its hands on its hips. "What're you doing here?" A deep voice. I screamed at the black hulk of man that stood in the walkway. He had to be a Saints football player, he was so big.

Merry picked me up, and I buried my face in his chest. The man shouted. "I said, what're you doing here?"

Merry shifted his feet and stood a little taller. "Working on our float for Mardi Gras?"

The man crossed his arms and sort of snarled. "Nice try. Wrong time of year."

"We're lost." Merry's voice shook a little when he fibbed.

"Well, consider yourself found. By the police. You come with me and wait while I call them."

I shrugged out of Merry's arms and stepped forward. "I'm looking for my—"

Merry got in front of me. "Well, you see. It's like this—"

"No. We just need to tell him about Daddy, Merry. He'll help us. I know it."

Merry's eyes got real wide, but he didn't shush me. I walked up to the muscley man. My neck ached when I looked all the way up to his eyes, but I knew that eye contact with a man was important. My mother always cleared her throat if I broke eye contact with one of her men, even when they looked at other parts of me. But this man's eyes held mine. "I ran away from home, because there's this bad man who's after me. I just need to get to my daddy. In Nashville. Merry found me and offered to take me there, even though he lost Daddy's letters."

He uncrossed his arms and squatted to help me see him better. I thought maybe it was a good sign, so I rushed on.

"The bad people are outside on the river, and we came in here to hide from them. We need to get away. If you call the police, they'll find me and give me to the bad man and I'll never, ever see my daddy again." I stepped closer to him. "Will you help us, Mister? Will you help me find my daddy?"

He scratched his bald-head and looked at Merry. "How do I know you aren't some kidnapper?"

I tugged at his pants leg. "I'm a little girl. Little girls are supposed to be afraid of kidnappers, but I'm not afraid of Merry. I told you. He's helping me find my daddy. Please *please*, help us."

He sucked in air until his cheeks were balloons and blew it out with a long pop, his eyes moving from Merry to me and back. When he talked again, I realized I was holding my breath. "Where you need to go?"

Merry stepped behind me and covered my shoulders with his hands. "Upriver. To Natchez, Mississippi."

He stood up, his massive hands on his hips. "What the hell you want to go there for? There's nothing in Natchez."

"Well. See, I think the Natchez Trace will be the safest way to get to Nashville. The folks after us will most likely focus on the river. But a forgotten roadway? I doubt they'll think to look for us there."

"I know the place you mean. Nothing there but ghosts." The man waved his beefy hand at the floats. "You like ghosts, little girl?"

"I don't know. I never met one."

He looked at the ceiling and laughed. His straight white teeth stood out against the rest of him. "Well, I reckon that's getting ready to change."

Merry took a couple of steps toward him. "Look—what's your name?"

"Jim. Jim Watson."

I couldn't hold my question anymore. "Are you a football player, Mister Jim?"

His eyes crinkled at the corners. "Nah. Never was much for all that. I'm retired. Used to run boats on the river. Now, what's your name?"

"I'm Emmaline, and this is Merry."

My hand was swallowed when he shook it. "I'm charmed, Miss Emmaline."

Merry put his hand on my head. "Jim, we need to get to Natchez. By water, if possible. Do you know anybody who might take us? Tonight?"

I watched his eyes and counted the seconds until he spoke. "I might be able to take you. Can you pay for the trip?"

Merry took some money from inside his coat, pulled out a few twenties and held them out to Mister Jim. He counted it, then stuffed it all in his shirt pocket.

I decided it was settled. "Will you take us? Right now, Mister Jim?"

The light flashed off his bald head when he nodded. "Maybe. Got a house-boat tied up out there. Past the last of the buildings yonder."

Merry held out his hand to shake Mister Jim's. "We can only travel at night."

"I don't want to know about it." He stopped and studied Merry's outstretched hand. "Let's just say I've done this sort of thing once before. Long time ago. Helped a boy run away from a bad papa. He turned out all right." Mister Jim grabbed Merry's hand and pumped it once. I put my palm on top of theirs to seal everything.

Almost like the Wonder Twins. They touched hands to become something else. We needed to become something else if we were going to get away from the Judge and his men.

Mister Jim pointed with his head. "Go that way. I'll get the lights and meet you at that door. Boat's through there. We'll have to walk a little ways."

"Follow me, Em." Merry picked our way through more Mardi Gras floats. More clowns. Dragons that spit fire. A woman with snakes for hair. Skeleton faces with big hats of flowers. A pirate with a patch over his eye.

I liked the pirate best, because he was like us. On the run. Hiding.

At the other end of the building, Mister Jim stood next to a switch. "Last one. I'll open the door. You go on out there and wait for me."

Merry nodded and led me through the slit in the door. It was darker than I remembered, cloudy again, and the wind was cold. Rain spattered onto the ground.

The door grinded shut and Mister Jim pointed toward the river. Next to the water, we found a ledge we could walk on. Merry picked me up and carried me to it. The river lapped against the sides as we stepped between it and another warehouse. Merry kept us close to the building as he inched along. Mister Jim's deep breathing followed us.

Around another corner, the path dead-ended at a broken fence and black water. Behind us, lights helicoptered over the river. I saw the muddy water and thought about swimming away. How far could I go? I strained my eyes at everything: the river and the shore. "Merry! Look!"

A twisty walkway floated below us. It snaked around the edge of the water between the warehouses and a marina, with lots and lots of boats.

Lights came close to Merry's head. I ran my hand around the edge of the building and pulled it back and shook it. "Around there, Merry. My hand hit something hard."

"It's a ladder, Em. It runs down to the walkway."

Mister Jim snickered. "I told you this was the way." He pushed past us and wrapped one leg around the corner of the building. When he got on top of a ladder, he reached out his hand to me. Lights lit up the wall next to where I stood. I stumbled a little, trying to get out of the way. "Come on, little lady. Climb on down with me. If you slip, I'll catch you."

A spotlight almost hit my toe when I slung it around the side of the building. I held my breath and waited for shouts from the water, for somebody to see me. Instead, the river lapped against the path. It masked our steps, maybe even helped us.

I put my feet on a slippery step and lowered myself to the dock, waiting for Merry to join Mister Jim and me. When the warmth from Merry's hand moved up my arm, his strength flowed into me. I followed Merry's fast steps and hoped the water and the sounds of the sirens would keep anyone from hearing us.

Mister Jim turned onto a ramp and climbed steps to another pier where the planks of wood snaked through boats: sailboats and motorboats and fancy boats. Which one was Mister Jim's?

He ran toward the end, leaving Merry and me to catch up, and jumped onto a houseboat, rattling the wood-and-glass doorway in front. He motioned for us to hop on board, and we followed him into the captain's wheel. A ladder went into a dark hole. I couldn't see below.

Merry panted when he spoke. "We can't risk turning on any lights, Jim. We don't need to draw attention."

"No problem. Been running this river in the dark as long as I can remember."

When Merry took my hand, it wasn't so scary to follow him down below. Everything sounded hollow inside the boat. Through a window, a smattering of stars winked above the water. No blue lights that far upriver.

"Merry, I think we tricked them."

"Maybe we did." He rubbed my head and pointed me toward a door. "There's probably a bed through there. You go on. Try to get some sleep. I'll keep Jim company until we get out of New Orleans."

He went up the ladder and left me to pull back the musty sheets and tuck myself in. I sank onto the hard mattress in my damp dress just as the boat's engine chugged to life. The reflection of the water made waves on the ceiling, and I wondered: what was the world like beyond New Orleans? I always dreamed of seeing other places, but would anywhere else ever feel like home? With its rowdy people. Its smell of mud and fertilizer. The perfume of Aunt Bertie's roses through the whirring blades of a fan.

If the Judge let us get out of New Orleans, I hoped I could come back someday. With Daddy.

THE JUDGE

I used to be a soldier. A military man. Leader of the whole American army. I served the first five Presidents of the United States, in some capacity or another. How many other men could say that?

Certainly not Meriwether Lewis. He sucked up to Jefferson and ignored the rest. Never understood the value of playing every political angle. We eke out success when we remain true to ourselves, whatever the cost to others.

I learned that early in my military career.

We had been marching all night. The Ohio River Valley, back in the 1790s.......well, it was wilderness. Trees crowded along the ground, too thick to walk through, all spangled with vines that choked out the sun. I didn't know what time it was when I smelled it, that first whiff of Death. It clogged up the air until I thought it would smite us all.

Seeing Death was worse.

We came upon the remains of another platoon. One of ours. I could still see ragged glimpses of the uniform in exposed bone and maggoty flesh. Heads void of scalps and mouths stuffed full of dirt.

The Natives were tenacious in defense of their land. And, it was theirs. We were the poachers, our true selves.

I vomited as I dragged mutilated body parts into a heap, especially when there was enough left to recognize someone. Would my Death be violent? I was young then, but I wondered. All the time.

When Death finally killed me, I remembered that scene from my youth. How the Natives fought to protect their turf. No act was unthinkable, no action undoable.

It's how I made Nowhere my home. My kingdom. My turf, the place where I could always find Ann again, if I was willing to do whatever it took to defend my space.

I looked sideways at Nadine Cagney, huddled in the passenger seat. Her fine nose and charcoal hair. Her chin trembled as she hugged her knees to her chest.

She perked up when I smiled. When I said I wouldn't take her to the station. We could go to my house instead.

EMMALINE

Sun hit my face, and I woke from a creepy sleep of bulldogs and running and water. When I rolled over, I knew it was all real, not a dream. I was on a houseboat, on the way to find my daddy, with Merry and a man named Mister Jim, who sort of looked like Aunt Bertie as a man.

I slid my feet to the floor. It shook with the hum of engines. The rocking of the boat made it hard to stand, but I moved my weight back and forth between my legs until I got used to it. Muddy air wafted through the open door at the top of the ladder. A bird floated through the square of sky.

I sniffed the air. Pe-ew. My filthy dirty dress just plain stunk. I had to find something else to wear.

Under the bunk beds, I found a clean white t-shirt, big enough for a grown-up. It hung to my knees when I put it on over my nasty dress. My mother would die if she saw me. Or smelled me. She never allowed me to look disheveled. Her word. At every moment, I was required to be pretty. To be ready for a visit from one of her men. When I looked down at myself, I realized I wasn't any man's little beauty anymore.

Especially not the Judge's. What did he mean when he said Merry killed his wife?

I called out his name, but it was lost in the hum of the engine and moving river. I opened and closed cabinets and turned on the water in the sink to see if it worked like the ones in real houses. The water that came out was river-brown. Yuck.

Still, my stomach rumbled, and I remembered I hadn't eaten since last night. Aunt Bertie brought a peanut butter and jelly sandwich up to my room. She even cut off the crusts and mixed the peanut butter and jelly together, just the way I liked it. Would anybody else ever know what I liked without me telling them? The world was a lonely place without anybody who knew me like Bertie. I could still see the look on her face—strength and caring. It followed me when I ran. I missed Bertie already. So much.

I blinked back tears and focused on another cabinet. Daddy would know what I liked. When I found him, he would know everything.

A plate. A plastic Mardi Gras cup. A string of green beads. Peanut butter. Yum. It was warm and sticky on my finger. I pretended it was an ice cream cone and licked layers with my tongue.

Behind the ladder, a door hid a shower and potty. I tugged a rusty chain and squealed when water fell all over my head. I ripped off all my clothes and stepped under the water. It soaked into my nooks and crannies and washed off my old life: my mother and tea with her men; the Judge and his fake smile; even Aunt Bertie and New Orleans. The water ran until my skin was red, and I figured I was clean. Still, I used a little bit of soap.

Just in case.

I studied my skin in the cloudy mirror above the sink, and I combed my hair with my fingers before it dried in knots. Dirt was crusted on my dress, but could I wear just the t-shirt? Would I still be me? The dress and the t-shirt were the Wonder Twins, hanging from the ends of my fingers.

The t-shirt was soft on my skin. I pulled it over my head and wadded up the dress. Before I threw it in a white trash bag next to the ladder, I stopped and pulled off a square of lace. Just a little bit of my old life. Still me, but different. New.

Sunlight made me squint at Mister Jim behind the wheel of the boat. His dark eyes looked bruised around the edges, but he smiled with big white teeth. "Thought you were going to sleep the morning away."

"Hi, Mister Jim. Where's Merry?"

"I'm right here, Em."

Merry stood in the pointy place at the front of the boat, his back to the wind, and watched Mister Jim steer the boat. Thick trees grew along the shore, all the way into the water. Mister Jim moved the boat into a spot behind an overgrown island near the shore. Everything went quiet, except for the slapping of water against the boat and the caw-caw of a black bird.

"Should be a good hiding place for the day. We'll cast off again at dusk." Mister Jim threw an anchor in the water. It splashed and made bubbles as it went down.

I pulled at the hem of my t-shirt, my mind racing with things to say. It was hard to believe all that had happened to me in one day. All the dreams about Daddy, and I really was on my way to find him. Even though we didn't have his letters, my heart knew where he was. It beat to bursting every time I thought about him.

Still, I couldn't erase the sound of my mother's voice, begging not to be hurt. I missed my mother. I didn't expect to miss her when I ran.

Embarrassed by the tears in my eyes, I turned away to study the black-ish water. The Mississippi always smelled funny around New Orleans, an oily smell. Away from the city, its brown surface was most of what I could see in every direction. Tree covered islands stuck up out of the water here and there, and the air smelled like dirt and leaves.

Merry's hand warmed up my shoulder. "We're still a night and a day from Natchez, by my calculations. If there's anything to eat down below, we won't have to stop." Laughter tinkled in his voice. "But, you can always do some fishing for your dinner.

The sun made a halo around his head, and I squinted up at him. "Fishing? Me?"

Mister Jim hooted, a deep bass like one of Daddy's band mates. "Got plenty of rods. Enough for all of us."

Merry's lips twitched. "There's nothing like slinging a line in the water, watching it disappear all blank-like and coming up with a squirming, scaly hunk of dinner. Between all of us, we could likely gut eight or ten fishes in thirty minutes, tops."

A yucky taste came up in the back of my throat. They were murderers, both of them. I crossed my arms and ground my feet into the sun-bleached deck. "I'm not killing a fish to eat. Yuck."

It was Mister Jim who taunted me. "Suit yourself. You can probably rustle up some berries or swamp weed to gnaw on. Just make sure it's not poisonous."

"How will I know whether something is poisonous or not, Mister Jim?"

Merry smiled. "Well, the poisonous stuff does give you the runs, and—"

"Ew!" I plugged my ears. Maybe I wasn't cut out to be a Wonder Twin tomboy, after all. I didn't want to kill my dinner or worry about which plant was poisonous. My voice rang between my fingers, like I was talking underwater. "What's wrong with going to the grocery store for food, huh?"

Merry picked up a pair of binoculars from the console and ran them over the skyline. "Not seeing any grocery stores out there, Em. Nope. Nary a one. It's a big fat nothing. What do you think people did before they could buy food at the store?"

I swatted a bug away from my face. "They killed it and ate it. That's what my history book says. But that was a million years ago, when they had to. We don't do it that way anymore. Because there are grocery stores. And McDonalds."

Merry and Mister Jim exchanged a look I didn't understand, and Mister Jim's voice was serious.

"Something about those folks before, though. They caught it themselves. They killed it themselves. They skinned it themselves. And they grew it themselves. Not a bad skill to have, scrounging your own vittles. You can always take care of yourself, wherever you're stranded."

I stomped my foot on the top of the ladder. "Well. I know I can find our not-breathing, not-swimming, not-poisonous breakfast from a not-scary box."

I huffed down the ladder into the broken light below, their laughter chasing me with each rung. Stupid men. Making fun of me. I'd show them

I could find something good to eat.

In the cooler, I found some milk. Cans toppled out of a cabinet and pinged around the floor, but I forgot to pick them up when I saw the box of Boo-Berry Cereal. My very favorite.

I pulled out the cereal and three glasses. Cereal always tasted best in a glass, not a bowl. I could pour more milk on it and drink the sugary purple liquid at the end. Plus, I didn't need a spoon to eat the cereal. It was what Aunt Bertie called "efficient."

Boo-Berry mounded in my glass all the way to the rim, because I loved it most. I triangled all three glasses in my hands and wobbled back up the ladder.

"Your breakfast." I gave them each a blue-ish glass.

"What is this stuff?" Merry closed one eye and stared at it with a doubtful expression.

"It's Boo-Berry, my favorite cereal in the whole world."

Mister Jim tipped the glass into his mouth. "Yeah. I love the ghost, too. My one weakness in life is a kiddie cereal."

Merry rolled his eyes. "I'm sure that's not true."

"All the same, don't tell anybody."

Merry dumped his glass into the river. "I can't believe you two would rather eat this sugary slop over a fresh piece of fish."

"It's good." Mister Jim and I said it together.

"My tongue is already turning blue. See?" I stuck out my tongue and crossed my eyes trying to see if it really was, but I couldn't tell.

"Jim, maybe we can get her to try some just-caught fish for dinner."

Cereal crunched in Mister Jim's mouth. "Poles are in that compartment, if you want to get started."

Merry looked back and forth over the top of the water. He started to reach for the place Mister Jim showed him, but instead he walked up to me. His tone was weird. "Um. Emmaline?"

"Uh-huh?" I crunched through my reply.

"We're going to find your daddy. You don't have to worry, all right?"

My eyes got all swimmy again, and I looked away to keep them from seeing. Since Daddy, I'd never met men who were so nice to me. At least, not without wanting to watch me serve them tea with my dress unbuttoned.

Another sound rippled across the water. A boat. It was going slow, like it was looking for something.

For me.

It was looking for me. It had to be. It turned and puttered our way. My glass crashed to the floor, splattering blue milk all over my legs.

"Get down below. Both of you." Mister Jim took a fishing rod from Merry and shooed us down the ladder. "You hide down there and don't come back 'til I say."

Sugar stuck my legs together when I snuggled up next to Merry on one of the beds. Merry hugged me to his side. I tried not to breathe loud, but my heart hurt my ribs from beating so fast. "I'm scared, Merry. Why would the Judge come this far?"

"This may have nothing to do with him. Just be still and stay quiet."

"But how did you know him? The Judge said he knew you, but—"

"Ssh. Not now."

A motor powered up beside us, and a smoky voice called out a greeting to Mister Jim. I listened as best I could over the splashing of water as our boat rocked from side to side.

"You all alone?"

Mister Jim grunted. "Yep. Don't like company when I fish."

"That's an awful big boat for one person."

"I like space. Obviously."

"Uh-huh. Well, you seen any other boats out today? Coming from New Orleans way?"

Mister Jim paused, and I held my breath. I counted ten bounces on waves before he spoke again. "A few. Natural on one of the busiest rivers in the country."

"Specifically, I'm looking for one with special cargo. A man and a little girl. Blonde. Almost ten. Wearing a blue dress."

Mister Jim splashed the rod into the water. It clinked along the side of the boat. It sounded like someone was knocking underwater. I held my breath and waited for Mister Jim's answer, but everything was lapping waves and birdsong. I squirmed against Merry, but he held me next to him and wouldn't let me move. I almost cheered when I heard Mister Jim's voice again.

"Like I said. Don't like company when I fish."

"So, you haven't seen anyone of that description?"

"Only seen you. All morning."

A shadow passed our grimy window, and I squirmed on the bed, trying to get free of Merry and close the curtain. He grabbed the hem of my t-shirt and held me close, and I buried my face in his chest to keep from seeing the man's eyes. His shadow rose and fell outside, right in front of the window. Blue and white and black pants. Any second, that man was going to shout that he saw us and come on board and take me away from Merry. Force me back to New Orleans and the sounds of my mother's house.

Make me be with the Judge forever.

MERRY

Wednesday. October 5, 1977. Somewhere along the Mississippi River, above New Orleans, Louisiana.

I held Emmaline next to me. Completely still. The man's cold eyes grazed over the dirt and spray on the window before he stood up and floated on. Thanked Jim for the chat and offered him a telephone number on a card.

Jim took it.

The boat creaked, and I imagined Jim leaning over the side, considering the number. Water dripped in the sink. I counted to twenty before Jim spoke again.

"This little girl. She in trouble?"

"She ran away from home, Sir, and her mother is desperate to locate her."

Emmaline squirmed beside me. As soon as she opened her mouth, I clamped my hand over it. Put a finger over my lips. Her cornflower eyes were etched with fear.

Still, Jim didn't betray us.

The boat motor sputtered, and the boat rocked in its wake as it motored away. Its hum faded, but I kept Em glued next to me until I couldn't hear it anymore. Steps sounded on the ladder, and Jim ducked through the doorway.

"All right. What have y'all gone and done?"

Emmaline bounced out of my arms and was in front of Jim before I could get a word out. "He was lying, Mister Jim. It's the Judge who wants me, not my mother!"

Jim crossed his arms over his burly chest. "Most mammas I know would miss their little girls if they ran away from home. If you've gotten me involved in something messy—"

"Mister Jim, I *promise*, cross-my-heart-and-hope-to-die. My mother only loved what I could do for her. She never loved me, not like Daddy did. That's why I've *got* to find him."

Jim cut his eyes at me. "She always this persistent?"

"Yep. Always."

I stood up, my mind spinning with alternate plans for escape, while she rocked her head back and forth between us. "What's 'persistent'?"

"I think it's the definition of your name, Em."

Jim smiled a little, but his chin was still rigid, his arms stiff. It never made it to his eyes. "Come on back up. Got a fish on the line during all that." He stomped up the ladder, sweat glistening on the muscles of his back.

I trotted back into morning. Em wrinkled her nose and followed.

Able hands that kill. They're good things to have. Would I have to use them if Jim turned on us?

I watched him from the corner of my eye. Staccato movements laced with anger, or maybe doubt. I didn't know how to reassure him. It was easier to focus on fishing. Something I knew how to do. I was always better with animals. People were tricky.

It took me five minutes of casting to snare a catfish. I looked into its eyes before I thwacked the whiskered head along the side of the boat. When I skinned it, I freed two long strips of white meat, still wiggling.

Em took one look and screeched like an Injun. Practically fell down into the hold and slammed a door. Her muffled protests wafted up the ladder, but when I went down, her door was locked, and she was quiet.

Just to spite her, I fried up our meal on the electric ring in the galley. Not the same as a campfire. Nothing tasted better than when it was seared with flame. I remembered the sizzle of trout and fire under the infinite Montana sky. Somebody strummed a guitar, and we dug into that tender meat. It tasted clean. One of our last good meals before winter made everything scarce.

I still missed Clark sometimes. Still wondered about the rest of them.

I rubbed my face with one hand to dispel ghosts. Maybe we'd have a campfire tomorrow. Or the next day.

I fanned the smell toward Em's closed door and chanted *smells so good*. With my ear against it, I couldn't hear a sound. I left her alone and went above deck with two plates. We watched the sun move behind scattered clouds. It would be hours until dark, until we could move again.

"We in pretty good shape here, I think." Jim licked fish from his fingers.

"Jim, I'm really sorry we dragged you into this whole thing."

"Merry—your name really is Merry, right?"

"It's my nickname, yes. Only name I use these days."

"Well, Merry. I don't do anything I don't want to do. Only wish you'd been straight up with me."

"I know this makes me look bad, but I swear, the people after Em are dangerous. They tried to shoot me, and Lord knows what they would do to her. I should've explained it all at the beginning, but, with you threatening to call the police and all, there really wasn't time."

He chewed. Avoided my eyes. "Nothing for it now but to get you two to Natchez."

My lips were a gloss of salty cornmeal and grease. I savored the sweet flavor of the fish on my tongue and studied a craft passing slow on the river. It moved along upstream but didn't pause. I watched until it slipped around a bend.

"I know just where to drop you in Natchez. You can get to town easy."

Jim leaned back on his elbows and studied the sky. His chocolate face was smooth, but age was tricky with some people. Like me.

I wondered how he knew the Mississippi so well. Was it a recent thing, his world of water? Or, had he been running it his whole life?

Turns out, it was the latter. As a boy, Jim built rafts out of sticks, lashed together with twine, he said. A craft I understood. My fingers itched to pull into some cove, to build with him. Later on, his knowledge of the shoals of the river landed him a job with a shipping company. He worked the river from Memphis to the delta. Started his own business and sold it several years before. The muscles in his chest expanded when he talked about living the American Dream. I thought I was the explorer, the personification of the American Dream. Compared to him, my story had to be secondary. A fragment. I couldn't believe anybody would care about it anymore.

He finished his biography. Shifted his weight on his elbows and looked at me. "So, you got one?"

"What?"

"A story?"

It wasn't that I didn't have a story. I had quite a life before Nowhere. A fine life, until it unraveled at the end. The trick with stories was how to seed them with flecks of truth without revealing anything. Knowing which bits to tell, what parts to conceal. I cleared my throat. My story was boring. The military. Some aimless wandering out West. Desk job in St. Louis for a while. Not nearly as interesting as his.

Or, maybe I projected how I knew history must see me.

Jim's eyes bored through me. Plumbed the depths of a life lived deeper than I let on.

I tipped my head back and studied the sky to avoid his stare. "It's going to be a long night. Mind if I take a nap?"

"I was thinking of taking one myself."

We left the boat anchored and stretched our limbs along the warm deck, and I covered my face with my hat. Some sleep would do us both good.

It was a creak that woke me. The boat moved in a gentle rhythm. Not fast. I blinked to clear the sleep from my eyes, because I couldn't see the shoreline, or even the front of the boat. When I was fully awake, I realized it wasn't bleary eyes. The sky was a white-out, a breath that ducked and swirled. An eerie light penetrated through the mist here and there.

Fog, smoky and rolling.

I felt along the side and stuck my head into the hold. Emmaline's door was still closed. Dinner dishes were strung around the kitchen where I'd left them. In the cockpit, I checked the time on the console. 6:22 PM. That much dead sleep would have to be enough.

I groped along the side of the boat, bumping into Jim on the way. The fog swirled over his skin, turning it lighter. He rubbed the nap from his eyes and blinked at me. Stirred. His muscles crippled with sleep.

When I leaned over to look at the river, fog was all I could see.

"Merry? Where are you?" Emmaline's hoarse voice drifted from the cockpit doorway. Her outline materialized when I approached.

"I'm right here, Em."

"I can't see anything."

Jim got up and lumbered to the controls, while I went over to Em and put an arm around her slight shoulders. She rested her tangled head on my waist. Her voice was raspy with exhaustion. "Did you eat all the fish?"

I had to smile, in spite of our circumstances. "Naw. I left you a little piece."

"Where?"

"In the cooler. Go on down and get it out, and I'll heat it up for you."

She put one dainty foot backwards on the top rung of the ladder and almost fell when a horn blasted through the shroud of air. Close. The approaching roar of multiple engines crescendoed along the surface of the water.

Em teetered, and I pulled her off the ladder and set her on the deck beside me. Her thin arms went around my waist, and her eyes were wide awake when she looked at me. She settled into me, and I accepted her weight. Like I imagined a father cared for his daughter. I'd never know. But I tried.

I slammed into the cockpit and studied the bank of instruments, alien things to a man like me. I knew how to use the sun and stars. New-fangled technology whipped me. Jim worked a knob with sausage fingers, and I watched him, helpless.

"Any of those things tell them we're here?"

"The radio, but it's a crapshoot to divine which frequency."

A horn sounded again, the strength of it vibrating our wooden deck.

"Can they see us, Merry?" Emmaline stood next to me. I never felt her slip her hand in mine, but I gripped it anyway. Empty reassurance: it was better than nothing from a leader, especially if it was swathed in a dose of honesty. My best, my only, answer.

Shouting wouldn't work—no one would hear us over the drone of engines and parting water. Sounds trapped in a blanket of white that played tricks on me.

"Get below, Em. Jim, you got any kind of raft or life jackets? Something that will keep us afloat if we get hit?"

"Yep. Someplace in back. Go have a look, Emmaline."

At least four separate engines rumbled through the mist, right on top of us. The wheel of our craft throbbed in Jim's hands. Tobacco smoke and engine oil drifted through the air. Somebody shouted, and laughter answered, almost close enough to make out conversation. Individual voices.

Emmaline tugged at my sleeve. "Nothing below, except this." She held a blown-up ring, pink on one side and clear on the other.

I looked at Jim. "Seriously? That's all you have? No life jackets?"

Jim shook his hairless head.

A child's doughnut wouldn't save us if we got hit. If the boat sank, we'd never be able to share that flimsy thing and float long enough to find the shore. I imagined the three of us, snared on a tree branch, clinging to a toy. What a ridiculous sight we would be to whoever found us.

If anyone found us.

The boat lurched. Violent. Em grabbed onto me, while I wrapped one arm around the console and sunk to the floor. Jim kept to the wheel, his big hands fighting through the commotion. I locked my arm around Emmaline, just as the boat rolled sideways. We hung there, frozen above the river. Waiting for impact. Jim bent his knees into the waves, and I slid along the flooring and rammed into the side, my beat-up body between it and Emmaline.

Our craft righted itself and surfed the barge's wake, tossing us around the floor. With another intense shift, I lost my grip and was sucked over the side. My feet toyed with the river, and I bit my tongue and gripped the railing. The barge drowned Em's scream.

My body swung like a pendulum above the churning water. On the uptake, I wedged one foot over the edge and hung there until Jim's hands steadied my foot. With traction, I was able to hoist up my other leg. When the boat leaned the other way, I fell into the cockpit beside him and Em.

I held Em to me while the boat continued to thrash. Glass rattled, and my teeth gnashed in my head. After a minute, the boat calmed down, and everything quieted. The water fell still. My breathing matched both Em and Jim, fast and spooked.

She pulled her head away from my stomach and looked up at me. "Are we okay, Merry? Did we make it?"

"Yep. We sure did. This time. That was some boat work, Jim."

He nodded and blew out air. "A miracle is what it was."

I watched as the fog swirled and parted to reveal a glimpse of water. Within the hour, it would be clear enough to use a compass and head upstream. Jim took his place behind the wheel. "Fog's lifting a little. Let me check things out before we move along."

"Do you think that boat was looking for me, Mister Jim?"

"Can't say, Em. Whether it was or no, I got to get you off this river before sunup tomorrow."

"Where will we be when we get there, Merry?"

"Natchez, Mississippi."

I shuddered, an involuntary reaction. I wasn't ready to walk through its gateway. To cover the miles that would carry me across my grave.

Not yet.

Perhaps not ever.

THE JUDGE

I tried to kill Lewis. He never knew.

Maybe that's because I always led others to carry out my desires. My evil deeds. Life was for preserving my name. For getting ahead. My reputation was on the line.

A double agent had to be cognizant of the stakes. Head of the United States Army. A spy for Spain as Agent Thirteen. Sometimes, I forgot the rules in my zeal to stroke every master.

When the Spanish army rode into the plains, they reminded me. I told them to intercept Lewis and Clark. Arrest them. Not kill them. But, the Spanish, they made my instructions the same thing. Sent three separate search parties into the Missouri watershed, trying to find Jefferson's great Corps of Discovery. All because I told them to.

Even as I sent bird claws and rocks to the President—stupid gee-gaws for an idiot man—I instructed the Spanish to annihilate his dream.

I wrote Meriwether Lewis's death sentence. In Spanish maps and cipher letters.

If the Spanish army had christened me head of a search party, I would've found him. Oh yes. And, I would've stood on the sidelines while they slaugh-

tered my nemesis.

I would've kept my job as governor of Upper Louisiana.

And my Ann wouldn't have died.

Nowhere gave me another chance to murder. At least, this time. I couldn't remember what came before.

Different, killing someone when they're already dead. I could give Lewis an unwanted immortality. My nerves pulsed with the chance to claim it.

For Ann and for me.

MERRY

Thursday. October 6, 1977. Outside Natchez, Mississippi.

A ragged, chalky cliff jutted out of the river on our starboard side. Dust to match my rotting memories. I knew where Natchez led: to the place that destroyed my life. A cabin in the middle of nowhere. An act that led me Nowhere.

I couldn't remember my time in Nowhere. It was all just random words and phrases, scribbled on the worn pages of a journal. Images I couldn't piece together. I never knew what I did. Who I'd been. Where I tried to make a difference. Every Nowhere outing was completely new. Things and places seemed familiar sometimes. I didn't even know why I bothered to record what happened. It was always stripped clean in the end. A blank journal and an inept man.

Journaling was a compulsion from life. I couldn't shake it. When I buried my journal under my mattress or pushed it over the edge of the boat and watched it bubble to the bottom of the river, I still woke up with it underneath my palm the next morning.

The engine coughed, and Jim stuck his head out of the cockpit. He pointed to the bluff. Natchez. Dead ahead.

This was one way to greet a sunrise. Light streaked over the bluffs. Burned my eyes. Hours of no sleep, leaning off the bow of the boat to help Jim navigate in the dark: the night did a job on me.

Emmaline watched a white gull fish off the front of the boat. When she wasn't scratching an angry sunburn, she giggled and waved with the freedom of a true child. I made a mental note to keep her sensitive skin covered for the rest of the trip. A serious case of sun poisoning could slow our progress a precious day or two. I called her to me, and she scurried to my side, her fingers scratching at her seared shoulder.

Her skin radiated heat against a white t-shirt, something Jim had in a corner of the boat, and her hair was a snarl down her back. She looked a sight, but it would have to do until I could get her something else. Jim turned the wheel toward shore, and I kneeled beside her. "See that spot? Jutting out in the river, just beyond the bridge?"

Her eyes followed my finger. "I see it."

"There's a ramp. Jim is going to drop us there, and we can head into town."

"Can we get something to eat first? At McDonald's? They must have one. Every place does."

"First things, Em. We've got to get you some decent clothes and find some scissors to cut all that hair."

She balled up her fists and wrapped her arms around her head. Fiery eyes poked through the crack betwixt her arms. Jim's laugh vibrated in his throat.

"You're NOT cutting my hair, Merry. No way." Emmaline grabbed up her tangled hair and stuffed it under her arms and down her shirt collar.

"Believe me. You don't want to be running a trail in the woods with all that mess."

Her red face grew even redder. "It's not a mess. It's NOT."

"Sorry. Sorry. Didn't mean to offend, Em."

"I'll find some rubber bands and keep it up. Pink. Or lavender." She grabbed at her hair and demonstrated a fat ponytail, but her hands were too small to hold it all. The longer she tried to keep it back, the more it blew around her face. In frustration, she spit a wad of it out of her mouth and stared at me, defiant.

Jim rolled his eyes and turned the wheel toward shore. Glad to have the easier task.

I sat beside her, Indian-style. Put myself in line with the stubborn set of her jaw. It wasn't just about hiking in the woods. She needed to look different. Putting her hair up wouldn't be enough. Somebody could see her. Call her mother and tell her where we were. And we always had to be careful of Wilkinson. The Judge.

She jumped in before I could finish. "How do you know the Judge, Merry?"

It was the question she couldn't forget. I knew it. Still, it caught me unawares.

White caps churned off the side of the boat as I remembered the first time I met James Wilkinson. His ready smile. The puff of his cigar when I shook his hand. Connection. He was Clark's superior in the Army. An example. I looked up to him.

It wasn't easy to accept how much I liked the man. At first, anyway. Until he undermined me in my job and revealed his duplicitous nature. That was his way: gain the trust of his target, and obliterate him. He did it, time and again, to become commander of the United States Army. Plowed through soldiers who were better than he was and took positions that should've belonged to greater men.

Why did my final assignment in Nowhere have to be mixed up with him?

I avoided her eyes when I answered. "I used to know him. A long time ago."

"How did you meet?"

"In the army, the first time."

Her eyes grew wide. "Did you kill people in Vietnam? I saw things about it on TV when I was little."

"I did my time before that war, so no. But I lost track of him for a while after I got out. I had a big job out west, and I was gone for over two years."

"What were you doing?"

"Exploring. Scientific research. When I got back, somebody gave me the Judge's job, because he wasn't suited for it."

"You were a judge, too?" She wrinkled her nose and took a step back, like being a judge was a disease. The way Wilkinson did it, I suppose it was.

"No. I was—I had a different position in government."

"And you got him fired?"

"Not on purpose, no. But, he always blamed me. Hated me, in fact."

"Does he hate you because you killed his wife?"

I flicked my eyes to Jim, but his hands were steady on the controls.

"I didn't kill his wife, Em."

"Why did he say you did?"

"I don't know. I met her a couple of times. Unforgettable woman. Even in straitened circumstances, she had a regal demeanor that forced every eye to follow her around a room. Not beauty, but........what's the word I'm looking for? Magnetism. She drew people in."

I looked out over the whipped-up river, and I saw her again. The last time. Wilkinson helped her onto a ship bound for Natchez. He had been reassigned to a different position. I only heard later that she had tuberculosis. She died on a plantation in Mississippi.

How was her death my fault?

Emmaline's touch feathered the back of my hand. "Merry, what's the matter?"

"What? Oh, it's nothing. I was just trying to work out why Wilkinson would believe I killed his wife. The truth is a convenient thing for a man like him. He twists it to justify everything he does. And now that I have you with me, he will use his every connection to find you."

"But we're, like, thousands of miles away from home. How can the Judge know people all the way up here?"

My knees popped when I pushed to my feet. I had little experience with children, almost none with girls. I ran my fingers along my scalp and sighed before turning around to face her. "New Orleans is probably two hours by car, Em. That's not very far for a powerful man who's been around a long time. Wilkinson has connections."

"How do you know that?"

"I know because I know, all right?"

"But—"

I clung to her hand. Forced her wandering attention back to the threat of Wilkinson. "Look. People are funny, especially where lost little girls are concerned. We already know one man is looking for you, and we don't know how many people he's talked to. There's no telling what somebody might do if they recognized you. All I know is I don't want you to see the Judge again. He would take you away. And that would be the end of your seeing your father. Don't jeopardize everything over a haircut."

She put one hand on her hip and gave me a skeptical squint. "Do you really think somebody in Natchez would know me by my hair?"

Jim swiveled around to look at her. "People remember pretty, Emma-line."

Underneath the sunburn, I could see her blush, and I used the opportunity to strike. "See? We've had no news for two nights and a day. We've been listening off-and-on to the radio. So far, there's been nothing about you, about us. We can't know about pictures in the newspaper or stories on the local news, not to mention the whereabouts of the man in the boat yesterday. Do you want to take the chance that somebody might recognize you? Turn us in?"

The motor sputtered. When I looked over Jim's shoulder, the needle on the gauge bounced below E. We had fumes to get us to the ramp. It was still a stretch to swim, but we were almost under the bridge. Jim kept his hands steady on the wheel. I wished I knew how to drive. I preferred negotiating with a dying boat to a nine-year-old girl.

She held a frayed chunk of hair. "If we cut it to my shoulders—like this much—would I look the same? Not like a boy? I could still pull it up when I had to, but it wouldn't be so ratty." She fought with the whole shambles and eyed her reflection in the window, to see what she might look like with shorter hair.

I paced to the front of the boat and back. Was the whole trek to Nashville going to be like this?

"Okay. I won't make you look like a boy. But, I'm going to buy you a couple of sturdy pairs of boy's blue jeans, the ones with reinforced knees, along with two or three long-sleeved shirts and a pair of sensible shoes for hiking."

"And pink rubber bands."

"Goddammit, Em." I took a deep breath and massaged my temples, while her jaw resumed its belligerent mask. We stared each other down while I gritted my teeth. In the end, she wore me out. "Fine. Yes. Pink rubber bands. If we can find some. Don't get carried away. You've got to tote your own gear."

She threw her arms up over her head and jumped around the deck. The thrill of victory.

Before her mood shifted, I went below and found some scissors in a drawer in the galley. They were dull, but they would have to do.

I worked the shears through the air while she danced down the ladder. She wiggled and scratched her sunburn the whole time I cut off hunks of her hair. When I was done, she sported an uneven bob, just above her shoulders, and it was curlier than ever. She closed her hands around it. "See? I can still make a ponytail, Merry. Just barely. I can't wait to have pink rubber bands."

I sighed and followed her back into the early morning sunshine. Together we threw her shorn hair over the side and watched it splay over the water, a mermaid princess swimming with the current. "Goodbye, hair." Emmaline laughed. She'd borne it with good spirit. I watched it float downstream, praying the loss of her hair would not equal the end of a little girl's magical, child-like wonder.

Not yet.

The water was still as Jim steered the boat close to the ramp. A row of abandoned buildings appeared above the incline. Jim jerked his head toward land. To our spot.

The boat sputtered again, but Jim got us close enough to lasso a wet line around a pile and tie a good knot. I grabbed a fishing pole and lowered it into the water, a crude depth gauge. It hit bottom after half its length went under. "Go grab your Sunday shoes and put them on, Em. They'll do until we can get to town. You can't go barefoot."

"But they're squishy. They make my feet feel weird."

"It's only until we can buy you something else. Now go."

She took her time going below. When she came back, she carried the shoes in one hand, her arm straight out from her body like they disgusted her. With a grunt, she sat on the floor and pulled them on, one at a time, without unbuckling them. When Jim cut the motor, the deep rumble of river life filled the silence. Toads. Tree frogs. Crickets.

Done with her shoes, Emmaline looped her arm through mine. I walked over to Jim and shook his hand. "Thanks for bringing us here."

Jim squatted in front of Em. In a beefy hand, he held a faded cap. He adjusted the plastic tabs in back and put it on her head.

Emmaline threw her arms around his thick waist and squeezed. "Thank you, Mister Jim. I'll never forget you."

"I won't forget you, Miss Emmaline. Not in the whole of my life."

When she broke free, I held my arms out, ignoring the fear on her face. "Climb into my arms. I'm going to carry you to shore. We'll wade a few yards, and I want you to hold on tight."

Cold water dragged my jeans when we splashed into the river. I gripped Em close and we quick-stepped toward the slick hump of concrete twenty yards ahead, slipping through muck on the river bottom. My boots squished onto the ramp, and I put Em down beside me.

Jim waved from the deck of the boat. "You be lucky."

"You be lucky, too, Mister Jim." Emmaline wagged her hand in the air.

I took her palm in mine. "Let's go find some pink rubber bands, Emmaline Cagney."

MERRY

Main Street. Natchez, Mississippi. A forgotten place in 1977. Just what I was hoping for. Dingy and empty, it was occupied by people too worn down by life to notice folks like me.

The few people we passed on the sidewalk stopped and stared at Emmaline, though. Who wouldn't take note of a child in a t-shirt and Sunday shoes, a baseball cap swallowing her head? I put my arm around her shoulders and scoped the street for any place that might sell what we needed.

In the next block, I pushed through a glass door.

"Gladstone's Department Store." Emmaline sounded out the words. "My mother used to buy my dresses at a place like this, Merry."

"Ssh, Em. Don't talk about that right now."

"Can I help you?"

An old man reclined on a glass case and gawked at Emmaline. Fine threads of hair swirled under the edges of Jim's cap. It was twice the size of her head. "Can I help you, Son?"

Son. He said it with a knowing emphasis that unnerved me.

When he said it again, I realized he was talking to me.

I opened my mouth. Told him we needed a few things. Some denims with reinforced knees, along with sturdy shoes and socks. A couple of long sleeved shirts. And the last thing on my list. "You got any camping equipment?"

He jerked his thumb. "In back. Know what size the boy needs? Looks like he's an eight to me."

"That's right. An eight."

While he went to find the clothes, I guided Em toward the camping supplies. "Don't say anything, and I mean *anything*, to that man, Em. You let me do the talking."

"But—"

"No buts. You stand right there while I grab what we need."

She whirled her arms from side to side. "Can we get the purple tent?"

"What?"

"The purple one. Right here." She picked up a box with the word 'Barbie' splattered across the front.

"No, Em. That's nothing but a toy. Now, *this* is a tent we can use in the woods." I shouldered a mud brown one that would blend in with the landscape. "Here. You carry these two sleeping bags, and I'll get the other stuff."

Her eyes were wide. "This already looks like too much to carry."

I waved two packs at her, one adult and the other her size. "We can fit everything in these. The tent will strap to the back of mine, and the sleeping bags will go on the bottom. See?"

Matches. A flashlight. A first-aid kit. All went in my bag. When I picked up a cooking ring with a small tank, Emmaline whispered something, panicked.

"What's that, Em?"

"When we're in the woods, where will I go to the bathroom?"

Terror etched the edges of her drawn face. I bit the inside of my cheek to keep from laughing. "Well, you can go any place you like. At the side of the trail. In a ditch. Behind a tree. Even on a rock. Shouldn't be too many snakes this time of year."

She dropped the sleeping bags on the floor and screeched, "Snakes!"

Before she could make any more noise, I shelved my supplies and pulled her to me. Her breath was ragged, and her whole body trembled. I cradled her chin and made her look into my eyes. "Em. I'm sorry. I didn't mean to scare you like that."

"I don't like snakes."

"I don't like them, either." I stroked her cheek and waited for her breath to slow. "Look, we'll be roughing it for the next few days. No way around it. It's going to be hard. I can't promise it won't be tough, that your feet won't hurt, that you won't get blisters on your hands or bites on your legs, but it will be an adventure. A new experience. Discovery."

"And, at the end, we'll find Daddy."

I kept my gaze steady and willed myself to believe. "Yes. Remember that. The end always makes the hardship worth it."

Her voice climbed higher. "But how will we find him? We can't go up to every house and knock on every door. Maybe he's not even there anymore." Her bottom lip trembled. "This whole idea was dumb and stupid. I'm never going to get to Daddy. I can't believe you ruined his letters, Merry. We will never, ever, *ever* find Daddy now, not before the Judge catches me and takes me away and hurts me and—"

I raised my voice a little to stave off her meltdown. It was all I could think to do. "Em, listen. Do you still have that two dollars I gave you?"

She drew in a breath and took off her cap. Tugged a wadded ball out of her hair. She held it out to me. I ran it through my fingers to straighten it. "Thanks. We're going to use it to pay for our supplies."

"But you gave it to me. It's our pact. You said." She crossed her arms, and her jawline was like marble.

My eyes lit around the store for an idea, anything to satisfy her. My eureka was a jar of pens, next to a cash register. Still holding her, I walked over and picked one up.

"Here. Take this pen and write a message on that two dollar bill. A note to your daddy. We'll spend it, and when we get to Nashville, he'll be waiting for us."

"Really? Money works that way? Like magic?"

"Yes, Em. I think it could." I had no idea, but as I watched her relax and accept it, I wanted it to be true.

Emmaline flattened the two dollars on the counter. Gentle-like. She chewed the purple cap and considered the blank surface.

"What should I write?"

Tricky question. I didn't know the answer. I bit my lip and waited for her to write something on her own.

"Merry, where will we end up in Nashville? When we get there?"

"The end of the Natchez Trace, somewhere close to the river."

"That won't fit." She gnawed on the pen again. "What day will it be?"

I licked a mental finger and threw it up in the air. "Wednesday."

"You mean next Wednesday?"

I never knew what I meant.

"Yes. Next Wednesday."

"How will Daddy know that?"

"He'll know."

"But how?"

"Some things, you just have to believe. Blind. It's called faith."

Emmaline closed her eyes, and her lips moved. A silent prayer, perhaps. When she opened them, she wrote the words *Daddy. End of Trace. Sunset. Wednesday. I love you. Emmaline.* At the end, she drew a little heart and colored it in.

"Perfect, Em. Now, give me that money. I'll include it when we pay."

She slid to the floor and picked up the sleeping bags, and I followed her tentative gait to the front of the store. Her posture was regal, and she held her head high. How much had that brave little girl bargained for when she ran? If she knew what lay ahead, she might've taken her chances with her mother and Wilkinson. Most lives were packed with disappointment.

Certainly, the end of my life had been.

The clerk held out a serviceable piece of denim with reinforced knees. Emmaline wrinkled her nose and fidgeted with her cap, trying to tuck a few long hairs back under it.

"Do you have corduroy Levi's? In powder blue?"

The man let the jeans fall to the counter to join our camping pile. His shock of white hair stuck out like he'd been electrocuted, but his smile was patient. He nodded and shuffled to the back wall, tortoise-like. While he scanned shelves in slow motion, I explored the glass case. When I found packs of boys' under drawers, I reached in and grabbed a couple. "Em, if they have powder blue, that's what we'll get. If they don't, anything will do. We don't have the luxury of being persnickety."

She tossed her head like a few women I'd known but didn't argue. I thumbed through our hill of stuff on the counter: shirts, socks, boys underwear, a backpack and a pair of hiking shoes, plus our camping gear. The pants would do it.

"Pink rubber bands, Merry. You promised." She threw a sweaty, wrinkled pack on the pile.

"Where did you find those?"

"Next to the door when we first came in."

The clerk came back with one pair of powder blue corduroys and another the color of dirt. "Only two in the boy's size, Son. You want 'em?"

"One pair will do. How much for all of it?" I dug around in the front pocket of my jacket for the rest of my money. Emmaline tugged my arm before I found it.

"But Merry. How will Daddy get the money in Nashville if you're spending it here in Mississippi?"

The old man's hand froze over the cash register. Milky eyes shifted from her to me over the top of his glasses. "On your way to Nashville? That where you're from?"

I pulled Em next to me and held her there. Gave him my biggest grin. "Virginia, actually."

"What are you doing here?"

I shook the wad of money in front of his face. "Got a final tally for how much I owe you?"

That Mississippi man's spine hunched a little, right in front of me, cowed at the sight of plenty. "Forty-two dollars even."

I counted out two twenties and threw in Emmaline's two dollar bill. "Exact change. Em, you grab that sack there, and let's get going."

I followed her without looking back. About halfway, the telephone rang, and the old man answered. "Hello? Yes, Thelma. So sorry I missed you earlier. Had my hands full with a couple of customers. A man. About six feet tall. And, a girlie boy..."

I pushed on the glass and took Emmaline's hand. A bell tinkled as the glass door slid shut. It was the only sign we'd been there.

EMMALINE

I jumped over the potholes in the road, trying to keep up with Merry. The longer we walked, the more my sunburn itched. I ran my fingernails across my arms and cheeks, mostly because it gave me an excuse to stop. We had been walking forever. My back was icky underneath my pack, and my shoulders hurt.

Plus, Merry walked too fast for me. He never wanted to slow down and look at stuff. When I picked a cottony flower by the side of the road, he told me it was a weed. I blew it, and a million tiny parts scattered everywhere. How could something so pretty be a weed? I picked another one and tucked it behind my ear without blowing on it. When I felt it, little white bits stuck to the ends of my fingers.

Anyway.

I was mad at Merry, because he walked right past a yummy-smelling place to eat on the way out of town. Drool rose up on my tongue when I thought about fried chicken and french fries, but when I asked him if we could stop, he just kept going.

Along the road, we passed big brick houses and some with wood on them, all pretty colors in the sunshine. I stuck my hands through a fence and touched soft petals. A rose bush just like Aunt Bertie's. The yellow flowers felt like her skin after her bath. When I smelled my fingers, it was like she was there.

Merry told me to hurry. I ran to catch up. His feet crunched on rocks next to the road, and I stretched to put my feet where his had been, but it was too hard. His legs were so much longer than mine.

"Wait for me, Merry!"

He kept looking around, like he was expecting something. He hadn't said a lot since we left the clothes store. When we heard car noises, he pulled me with him into the bushes on the side of the road. Once the car sounds went away, he stepped back onto the road and kept walking.

I couldn't run very fast in my new shoes. The bottoms were slick, and they didn't bend at the toes. They were heavier than the mary janes I was used to. My legs were already tired from picking up my feet higher, and I felt a big blister on the back of my heel. But I'd get used to it. The pain was nothing if it meant finding Daddy.

Merry stopped, and I tripped over the last few steps to stand next to him, panting hard.

He kneeled on the dirt, his face close to mine. "We're over halfway to our camping spot for the night. I know I'm pushing you, Em, but if we're going to get to Nashville by Wednesday, we've got to make time. You're doing great."

I wet my lips. "It's okay for you to hurry, Merry. I'm just a little bit hungry is all." Better not to mention how tired I was when he was saying nice things. Adults always got mad when kids whined, and I couldn't understand why, because they whined all the time about money and jobs and other people and stuff.

Merry was different, though. He didn't complain about anything. Like right then, with his sweaty face and blank eyes, he kept going. His batteries never ran out.

He dropped his pack on the ground and unzipped a pocket. "Well, I have a little surprise for you, Em. Close your eyes and hold out your hands."

A rectangle hit my palms, and when I opened my eyes, I shrieked. "A Snickers bar! Merry, how did you know it was my favorite candy bar ever?" I ripped the cover down one side and bit into the chewy sweetness before it was open all the way.

"I'm sort of partial to them myself. A recent thing." He pulled out another one, and we munched on them together. A bee circled through the weeds, its wings whirring in the sunlight.

"Merry?"

"Uh-huh?"

"Are you really from Virginia?"

He sat down on top of his pack, and I dropped mine to copy him, light enough to float. Merry licked chocolate off his fingers. "I was born there, yes."

"What's it like?"

"I haven't been back in a long time, but the part I'm from was rolling hills and green."

Merry's empty eyes were faraway, unfocused, like he could almost see Virginia. What was it about his eyes? They were funny. Different from mine, but I couldn't figure out how.

I stared off in the same direction and tried to imagine home again. My bedroom under the eaves. The fountain in Jackson Square. The perfume of Bertie's rose garden. "I hope I don't forget New Orleans. It's the only place I've ever been, besides here."

"Well, I've been all over, Em, but I've never forgotten home."

"But how do you remember it?" I closed my eyes and imagined my mother's house. I tried to see Aunt Bertie's face, but it was blurry. When I thought about it, everything was out of focus. My eyelids hurt. "I'm afraid I'm already forgetting, Merry. It's scary to not have a home anymore."

He scooted closer to me and put his strong arm around my shoulders. "You have a home. With your Daddy. You just can't picture it yet. And, when you can, it will dim New Orleans for you. It won't make it go away, because life doesn't work like that, but maybe it will make it bittersweet."

"What does that mean, bittersweet?"

"It means happy and sad at the same time. Equal parts, so the happy cancels out the sad."

"Oh, like when I think about Mister Jim now? I'm happy I met him, but sad we had to say goodbye."

"Precisely. And, any time you want to see him, you can close your eyes and dream."

"I do that with Daddy. I see him all the time when I sleep. But sometimes, when he isn't there for a night or two, I get scared. I don't want to dream if it means that I won't see him ever again."

Merry hugged me to him, and I turned to look into his eyes. Sort of like mine, except flat. "Don't be afraid of your dreams, Emmaline. Sometimes, they're the only things that make life real."

MERRY

A specter stepped through me when my foot hit the soil of the Natchez Trace, ghosts whispering among the leaves. It was the same. And not. Its rutted dirt was the way of violence. Of possibility. A pathway to a dream. Witness to a multitude of lonesome deaths, including mine.

If I was dead. Somehow, Nowhere was worse.

The Trace was a tunnel through time.

Sunlight cast shadows through the timber, and a squirrel scampered across the trail ahead of us. I breathed in the rich smell of earth and rotting leaves and tried to remember what it felt like to lead. To be fearless, decisive. To guide another person through the unknown.

The last time I remembered having true confidence, I stood at the junction of two rivers. One was clear and rocky, like it flowed from the mountains we sought. The other was brown, unfathomable. All the men, including Clark, were con-

vinced the rock-strewn stream was the Missouri.

Not me.

I walked along the shores of both waterways. Made calculations and studied the terrain. When I returned to camp, I knew the muddy ooze was the way. My men followed me even when they believed I was wrong, because they knew every other time, I had been right. My confidence made them believe.

I wasn't that man anymore.

Emmaline's step was uncertain. She picked her way through knee-high weeds at the start of the trail and slipped her hand in mine. "Where are we, Merry?"

"The Natchez Trace. A very old road."

"If it's a road, why isn't it paved?"

"Roads haven't always been paved, Em. A lot of the roads we have now started out just like this one, a ribbon of dirt through some trees."

"Have you been here before?" She swung our arms together.

"Not here, no. Further on up."

"What's it like there?"

I rubbed my forehead and squinted into the trees ahead. Kids. They asked too many questions, but when they stopped wondering, they became jaded people pretending to enjoy the motions of life. I wished I could still see the world with the hue of childhood magic.

"It's not as flat as here. The trees are different. You'll see when we get there."

"How long will it take?"

"I don't know."

My nerves twinged every time I thought about that place I never wanted to see again. The place where I died. Grinder's Stand in Tennessee. When I closed my eyes, I could see it imprinted on the backs of my eyelids. Would it still be a wooden cabin and some outbuildings? Would I even recognize it when we got there?

Could I skip it? Or was walking over my own grave the final challenge, the last insult of Nowhere?

I let go of her hand and walked ahead. "If we don't stop, we should make it to Nashville by next Wednesday."

"In time to meet Daddy?"

"Yes, but we can't dawdle. That's a lot of ground to cover. Almost 500 miles."

"Are we going to walk the whole way?"

"People have done."

"Did you, when you were here before?"

"No."

"So, you went in a car?"

"Something like that."

"Will we get a car?"

"I hope we can find a ride once we get a little further from Natchez."

"Like hitchhiking?" She practiced her stance, her thumb out and her face lit up with a smile that tugged at my insides. I had to get my mission right for that hopeful girl.

"I'll take care of it when the time comes, Em. If I deem it safe. For now, we've got to make tracks and find a place to pitch camp for the night."

Emmaline butterflied around me, firing questions into the fall breeze. "What kind of bird is that, Merry? Can I eat this mushroom? Why does the ground stink right here? How much further is it? What do you think Daddy will say when he sees me again? Do you think he's already gotten my message?"

Her chatter was my lifeline. It distracted me from darker thoughts buried in dirt and leaves. "I think your father will tell you he loves you, Em, as soon as he sees you."

"So, you *do* think he got my message."

"It hasn't even been a day yet."

The wind blew hair around her face. "Do you think I'll feel it? When he gets the two dollars? Feel it in my heart?"

Please, don't ever rob that child of her hope.

I swallowed. "Maybe you will, Em."

Off in the trees, dry leaves rustled, and wood snapped. Em snaked her hand into mine and whispered. "Merry. What was that?"

"An animal of some kind."

"Will it hurt me?"

I pulled her closer. I could feel her heart hammering against my hip. "Most animals in this neighborhood don't bother people unless we bother them. Besides, it was probably a deer, and deer don't eat people."

"A deer like Bambi?" She broke away and skipped around the path. "Oh, I would *love* to pet little Bambi. Can we go find it?"

"What did I just say? About bothering the animals?"

"That we shouldn't. But I just want to pet it, and petting means love."

"Em, to a wild animal, people mean death. I doubt a deer would let you get close enough to pet it anyway. If we see a deer, just look, all right?"

She kicked through leaves and swung her hand in mine. "Okay. How do you know so much about animals, Merry? And the woods and stuff?"

"Remember when I told you about going out West? Part of my job was to find new plants and animals and record them for science."

"Really? Were you scared of any of them?"

Was I scared? Of course I was. Once, a grizzly took after me. My gun locked up when I tried to shoot. I never knew how fast an angry bear could run until I took off with its breath on my back. When I splashed into the river, it stopped, like it was afraid of the water. I still didn't know why that bear ran off when it could've made a decent meal of me. It was one of the most frightening moments of the expedition.

Emmaline punched my side. "I bet he knew you wouldn't taste very good."

I had to laugh along with her.

Late afternoon, we pushed into a clearing. I sneezed when I caught a whiff of mown grass.

"God bless you, Merry."

I bit my tongue to keep from telling her whatever god there was abandoned me, left me Nowhere, a long time ago. Instead, I focused on picking our campsite. Set off from the road, surrounded by thick trees. If cars went by overnight, they wouldn't see our fire. The grassy space was open enough for a tent, and in the middle, a ruined brick wall cut through it. I looked through one of two window holes and found a ground down hearth set off by jagged brick and Virginia creeper.

A monument to "forgotten."

Free of my pack, the light breeze cooled the sweat ring on the back of my shirt. When I pitched the canvas tent I bought for Emmaline, it made a crude palace for the princess of the rambling wall. Inside, I set up her sleeping bag and arranged her pack along the back. Even zipped open a flap, a window to let the stars lull her to sleep. I couldn't wait to show her how much I knew about trail life. I surveyed the inside of her tent, capable again for the first time since the bar. Since New Orleans.

Her voice floated to me with the wind. I stuck my head out of the opening.

"Em?"

No answer.

I ducked out of the tent and poked around the clearing. On the other side of the wall, blank space greeted me. Beyond it, smashed bricks broke through the soil next to the tree line. I took a few paces into the forest. "Emmaline! Where are you?"

The leaves applauded her disappearing act.

I ran to the line of trees on the other side and cupped my hands to shout again. That's when I saw her. She stood on the trail we walked earlier, waving her arms and talking to a tall wisp of a man. White hair and a matching handlebar mustache.

I never liked men with fancy facial hair. Couldn't trust them.

My heart pumping, I crouched low and crept, silent, through the brush. Always was a talent of mine, hiding my tracks in the woods. As I stalked closer, I sized up the intruder. Had I seen him before? How long had he been following us? Dammit. I should have kept off the road.

I rubbed my face to arrest my wandering thoughts. Em's voice was childlike innocence.

I stepped out of the trees and put myself between her and the stranger.

"*Merde!*" He staggered back. Put his hands on his knees and breathed through the scare I gave him. His bright eyes went from Emmaline's face to mine, while I studied him for tell-tale bulges in his khakis. With his skinny build, how many steps would it take to overpower him, if he had a gun?

"Merry, why did you have to scare us like that?" Before I could stop her, she walked over to him and patted his shoulder. "I'm sorry, Mister Jack. Grown-ups can be really rude sometimes. That's Merry. He's like my father. Merry, this is Mister Jack. When I found him, he was close enough to a deer that he could almost pet it. He held out my hand to it, and I felt its breath on my fingers. It was amazing."

The stranger's mustache stretched across his lip when he smiled. Good or ill, I couldn't decipher. When he straightened, he adjusted the binoculars and camera that hung from his neck. No backpack. No other visible supplies. He was unprepared for more than a few hours on the trail.

Cajun music lit up his voice. "Pardon, *pischouette*. The birds, they captivate me so. Coupled with your exquisite beauty, it's enough to distract me from approaching strangers."

Emmaline blushed through her sunburn, and I stepped forward and took her hand. "This is how you bird watch? By sneaking up on people in the woods?"

"Bird watching is a lonesome business. Too much noise scatters the birds."

I pulled Emmaline's hand to lead her away. "Let's go, Em. We need to find another place to camp."

She planted her feet and put one hand on her hip. Her jaw hardened. Stubborn. "What did you call me, Mister Jack? That p word?"

"Ah. *Pischouette*. Cajun for little girl. Or, in your case, beautiful little girl."

The Cajun bowed from his scrawny waist and looked up at me. "My name is Jacques, but everyone calls me Jack." He shifted to Em. "And, what are you called, *pischouette*?"

"My name is Emmaline. I already told you about Merry." She waved me back with her free hand.

I grabbed it, insistent. "Nice to meet you, Jack. We've got to get moving now."

He ignored me. "A pleasure to meet you. Both of you." He stopped and scanned the tree tops, his long fingers drumming along the side of his binoculars. I could hear his breath. Deep. Even. His voice sported a reverence that was magic. "I love this spot. I started coming here several years ago. Sudden-sudden, it was. The urge to see the birds. The place called to me, with the lingering tease of the female."

"What does that mean?"

"It means he's a dirty old man, Em."

He laughed, cordial-like. "Ah. Perhaps I am. Harmless, at my age. Birds turn my head now."

Emmaline took his hand and walked toward our camp site. "So, you come here all the time?"

"Once a month. I visit and watch the birds flutter in and out of the trees. Sometimes, I bring my camera. Alas, as a photographer, I am bad-bad."

"Do you live nearby?" She dragged her feet through leaves. Carefree.

"*Oui*. Outside New Orleans. Cajun the whole of my life."

"New Orleans! That's—"

"Em—" I tried to cut her off. I stepped in front of her and smiled at Jack. "This child will talk your leg off if you get her started. I'm sure we are scaring your birds away. We'll find another spot."

Jack took off his round hat and sun caught in his white hair. I squinted into the light that shimmered all around him. Was he following us?

The lilt of his voice made me focus. "Nonsense. I have always wanted to camp here, but I never had the courage to spend the night alone with so tangible a ghost." He gestured to the wrecked wall. "I left my car at the pull-off, further on. If you don't mind company, I'd enjoy camping with you."

"Can he, Merry? Please?"

Know your enemy. Fighting tactics from long ago echoed through my mind. It was always easier to camp close to the natives out West. Whether friend or foe, I could watch them. Learn their habits. Note their weaknesses. Most times, they were friendly.

But, if Jack was Wilkinson's man, keeping him close might be the best way to defeat him. To learn whether Wilkinson was on our tail.

I shook off my misgivings and gripped the man's hand. "Jack might have a time following your chatter, Em. But, another hand for the fire might be nice."

"Good-good. Glad it's settled. I've got provisions in the car. A sleeping pallet and a can of red beans we can share." Leaning over to Emmaline, he winked. "I believe I have some marshmallows, too." In four strides, he was in the trees, singing baritone.

Way down yonder in the bayou country in dear old Louisianne......

Emmaline clapped her hands. "He's singing *Cajun Baby*! Daddy used to sing that song to me. Merry, isn't Mister Jack handsome?"

I rolled my eyes and waited for his voice to peter out before kneeling in front of her. "Emmaline, you can't tell everyone we meet who you are and where you're from. We don't know anything about Jack. He could be dangerous."

"But if I had been unfriendly like that when you found me, we wouldn't be here together. Would we?"

She had a point.

"Doesn't matter. For all we know, he works for the Judge. He could be going back to his car right now to load a pistol and force us to go back to New Orleans with him." I stopped when she gasped. Held her eyes and let the impact of my words sink in. "This world can be pretty small. You can't trust anybody."

Whistling wafted out of the woods. I got up, put Emmaline behind the wall and braced myself for whatever menace Jack might bring from the car.

EMMALINE

Mister Jack was a nice man, not bad like Merry thought. He brought marshmallows just for me, plus his rolled-up sleeping bag. I grabbed the marshmallows, the squishy jumbo kind, and stuffed three of them in my mouth. Sugar stuck my lips together, and my cheeks got fat. Even Merry smiled a little bit.

I played with Mister Jack until it got dark. He let me look through his binoculars, and when different birds sang out, he told me their names from their sounds. After a few tries, I could even name one or two. He patted me on the head and called me *chérie*, and my heart felt funny, like it would beat right out of my chest.

When it got dark, I crammed myself into my tent face first and kicked my feet through the opening.

Thinking.

Merry was right. Even though Mister Jack turned out to be my friend, I had to be careful with strangers, but sometimes I wanted to say hello so much I thought I would blow up, especially after Mister Jack got so close to the deer.

I scratched at mosquito bites on my hands and legs. Rolled up pants were a bad idea. My heavy shirt had long sleeves and my thick corduroy pants made my sunburn hotter, but I was protected from most of the bitey bugs.

Merry was right about that, too.

I flipped onto my back and admired myself in boys' clothes. The cut of the pants made my legs look strong, and the cuff on my shirt didn't itch. Boys' clothes were definitely easier to wear.

My mother's rules exhausted me, dressing up every day, always having to look girly. Ruffles and lace might make a girl pretty, but beauty was on the inside. That's what Daddy always said. If my heart was ugly, it would make all of me ugly in the end. Maybe that's why he came to hate my mother. No matter what she wore or how she fixed her hair, her heart was mostly rotten, and he couldn't find anything to love in the end.

Did I ever love her? I didn't know.

I closed my eyes and imagined Daddy. Did he still wear the white suits of his Dixieland days? Would he smell like smoke and wood? Would his fingers be rough from hours of playing his upright bass?

Would he know me when he saw me? Even without my fancy dresses and long hair?

I slid out of the tent and stretched in falling darkness. Merry and Mister Jack sat on the ground, leaning their backs against a dead log near the edge of the trees. A small campfire popped and flickered in front of them, and Mister Jack was on his knees, working a small tank. I rubbed my eyes and wandered across the dewy grass.

When I felt the heat from the fire on my face, I heard Merry's voice. "And that's how I thought I knew you, I guess."

I stopped, and my throat closed. Who was Mister Jack, really? Would he tell anyone about Merry and me? If he did, it would be all my fault. If I hadn't run up to him and the deer in the woods, he might've walked right on by instead of coming through the clearing. Were the marshmallows part of his trap?

I blinked my eyes and focused. Merry's legs made a lazy line in front of him, and he threw one arm back over the dead tree. Relaxed. Not worried.

His mouth turned up in a smile. If Merry thought Mister Jack was our friend, then he had to be. Merry wouldn't sit there and let something bad happen to me. To us. I let out a long breath of relief and tried to forget my hyperactive imagination for one night.

Mister Jack pushed a button on the tank, and a circle of blue fire shot up through the top.

"*Et voila*. I may be as dull as a beetle, but I do have my uses."

"That you do, Jack." Merry threw another stick of wood on the fire. "It's been good for me to have a spell of manly conversation. I'm glad you understand my predicament."

Predicament? Was I his predicament? Was that how Merry saw me? As something bad?

Before I could ask, Merry patted the ground next to him. "Hi, Em. I missed you while you napped."

"I wasn't sleeping."

I ignored Merry and watched Mister Jack turn a can opener around the top of the biggest tin of red beans I ever saw. It was enough to feed us for two days, a whole week even. He dumped it into a pot and stuck it on top of the ring of blue fire. With a flick of his hand, he added other things: salt, lots of pepper and a heap of brown sugar.

He handed me a flat wooden spoon. "Stir?"

"Oh, yes. Can I be the taster? Aunt Ber—I mean—I always get to taste when I help cook."

He nudged the spoon into my hand and sat back. "By all means, *chérie*. Taste as much as you like."

I stuck the end of the paddle into the beans and moved my arms in a slow pattern. The more I stirred, the better they smelled. I stuck my nose in peppery steam that made my tummy turn a hungry cartwheel.

"So. You know something of the history of this place, then." Merry just said it, not as a question.

Mister Jack gave him a funny look and nodded. "*Oui*. A recent favorite of mine. A shame, the ruined state of it." His face grew slack when he angled it at the broken wall. "When I turn my head just right, my eyes play tricks on me. I don't know why, but I can almost see it whole."

Mister Jack moved his head, and his mustache twitched a little. Merry's voice sounded weird when he spoke.

"What can you see when that happens? Do you see the school?"

"This was a school, Mister Jack?"

Mister Jack nodded. His voice was even more Cajun when he continued. He told us the Elizabeth Female Academy was one of the first colleges for women in America. A long time ago. Buildings circled the entire clearing. They fanned out from the center in joined hallways. Craftsmanship of the highest calling, he called it. The pinnacle. All left to rot away. He blinked. "Sometimes, when it's quiet, when the birds don't cooperate, I hear them. The girls."

Shadows fluttered on the brick wall, and smoke danced around the flames. If I squinted, a couple of the poufs floated along the ground. Pretty hair. Long skirts. One turned her head and winked at me.

I swallowed. "What girls?"

"Why, girls like you, *chérie*. Laughing and whispering. Telling stories about boys. Passing notes and crying over letters from home. Asking hard questions in the classroom, pushing themselves to a better station in life. A lost opportunity for women, the day they closed the academy."

I stirred the spoon in the other direction. "Why couldn't they just go to school somewhere else? I mean, almost every school takes girls. They have to, don't they?"

"They haven't always, *chérie*. You are lucky-lucky to be born when you were, right now." He took a deep breath and stopped. His smile was normal again when he looked at Merry. "Perhaps figments of my imagination are too heavy for dinnertime. I don't know what comes over me sometimes. When I am here."

Merry cleared his throat and handed me three thin paper plates. "Those beans smell delicious, Em. Let me take over for you, and I'll serve them out when they're done."

He crawled over and took the paddle from my hands and stirred slower, while I leaned close beside Mister Jack. I sighed when he put his arm around my shoulders. He was so sophisticated and dreamy, with his accent, tanned face and twinkly eyes.

The fire made orange light dance on Merry's face when he talked. He said the Natchez Trace used to be a busy highway. A long time ago. Nobody knew for sure how old it was. Animals used it, way back before there were people here. They migrated south along its natural ridge line, stampeding herds of buffalo and bear, deer and elk.

When the Indians came along, migration made the Trace a natural hunting ground, with food aplenty. They settled all along it and adopted the pounded ground as their own road. Early settlers used it as a way to get home after they sold their goods down in Natchez or New Orleans. Merry stirred the fire. "A lonesome trip, dogged by rainstorms and poisonous snakes and robbers. Men were almost relieved when the invention of the steamboat killed the Trace."

"The steamboat? Like the one we rode when we—to get here?"

"Yes, Em. Just like the one we rode. Nobody much came this way when they could just power upriver like we did."

Mister Jack hugged me to him, and my heart was in heaven. "Yes, Merry. A shame so many wonderful things died with the Trace."

"But, in the gamut of forgotten places, I probably chose the best neighborhood for exploration. Camping. All that." Merry scooped the paddle to his lips and tasted a bite of beans. "Mmmm. Perfect, Em. Jack here is definitely an expert of camp cooking."

He piled them onto each plate and passed one to Mister Jack and me, followed by white plastic spoons. We chewed the first spicy bites in silence, because we were all really hungry.

Mister Jack swallowed a mouthful of beans and laid a hand on Merry's arm. "Do you think you can make it all the way, *mon ami*? To Nashville?"

"I have to, Jack. It's the only way."

Mister Jack shook his head and sighed. "I can take you as far as the bus station in Jackson tomorrow morning, if you'll indulge me with one stop along the way. Sorry I can't help you to the end."

"The end. I don't know what comes at the end."

"I don't know the answer, *mon ami*, but have hope. Hope is like the shy birds. They fly at a great distance, where they are seldom reached by the best of guns. They always make it home. I think, if we can only learn to fly the right way, then we will all find our way home."

I put my empty plate on the stubby grass and leaned over to fling my arms around Merry. I hugged him as hard as I could.

"Thank you for helping me find my daddy," I whispered. Before he said anything, I looked over his head at Mister Jack. "Don't we have more marshmallows? Marshmallows make everything all right, don't they?"

The two men laughed with me, and it echoed under the stars and through the trees, all the way into my heart.

EMMALINE

It was my tummy that woke me. Too many of Mister Jack's beans. I rolled away from my sleeping bag and slipped out of the tent. Both Merry and Mister Jack slept outside, close to the dying fire. When I looked up, the sky was black and sparkly, and the night bugs honked and croaked and cricketed, their sounds coming from everywhere at once.

I had to go, but where? If Mister Jack or Merry woke up and saw me with my pants down, I would die. I didn't want them to hear me, either.

With my Wonder Twin powers, I tippy-toed past them. A few steps into the woods, and I would have enough privacy. Leaves crunched under my feet, and I blinked my eyes to see better in the dark. The ground was uneven, and I couldn't remember what Merry said about going in the woods. Did he say rocks were good? Or was that where the snakes were?

A branch broke off somewhere behind me, and I froze. In the dark, tracks thudded along the ground, close to me. A dirty smell came with a sudden breeze, and I pinched my nose together.

Feet scraped at leaves and dirt, a bull getting ready to charge. To ram his horns into me. To trample me like I once saw happen to a cowboy on television. Every way I turned, I heard it, grunting, pawing at the ground, not like it was going to run over me, but like it was going to eat me.

I shuddered.

It was a monster, not a bull. A nighttime woods monster, and it could see me in the dark, and its squinty eyes locked onto me, and it licked its fangs and got ready for its dumb-little-girl-lost-in-the-woods dinner.

When its shadow charged, I screamed and ran as fast as I could. Through the leaves. Over a dead tree. I fell in a ditch, and it kept coming. Stinking wetness ran down my cheek, but I ran again, up the other side of the ditch. Further into the woods. If I could just get far enough away, the monster couldn't catch me.

My chest hurt. A long ropey thing wrapped around one of my arms. I jerked to a stop. Monster jaws...or snakes. It was snakes. Merry said snakes were everywhere in the woods. One had its drippy fangs around me. I thrashed against it, but it was no use. I could feel its mouth stretching. It was going to put its icky lips all the way over my head and eat me, head first. If it ate me that way, I wouldn't be able to scream, so I screamed and screamed and screamed until my throat hurt, and I hit and kicked and fell down on the ground and bit the snake's scaly skin as hard as I could.

"Emmaline! Where are you?"

"Merry! Help me! A snake! It's eating my head! Hurry!"

My mouth tasted dirty, but I kept fighting that old snake. I scratched it with my fingernails, and I even pulled a piece of it apart in my hands. If I could just keep it from eating me until Merry got there, he would kill it and send it all the way to hell.

A weird light shot through the trees. I screamed again. Strong tentacles went around me, with a light at one end. I kicked at the new creature and bit into the flesh that held the light.

"Ow, Em."

Merry.

He let go of the flashlight, and it dropped on the ground with a dull thud. "Why did you bite me?"

Merry sat on the ground, rubbing his hand. Mister Jack ran up behind him, panting hard. "*Chérie*, there you are."

The flashlight beam lit up a clearing. Lots of vines hung from the trees, the same ones I saw during the day. Merry motioned to them. "Meet your snake, Em. What are you doing, tearing up the forest in the middle of the night?"

"I didn't mean—"

"Do you know how far away from camp you are?"

"I'm sorry, Merry. I, um. I—" I couldn't talk anymore, because I was crying. When Merry hugged me to him, I wiped my nose with the back of my filthy hand.

"Em, the woods are dangerous at night. You can't just go wandering off by yourself."

"But I—I. Um. This is s-s-so embarrassing."

"What is? That you got lost?"

"N-n-n-n-no! I had to g-g-go a lot—it was the b-b-beans—and I d-d-didn't want you to s-s-s-see."

Mister Jack's mustache shook when he laughed, and Merry chuckled and ran his hand through my hair. "Aw, Em. I never thought about bathroom etiquette on the trail. When you went earlier today, you just walked off in the trees, so I figured you were okay with the whole thing."

"But that was d-different. It was only number one."

"Okay. Okay. I understand. Still, if you have to go at night, you need to wake me up and let me know, all right? I can go with you, help you find a spot, and wait a little ways away to give you some privacy."

"C-c-c-can you and M-Mister Jack do that n-now?"

Merry stood up, still holding me. He rubbed my tears away and set me on the ground. "Sure, Em. We'll be right over there, behind those bushes. Give a shout when you're done, and we'll come back."

When I couldn't see them anymore, I pulled my pants down and did what I had to do. It wasn't nearly as hard as I expected it to be. If I didn't get ahold of myself, I might make Merry mad enough to stop helping me, and if he stopped helping me, I wouldn't find Daddy, ever. I looked up at the stars, shining through the trees, and I decided, right then, that I had to grow up. To stop crying when I was scared. I needed to be brave.

Like Merry. If I could be like him, I knew I'd find my daddy.

I cleaned myself up and stood tall. My breath was misty when I spoke. I watched it shimmer and disappear into the night. Remnants of the old me.

"Okay, Merry. Mister Jack. I'm ready."

THE JUDGE

Words remain behind. To glorify us. To betray us. I understood why George Washington wanted his papers burned after his death. Words betray weakness. They illumine the soul.

Always, I tried to be careful with words. To write in cipher. My own private code.

Like this:

μ Δ μ ¤ ∏

It didn't help me in the end. The Spanish saved a record of payments to me, money I earned for selling my government's secrets. Plans for expansion. Military outposts. Even the famed trek to the Pacific by Lewis and Clark. After I died, I feared their carelessness would betray me and smear my name across the pages of history.

In Nowhere, I was more circumspect. It's how I managed to elude my assignment. To disappear into the ether. To recreate myself as the man I lived to be.

A man of reckoning.

Nadine, with all her cunning and trickery, she learned the manner of man I am.

I shook my head to banish images of her. It was time to focus. To find Lewis and my darling little beauty.

To delve into her and release my Ann. To make her mine again.

I sat down at my roll top desk and pushed the mechanism for the hidden compartment. My stash of parchment. I fingered its raw edges and picked up my fountain pen.

Brevity lent weight to orders. And, I had only one directive to send.

Δ 〒 ■ Δ

(Wait for me.)

EMMALINE

Mister Jack swung his car door shut and stepped onto the dirt path that led through the woods. If I walked behind him, he would smile and show new birds to me. A bald eagle perched at the top of a tree. The black-and-blue feathers of a blue jay.

Merry followed us, his steps so quiet I almost forgot he was there. The sun got dark behind the leaves and ropey vines and Spanish moss, and the trail became a deep ditch with sides higher than my head. Tree roots clung to the dirt like claws. I could even swing from some of them if I tried, but I didn't, because that would make noise. I had to start acting like a grown-up.

I dug in my heels. I would do it. Somehow.

"The Sunken Trace." Mister Jack opened his arms like ladies did on television game shows. He tiptoed ahead of us. The ditch was deep enough to feel like we were being buried alive. I shuddered and took Merry's hand.

I remembered to whisper. "Why is it a ditch, Merry?"

Mister Jack looked into the trees and held up his hand, moving it back and forth through the air like he wanted me to be quiet. Merry squeezed my shoulder. I leaned my head into his solid stomach and thought about how brave he was. He was never afraid of anything, while I thought vines in the trees were snakes and the animals were monsters. He would never be that stupid. I wanted to be as brave as Merry, because Daddy would be super-proud of me.

I looked up the trail and saw Mister Jack freeze. He put his hand in a pocket on the side of his pants leg and pulled out a small camera. When he raised it to his face, the snap made me jump, and I let out a little yelp. Something moved through the branches and went further into the forest.

"*Merde!*" Mister Jack hopped from foot to foot, like I did during one of my tantrums. I didn't realize adults threw tantrums, too. Maybe I was more grown-up than I thought. "*MerdeMerdeMerde!* Did you see it?"

"What?" Merry whispered.

Mister Jack got even more excited in a mad way. He bent over, his hands on his knees, breathing really fast.

"An ivory billed woodpecker. I'm sure of it. Rare-rare."

I started to ask another question, but when I opened my mouth, Mister Jack threw up his hand. He wanted no more talking. He put an elegant finger over his lips, and his mustache twitched. After he caught my eye, he turned and continued down the trail. His steps made no sound.

I motioned for Merry to lean closer to my head. With my hand, I covered my mouth and asked my question close to his ear. "What is an ivory-whatever woodpecker?"

"Silence!" Mister Jack roared, causing both Merry and me to jump. He put his camera back in his pants pocket, and he charged down the path to find the ivory-whatever bird.

Merry just looked at me and smiled like he knew a secret. "Bird watchers are funny, Em. I've known a few. Wait here."

I asked him where he met other bird watchers, but he didn't answer. He just mouthed the words *wait here* again to make sure I understood. I was a little scared, but I nodded anyhow. The dead quiet of the forest wasn't spooky.

It wasn't.

Merry tip-toed along the trail up ahead, making no sound. It was almost like he wasn't even there. I had to keep looking to remember I wasn't alone.

Breath blew my hair, and I looked up to see faces in the tree trunks and snakes wrapped around the limbs, so long they almost reached the ground. In the bark, kinky grey hair blew around witches' snarling, toothless mouths. I took a step back, but everything closed in on me. Taunting. When I closed my eyes, the witches and snakes crashed in my mind. They were all around me. On top of me. Suffocating me. One witch licked her lips and eyed my arm. Hungry for a piece of dead little girl.

"It's not real. It's my hyperactive imagination. Wonder Twin powers. Activate." I whispered it, over the heavy breathing and hissing and—

I couldn't help it. It was hard to be a grown-up. I screamed.

"*Merde!*" Jack shouted from around a bend in the deep gouge. Feet pounded into the dirt, and Merry appeared around the curve of the trail.

"What is it, Em? What did you see?"

He pulled me to his chest, but I was so embarrassed. I buried my head and wouldn't look at him. Stupid Wonder Twins. No matter how much I thought I wasn't scared, their powers didn't work to make me not scared for real. I was such a fraidy-cat girl. I couldn't even be left alone in the woods. I was never going to find Daddy if I was afraid of everything.

Merry held the back of my head and ran his fingers through my tangled hair. "Really, Em. It's okay. The first time I encountered an unknown wilderness, I was mighty scared, too."

Merry? Scared? Like me? I looked up at him and spoke through shaky breath. "Where was that?"

He smiled, but his eyes were sad. "In a lot of ways, it was a place just like this."

"This very place?"

"Not exactly here, no. But it was close to a river not unlike the Mississippi. You know, the stuff that scares us is all the same in the end. It doesn't matter where it is."

He gave me a squeeze and set me on my feet. I stood as tall as I could, to make him proud of me. "Cross-my-heart-and-hope-to-die. I'm going to be more grown-up from now on."

"Aw, Em. It's okay if you're scared. This whole adventure is a lot for a kid, especially one who's always lived in a city. Never been anywhere."

"Well, I'm going to be a brave. It will make Daddy proud when he sees me."

He patted my head. "I want you to crawl up on my back, all right? I think I can track with you there, and it will keep you close to me."

He turned, and I felt his muscles strain when I climbed onto his back. I crossed my legs around his waist and locked my fingers around the front of his neck. He stood, and everything in the forest got smaller: the trees were thinner, the vines not so snakey, the Trace even looked peaceful. Kind of pretty.

I clung to Merry while he snuck around the bend to join Mister Jack, who sat along the side of the path. Merry made a hand signal to him, and Mister Jack shrugged, frowning. Merry shook me higher on his back and crouched on the ground. He moved ahead slow, the sound of his feet lost in the old dirt.

Quick, he stood and studied a thick tree that rose up tall beside us. Rough bark became high branches with long green needles. Merry tapped two fingers to his eyes before he pointed up. I followed the line from the end of his fingers up the side of the tree.

Plockplockplockplock.

A black-and-white bird with a white blotch on the side of its head was pecking its beak into the bark. I bit my tongue to keep from shrieking with excitement. Merry found Jack's bird. It drilled into the wood, its feathers moving with its head. It made a lot of noise for such a small thing.

Mister Jack came up beside us, a sketch pad in his hand. His handlebar mustache twitched as he worked a pencil in graceful strokes across heavy cream paper and made the bird appear right before my eyes. In no time, he finished and held it out at arm's length. His picture of the bird looked real enough to fly off the page. With big swirlies, he signed it, tore it from the pad, handed it to me and bowed.

An ivory-billed woodpecker of my very own.

I took it from his hand and showed it to Merry. He held it for me while

I slid down from his back. When I took it from him, I fingered its edges, afraid I would tear it. The bird watched us from the tree for a second before flying into the woods.

"A treat to see one these days, so I'm told." Merry kneeled to admire Mister Jack's artwork.

"*Oui.* They are rarer than they used to be."

Merry sighed. "Many things are."

I looked up at Mister Jack. "It's so pretty. May I really keep it?"

He touched my face with his long fingers. "But of course. It pleases me that she was present for you." Looking at Merry, he continued. "Expert tracking. You're sharp-sharp, *mon ami.* I know you'll make it to Nashville. And, speaking of that city, we must return to the road. I can get you to Jackson by twilight, but only if we hurry."

I squinted at Mister Jack's signature again and recognized the name. "Mister Jack, is your last name Audubon? Like the park in New Orleans?"

But he was already halfway down the trail, his straight back weaving through the trees.

He never answered me.

ivory billed woodpecker

MERRY

Friday. October 7, 1977. Evening. Jackson, Mississippi.

Doughnuts. Em's eyes lit up with red neon and sugar. She looked through the window of the Peoples Cafe in Jackson, next to the bus station, where Jack left us.

Me, I watched Jack's oblong tail lights fade down Main Street. I was sad to see him go. It was always hard to lose a friend. Connections were rare in Nowhere.

Jack's spirit reminded me of someone I met in life. He was a bird lover, too. A Frenchman. The drawing he gave Em was so like the style of the man I knew. I wished my expedition drawings rose to his level of artistry. Instead, they were just doodles in the margins, crude images captured in a hurry. I still didn't get them right.

Emmaline's voice dragged me back to the present. "Can I have three cinnamon twists if they sell them, Merry? Please? I promise I can eat them all."

I looked over at the brick bus station. "We need to get our tickets and head on, Em. We don't know who may be after us."

"We can get them to go, Merry. Like Aunt Bertie used to get her cocktails. Pretty please?"

Before I could answer, Emmaline took my hand and barreled through the heavy glass door. Sweetness mingled with hot grease and brewing coffee. She climbed up on a stool in front of a counter, and I sat beside her. The metal seats were bolted to the floor, and Em started turning around and around. She used her feet to push off the base of the counter with every twirl, her head thrown back and her eyes glazed.

So much for doughnuts to go.

"This is fun, Merry. You do it, too."

"Nah. Might make me too dizzy to enjoy my—what am I having again?"

"A cinnamon twist doughnut." She kept her eyes on the ceiling and grinned like she was on the back of a wild horse.

A woman in a tight green uniform appeared from the back, her chocolate hair peeking through a hair net. "Maxine" was printed in red letters on her name tag.

"Coffee?" She raised the pot in her hand.

"Em. That's enough with the turning." I winked at Maxine. "She doesn't need any, clearly, but I could sure use a hot one."

She sloshed some coffee into a mug and pushed the sugar and cream my way. "And what will you have, kid?"

"Three cinnamon twist doughnuts please."

"Uh-huh. And to drink?"

Emmaline stopped spinning. She wobbled a little on the stool and held onto the edge of the counter. "Nothing."

Maxine piled fried dough on a white plate. A shower of sugar and cinnamon littered the counter when she plopped it down in front of Emmaline and looked at me. "Anything else?"

"You got a paper?"

"Got several of them right there. End of the counter. Help yourself. Most of the news is old by now, though." She swung through a door, into the back.

Emmaline crammed almost half a doughnut into her mouth. I lost a little piece of my heart to her puffy cheeks and cinnamon sugar smile. Her love of sweets almost made them palatable.

Amongst the newspapers, I found one from New Orleans, dated the previous morning.

"These are so good, Merry. Why aren't you eating one?"

I mussed her hair and sat down beside her, paper in hand. "The way you're tearing into that plate, I might lose a digit if I try."

Sugar and spice rained all over me as she held out a doughnut with sticky fingers. Unappetizing presentation, but I took it from her and put it on a paper napkin. Licked my fingers and scanned the front page.

Under the fold, I saw it. A headline.

Decapitated Body Found in Mississippi River

New Orleans - The headless body of a woman was dragged out of the Mississippi River above New Orleans early Tuesday. Two teens, Wilbur Pollack, 15, and Bubba Overton, also 15, were fishing in a small boat along a bend in the river near Montz, LA when a large object got caught in their net. It took both of them to pull it out of the water, revealing a grisly catch. They returned to shore and contacted local authorities, who notified New Orleans PD. The teens are not suspects in the case.

Sources in the New Orleans Police Department have identified the woman as one Nadine Houghton Cagney, 36, formerly of the French Quarter. She was reported missing from her home late Tuesday night. Cagney ran a boardinghouse off Bourbon and St Philip and was reported missing by one of her lodgers.

A spokesman for the NOPD reports that the body had not been long in the river. Fingerprints were intact. Comparison with those on file for Nadine Houghton Cagney matched the prints of the victim. Cagney was divorced and had no immediate family in the area.

Authorities have no leads. The death has been ruled a homicide. If you have any information regarding this case, please contact the NOPD Tip Line at 800 735 3114.

My hands shook, knocking coffee all over the newspaper. I pulled a few thin paper napkins from the dispenser and blotted, trying to save the story to read it again, but it was no use.

Emmaline stopped eating and watched me, her mouth a ring of crusty

To Live Forever

brown. "What's the matter, Merry?"

I wadded the paper into a ball and walked over to the trash can. After a quick shove, I turned to her. "Come on, Em. We have to go. Now." I gestured with inky fingers, a blood-like stain.

"Aren't you going to pay, Merry?" She slid off the stool and wiped her hands on her pants.

Maxine was still somewhere in back. No time.

I pushed Em through the door. The autumn air nipped us as we stepped onto the sidewalk. Around the corner, the bus station glowed with lights. Buses, coming and going. We crossed the street and pushed through the heavy wood doors into the sparse lobby.

Our footsteps echoed on the tiles. I imagined every eye in the place, following us. Questioning us.

Knowing us.

On the other side of the ticket window, a baggy-eyed man didn't even look up when I tapped on the glass. "Where to?"

"You got a route to Nashville from here?"

He thumbed through dog-eared papers. "Yep. Leaves in ten minutes."

"I'll take one adult ticket and one child, please." I counted out the money and shoved it through the slot.

"Boarding's over there. In the far corner. Safe travels." He punched my tickets and handed them through.

I grabbed Em's hand and steered us toward the line of passengers, still holding my breath.

"Merry, you're hurting my hand."

"Sorry. Preoccupied." I relaxed my grip, and she wiggled her fingers.

"What's the matter, Merry?"

I stopped a few paces from the small group of people waiting for the Nashville bus. Bedraggled, most of them. A couple were asleep. Nobody paid us any attention. I unwound a little.

"Nothing is the matter, Em. We just need to be alert. Watchful."

"In case the Judge is looking for me?"

"Yes." Another sweep of the territory. New people, in and out.

"Do you think he would come this far?"

"Probably not. But he might have people looking for us. A network can help a person be in many places at once, if that makes sense."

All aboard the Nashville bus. First call. I threw our gear over my shoulder. The baggage holds were open along the side of the bus, but I skipped them. Better to keep our things with me. With a tap on her arm, I pointed Emmaline up the stairs and onto the bus. I guided her into a space two rows from the door.

She took the seat next to the window and turned her face away. I followed her gaze, sizing up the line of folks waiting to board. A woman with a baby. A man and his family. A couple of teenagers. They all filed on and squeezed past us.

The driver stood at the front. "Jackson bus to Nashville. All are aboard." His dimpled hand moved to shut the door, but a latecomer stopped him with a rap on the window glass. A man. The driver hauled the door open again. Asked if he was headed to Nashville.

I didn't hear the man's reply, but as he handed the driver his ticket and climbed aboard, his eyes scanned the passengers. When they lit on mine, he smiled. Lopsided. He walked down the aisle and took the seat behind us. Before we moved, his foot hit the back of my seat. A mindless rhythm.

Or a threat.

I started to get up, but we were already moving. The lights of Main Street scrolled by the windows in time with the stranger's tapping foot on my seat. When I caught a glimpse of his reflection in the window, he mouthed a few words. I couldn't make them out, but I thought he said, "Gotcha."

To Live Forever

EMMALINE

"We've got to get off the bus." Merry whispered in my ear. "Have your stuff ready and follow me when I get up."

My whole body clenched. When I tried to turn around in my seat, Merry's hand stopped me. My heartbeat hurt my chest, and I hugged my pack and scooted closer to Merry. If one of the Judge's men got on the bus, would he stop us from leaving? Make a scene and try to take me with him? I squeezed my eyes shut to block out bad thoughts and tried to think about doing everything right when Merry gave the signal.

Help me, Daddy. I whispered it as low as I could.

Merry waited until the bus slowed down at an intersection. When he jumped out of his seat, he pushed me into the aisle in front of him and followed me to the door. I veered into a bank of seats because the bus was still moving, but I ignored the pain in my shoulder and kept going. It was what Merry would do.

The driver looked at us with tired eyes. "Gonna be a rough night to be out there. Sure you want to get off here?"

Merry nodded. "We're sure."

I tried not to look at the people on the bus when the driver slid a bar, and the door squeaked open. My feet slipped on mud, but I picked them up and ran beside Merry. While the bus rattled, I pushed my hair out of my eyes and ran as fast as I could. As long as I could stay with Merry, I would be okay. He wouldn't let anybody take me away from him.

We hurried toward a thick line of trees. Before I got there, I stopped and looked back. The headlights of the bus made spooky shadows on the road. I shuddered. *It's only your imagination, Silly. There are no ghosts.*

When I looked at the bus again, the door was blocked by a man.

He watched me, and I scraped my arm against a tree when I turned to run. With every splat of my feet, I could see the man's slow, lopsided smile.

The man on the bus worked for the Judge. He was still after me. I just knew it.

I felt Merry's hand on my shoulder. His voice encouraged me to keep going. He told me I was doing well.

My feet slipped in ruts on the dirt path, and my legs burned inside my wet jeans. My lungs ached from trying to keep up with Merry. He ran next to me, almost like he had night vision power, never missing a step. Every few feet, he told me to hurry. With almost every footfall, puddles sucked at my shoes, and roots tripped me. Once, I fell hard on my knees, and I bit my lips together to keep from crying.

"Hurry up, Em. Keep moving."

I stood up and brushed mud off my jeans. "I saw the man on the bus, Merry."

"Yeah. He followed us on. I didn't want to stay and find out his intentions."

"He stood in the door when the bus drove off. It was creepy when he waved."

"All the more reason to stop talking and keep moving. Come on."

I concentrated all my energy on my Wonder Twin power. When I touched my fists together, I wasn't tired anymore, because being tired was not grown-up. Adults had to do things, even when they didn't feel like it, and I was a grown-up now.

Wispy stuff clung to my face and hair, but I didn't scream. When the top of the grass scratched against my waist, I didn't even think about the critters that might be there, waiting to bite me. I gritted my teeth and ran around a turn, to find a narrow beach that went down into water. Here and there, picnic tables peeked through the dark.

Merry sat with me on top of one of them. Stars twinkled through the clouds and sparkled on the water. I rested beside him and let my fingers trace the names carved in the wood.

"Is this a lake?" I wasn't too out of breath.

"Reservoir, I think. We should be able to find a decent campsite around here somewhere."

"Can we camp here? I'm so tired, Merry."

"Too public. If that man leaves the bus and loops back, this will be one of the first places he'll look."

"How much further do I have to run?" I checked the whine in my voice. "I'll try to go as far as you say, Merry."

"Should be around a couple more bends, right over there."

He waved into the darkness and moved again. He followed a sign to a trail along the shoreline, his head down and his hands in his pockets, like he had something really heavy on his mind.

"What's wrong, Merry?"

He didn't answer. Just kept walking into the world beyond the weak starlight. Since the doughnut place, Merry had been acting funny. It wasn't just the man from the bus. Something else was bothering him. Why did he have to be like every other adult, deciding when I was too little to know things?

I smelled the rain before the first drop fell. It hit me in the right eye. After a few random drops pinged across the top of the picnic table, the sky opened up and buckets of water poured down, even though I could still see a few stars through the clouds. God crying. That's what Aunt Bertie always said when it rained but the clouds didn't cover the sky. I sloshed through the mud and shouted into the storm, but it was like the raindrops trapped my voice and forced it into the ground.

Thunder rattled my insides. I ran along the mucky trail to where I last saw Merry. Around a finger of land, I stopped. The lake was swallowed up by thick trees planted in black water. In the weak light, their bottoms looked like fancy skirts that twirled across the dance floor at Cinderella's ball.

A swamp. No matter how much I thought not-scared things, swamps were the scariest places ever. The water was too black to see the bottom, and stuff hung out of the trees. Sometimes, people went into swamps and were never, ever seen again.

I slipped on wet dirt as I felt my way along the path. Under the big trees, the rain didn't fall as hard. I wiped more water out of my eyes and looked around me. I stood on a soupy path. Everything smelled rotten. Holding my breath, I slid one foot ahead of the other. Drenched soil sucked at my shoes like a vacuum cleaner.

My eyes hurt from holding back tears, but I blinked fast to keep from crying. I would not be a baby. Not this time. If I was always scared and couldn't keep up with Merry, how could I expect to find Daddy? I stood taller and swallowed my fear.

The path went up a hill that overlooked the water. With both hands and feet, I grabbed fists full of mud and climbed through a waterfall of ooze. At the top, the tree branches made a ceiling overhead, a tunnel that opened into a clear spot, sort of like an island in the middle of the swamp.

Merry.

He was there, waiting with my tent. It was almost set up.

I was so happy to see him that I ran down the hill, until two yellow eyeballs stopped me. They glowed in the path between Merry and me. When it moved its head and opened its triangle mouth, sharp teeth were everywhere. I stared into the squinty eyes of an alligator. Its tail slashed at the weeds and grasses as it came at me, faster than I thought it could.

I screamed.

Inches from my feet, the gator opened its jaws wide and bellowed. Really, really mad. It was going to eat me. It locked eyes with mine and charged at me, a mouth like scissors the whole way.

I kicked muddy water in its face to keep moving, but it was no use. The alligator was going to eat me. Its stinky breath was already on my skin and its teeth were closer and closer, and it was going to drag me—

Before the gator got its jaws around my foot, strong arms lifted me, and I flew through the air, landing hard in the weeds along the path. When I stopped rolling and got up, Merry circled the alligator with a long stick in one hand.

The gator threw back its head and bellowed before it charged Merry. With a shout, Merry swung the stick and hit the gator in the middle of the head. It stopped for a few seconds, stunned.

He yelled over his shoulder, "Emmaline! Run to the camp! Now!"

But I couldn't leave Merry to fight the alligator all alone. I would not run away and be a baby. That wasn't what Daddy or Merry would do.

I slid to my feet and watched, my shirt sticky with mud. The alligator shook its bumpy head and charged Merry again. It hit Merry sideways, knocking him to the ground. When I shouted, the gator started my way, right before Merry rolled over on his knees, the stick still in his hand.

"Eat this, you monster."

His hand moved quick like lightning and shoved the stick into the gator's open mouth. It went in so far that most of it disappeared. The gator staggered to one side and made a gurgling noise before sliding into the black water with a loud splash. Merry fell to his back, panting. His jeans were torn at one knee, and his white t-shirt was stained the color of tea.

I ran to him and held his hand while he wheezed. "Thought. You. Were. A goner, Em."

I reached out my fingers to stroke his greasy blonde hair. "I couldn't see so good in the rain and the dark, but I found you. And I didn't cry. Not even when I saw the gator."

He gripped my arm with his filthy dirty hand. "I'm proud of you." He struggled to sit up and wipe his muddy face.

"Really? But I couldn't keep up with you or anything."

He sighed and stared into the black water. I took his face in my hands and turned his head to me.

"What's the matter, Merry?"

"What do you mean?"

"Ever since we left the cafe and went to the bus station, you've been different. Quiet. Not answering my questions like you usually do. Did I do something wrong?"

"Aw, Em. You didn't do anything wrong. We've just got to keep moving. That's all."

I hit his arm with my fist. Hard. "That is *not* all. You're not telling me something."

"You're too young to understand, Em."

"I'm big enough to be out here in the middle of the night, facing down an alligator. Don't treat me like a little girl when I'm trying so hard to be big."

He put his hand on the back of my neck and put his face close to mine. "I read something. In the paper back in Jackson. It changes everything."

EMMALINE

I watched two turtles on a log in a strip of sunlight at the edge of the black water. One big. One little. Maybe mother and child. Would the baby turtle feel as bad as I did when it found out its mother was dead?

My cheeks were still hot, and my heart beat so hard it hurt my chest. After crying most of the night, I didn't think I had any more tears left. Grown-up tears. That's what I cried.

Merry put more wood on the fire. The wet wood spewed smoke through the trees all the way to heaven.

Was my mother in heaven?

"Your mother is dead, Em. I read it in the paper back at that cafe in Jackson. That's why I hightailed it out of there and went for the bus."

"But you won't tell me how she died."

"The paper didn't spell it out. Besides, knowing some things makes a child a grow up too fast. This is one of those things."

"I have a right to know. She was my mother."

He pulled me to him and wiped the hair out of my face. "Emmaline. Look at me. If your father thinks it's all right to tell you someday, then he can. I'll leave that up to him."

"What about Aunt Bertie? Is she okay? Did the paper say anything about her? She's not dead, too, is she?"

My voice cracked at the end. Even though my mother could be mean sometimes, she was still my mother. I loved her even when I hated her.

Aunt Bertie, I just loved. She was everywhere in my heart. If she was dead, I didn't know what I would do. Tears ran down my face as I thought about the last time I saw her, right after I popped out from under her robe and ran. I shouldn't have run away. It was all my fault. My mother and Aunt Bertie died because of me.

Merry's strong arms closed around me, and he held me close while I cried into his stained t-shirt. He rocked me back and forth like a baby, like Daddy used to a long time ago.

A squirrel chattered somewhere, kind of like a scared bird. I leaned into Merry and let all my fears come out: that I would never find Daddy, that the Judge would somehow catch us and do bad things to me, that Merry would leave me, that I would be alone, sucked into the grimy swamp, that I would never see Bertie again.

Merry wiped my face. His fingers were tough. Like old leather. But it made me feel better all the same.

"Em, the paper didn't say anything about Bertie. The article said your mom didn't have any family. It didn't mention you at all."

"Why won't you tell me how my mother died? I'm big enough to know."

"I already told you nobody knows what happened. That was the point of the article. The police are asking the public for clues, because they don't have any leads about who killed her."

I pushed away from him to stand up. "But we know what happened to her. We have to tell them, Merry. We have to."

"Em—"

"The Judge did it. We know he did."

When I thought about the Judge, he was like the black hole we learned about in science class. Sister Mary Catherine called it a void that sucked up everything in its path. That's what the Judge did. He took me from Daddy and killed my mother. Who knew what he did with Aunt Bertie. A deep chill ripped through me, mixing with the memory of cigar smoke. There was no way to escape him. In the end, I knew the Judge would take me, too.

Merry took one of my shaking hands and made a sandwich between his palms. "We may know he did it, Em, but we can't prove it."

"We can call the number for the police. The one in the paper. We can—"

"We can't trust the police, Em. He had police with him the other night, remember? They were the ones chasing us. If we called that number, we'd have no way of knowing who might answer."

"But if they didn't know it was us—"

"It would be the end, Em. You'd never see your father again."

"But how can the Judge get away with being so bad? Why can he kill people and chase little girls like me?"

Merry pulled his knees to his chest and watched the turtles splash into the water. "Wilkinson always ruled himself by a different code, one of absolute self-interest. He was like that when I knew him, since the beginning, but he's gotten meaner, more ruthless, over the years."

"You talk about the Judge like he's been around forever."

"Well, he's been around long enough to amass a lot of power. To build the empire he always wanted."

"I don't understand why he wants me."

"Em, I don't know how to describe the world he inhabits. He.......it's tough to explain."

"You make him sound super human, like one of the bad guys the Wonder Twins fight."

"Oh, he's human, all right. Much as I am. When I look at you, I try to see what he sees."

"What do you think he sees in me?"

"I don't know what he sees, and that's what's got me worried."

"Why?"

"Em, it's too complicated. People like Wilkinson are capable of anything. We've got to stay ahead of him. Okay?"

I picked up a stick and threw it into the water. Ripples played with the sunlight and shadows. "But how do I stay ahead of him if he wants to find me, Merry?"

"That's why we have to keep moving. Keep switching things up so nobody can follow us."

He stood up and brushed the seat of his jeans. The fire smoked when he kicked dirt onto it. Most of our gear was packed, but Merry picked up the last few things and stuffed them into our backpacks. He shuffled the dirt to scatter leaves over where we'd been. When he finished, he turned to me. "I'm sorry about your mom. About Bertie. I wish I could protect you from everything bad, Em, but I can't. All I can do is try to get you to your father before Wilkinson and his men find you. On that, I'll do everything I can. I promise."

As I closed the space between us and hugged him, I wondered: what made Merry help me? Why was he risking everything to find my daddy? Didn't he have a home full of people who loved him? I couldn't understand why he would be in the middle of nowhere with me. But before I could ask him more questions, he started walking.

"Through there about a hundred yards is a boardwalk. If we follow it, there's a small campground with some showers."

"With running water and everything?"

"Yes. One for girls and one for boys, with running water and everything. It was abandoned when I went over there about an hour ago. Let's go and wash up. I'll meet you outside the ladies when you're done."

I looked at his filthy clothes. "You sure do stink, Merry."

He smiled. "We're both pretty ripe. I'll break out a fresh set of clothes for each of us."

"I want the powder blue corduroys."

"Done. Hurry up, now. We've got some ground to cover today if we want to make a decent campsite before dark."

I picked up my small backpack and threw it over my shoulder. "How far are we going, Merry?"

"Depends."

"On what?"

"On how fast you can trek through this swamp. And what's beyond it."

Beyond? I looked around at the fluttering trees and black water and listened to the creaks and groans of the swamp. I didn't even want to imagine the only thing that could be scarier.

But before I could stop myself, I thought of the Judge. He leaned over the horizon. His meaty hands parted the trees. A cigar blew through the air when he waved. His lips moved around the cigar, but I ran into the bathroom to keep from seeing what he said. When I peeked outside, the forest was thick again. No gaps.

Still, I knew the Judge was out there.

Somewhere.

MERRY

Saturday. October 8, 1977. Near Kosciusko, Mississippi.

Emmaline trawled her feet on the trail ahead of me. She'd been happy to walk when we broke camp, but as the day wore on, the monotony of hiking blighted her disposition. She wove from side to side on the trail, idle hands pulling at dry leaves and slapping at vines. Once, she even started limping.

I wrapped my arms around Em's waist and lifted her off the ground, backpack and all. "Let's give you a little rest, Em. I've pushed you hard today, but it couldn't be helped."

"You don't have to carry me, Merry. I can walk. Clearly. I've walked the skin off the bottoms of my feet today."

"You're limping. Does your leg hurt?"

"It's sort of a come-and-go pain. It moves around. But it's all better now. Will you put me down?"

I lowered her feet to the rutted ground beside me. The caw-caw of a crow sounded in the distance, filtered through leaves that rustled in the wind. The scent of earth and pine.

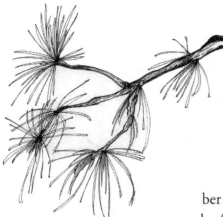

I breathed deep, willing us both to relax, to break through Emmaline's frustrations, to bring us both a bit of calm. After a minute or two of walking, Emmaline took my hand. Her deep breaths matched my own. Cleansed. Together.

I cleared my throat. "I remember the first time I had to do a long stretch of hiking."

"How old were you?"

"Five or six. I don't remember exactly. Younger than you, though."

She peered up at me. "Did your daddy teach you?"

"My step-father. That man loved to be out in the woods. Taught me to understand it like he did."

"Step-father? Did your parents get a divorce like mine?"

"No. My dad died when I was a little guy. I don't really remember him."

"Oh. Like my mother." She sniffed but kept her eyes trained on the trail ahead.

"After a fashion, yes."

"What happened to him?"

I listened to my breath. In and out. "Pneumonia killed my father." I remembered hearing air rattle in his chest. From the doorway, I watched him drown in his own juices, saw his chest labor to rise and fall. My head barely came as high as the door knob. I stood at attention until my legs cramped, but I wanted him to look at me. To see me, one more time.

He never acknowledged me before life wheezed out of him. I sat on the edge of the bed. Pretended those glassy eyes could see. They followed me the whole of my life.

Em's voice nudged me back. "Were you close to him?"

"Not really, but he was my father, and I respected him. He'd been away a while before he got sick. Was gone a lot, actually. Must have caught the lung fever during his travels."

"I thought you said he got pneumonia."

"Lung fever. Pneumonia. Same thing. Lung fever is… an older term for it."

"Oh. I never heard it before. So, were you there when he died?"

I couldn't tell her how much his eyes haunted me. How I saw them change the moment his spirit fled. I didn't want her to imagine her mother that way. Our walk through Nowhere was nightmare enough.

I picked up a stick and threw it. Watched it run aground. "I remember seeing him lie in state in the front parlor. People came over to the house to pay their respects. I stood next to him until my little legs ached. Even fought my mother when she tried to make me go to bed. I wanted to keep him with me for as long as possible. When I touched his skin, it was as cold as the chill in the room. I never could get warm in that house after that."

"When my friend at school's aunt died, we went to a fancy funeral home. Why did they come to your house?"

"Uh. Well, when there aren't any fancy funeral homes around, the house has to do."

"I guess you still miss him, huh? It sounds like you really loved him."

"The loss of a parent is always a hole, Em. It never quite fills up."

"That's why you understand how I feel about my daddy, right?"

I helped Emmaline step over a fallen log. Its rotting core was shredded around an empty chasm that rang hollow when I kicked it with the toe of my boot.

"Perhaps it is. I was lucky, though. My step-father came along and took care of me. He's the one that turned me into a man."

"So, he was the one you loved like your daddy? The way I loved Aunt Bertie like she was my real mother?"

"Over time, I grew to see him as my father, yes, and I loved him just as much. Could be why I understand how you miss your dad so much."

She picked a spray of yellow ragweed. Pulled at the individual buds and let them trail in the breeze. "I bet my daddy could hike for days and days without getting tired like me. I'm such a baby sometimes."

I hugged her to me, a quick gesture of reassurance to keep from telling her how much I admired her mettle. It made people aspire to things, but determination fueled their footsteps, even when the ground ran out. She was both a dreamer and a doer.

Like me. In a lot of ways, she was just like me.

"You want to hear tired, Em? The first time I went hiking with my step-dad, I walked right off the edge of a cliff. Only fell a few feet, into some bramble, but my ego took a bigger tumble. My step-dad had to rescue me and carry my crumpled up and howling self right back into the house. Everybody laughed at me. It took me a whole day to recover."

"Were you scared to hike after that?"

"Sure I was. But, the next morning, I was out there. Trying again. My step-dad was big on not letting a thing whip you."

"Did you fall that time?"

"Not in the same place, but I fell. Got lost, too. Lots of times. The bad things are all part of the experience, Em. You can't see the things a trail has to offer if you aren't willing to take on the worst of it. Think of everything we'd miss if we avoided life's trials: the river trip with Mister Jim, the birds with Jack, the turtles in the swamp, the pink sky at sunset and the boom of night noise."

She sunk into a mound of dirt on the side of the trail, and I eased down beside her. Shadows danced on her hand when I took it. The black wingspan of a vulture swooped down and slipped out of view. Her voice was diminished by defeat. "I feel so stupid. About everything. You always know the right things to do, and I never know anything. I thought it would be so easy to get to Daddy, but it's not."

"Emmaline, does anybody know the first thing about anything? I mean, I don't ever know how a day is going to turn out when I get up in the morning, but that doesn't stop me from tackling it. I seldom know what I'm doing, but I figure it out as I go along."

"But I'm never going to be able to hike in the woods like you, Merry. Never in a million years. Everything scares me, and I get so tired, and then I get mad at myself for being scared and tired."

"You won't be able to master it if you don't keep trying. Look. These woods are a part of life right now, and if you keep pushing, you'll figure them out. Don't expect to know everything all at once. Just let the bits and pieces be enough."

She let off a shaky exhale, but she never cried. Progress. I could see her growing, that stubborn set to her chin. "Bits and pieces. For the past few months, I've only had little pieces of Daddy. Letters he wrote me. A few pictures. The bits and pieces were never enough, because here I am. No matter how hard it is or how tired I get or how scared I am. I'm going to find Daddy. With you."

"I'm glad, Em. I'm glad you're with me."

"Let's go on, Merry. I'm ready. I promise I won't be such a baby anymore."

Her promise was lost when a thunderous boom shook the ground, followed by rapid gunfire. I jumped to my feet, with Emmaline clinging to my leg.

"What's that?"

"It sounds like cannon fire to me. Through there. Other side of those trees."

"Are they firing at us?"

"Ssh. Let's creep over to the tree line. See what's going on. Stay behind me."

EMMALINE

My legs couldn't keep up with Merry. But I ran behind him through the trees, toward the booming sounds. My nose burned, like the time we shot Mardi Gras fireworks in the courtyard behind the house, and the colored smoke hung in the air. I liked the glow worms best, because they laced out from a tiny button we set on fire. Some of the shapes were pretty, and they didn't stink like firecrackers.

"Gunpowder." Merry stopped and held up his fist, his signal for me to stop, too. "I think they're shooting over there, beyond that line of trees. Stay behind me, and be quiet."

Another blast lifted me off the ground, making my ears ring. When I screamed, my voice was lost in another roar like thunder. With my palms over my ears, I mouthed *sorry* and stumbled behind Merry. Loudness like that was really exciting-scary, because I didn't know when the next explosion was coming, and it was hard not to react. When I tried to hold in my screams, they always came out even louder. I bit my lips together, my mind on Daddy's face. What it would look like when he saw me.

Merry mashed his body flat against the trunk of a thick tree and pulled me beside him. Beyond the twisting branches and weeds, a small clearing opened into a rolling field that crawled with people. The men were dressed in knee-length pants with navy blue coats, and they wore triangle hats on their pony-tailed heads. Some of the men walked in a single line, and their guns had swords coming out of the ends. Other groups of soldiers stood around cannons that rolled on giant spoked wheels. Tents dotted the site, with bonfires near their openings.

"Merry, what are they—"

"Ssssh." He pulled me closer to him. I could almost hear his heartbeat through the front of his shirt.

When I smelled meat, I realized they were cooking fires. A woman in a long dress stirred a steaming black pot with a witchy wooden paddle. My stomach cartwheeled. Food didn't stay with me on the trail. I was always hungry.

Merry's bird-like eyes followed a man's march around the edge of the field, next to the trees. He had a gun slung over one fat shoulder, and his face was slack, sort of like mine felt when I was bored in school.

When the man came close to our hiding place, he weaved into the trees. A stick cracked behind us. Before Merry could turn around, the tip of a gun tapped him on the shoulder. "Get up."

Merry shielded me with his body. The soldier looked over his shoulder and spat, still pointing a gun at Merry's chest.

Merry stood a little taller. "My daughter and I, we're just a couple of hikers, out for the afternoon. We're not part of whatever it is you're doing here."

The man leaned over his round belly and spat on the ground again. I tried not to make a face when I saw that his teeth were crooked and brown. "We're mustering. War of 1812. And, we don't allow people to snoop around the perimeter."

"We're not snooping. I already told you. We're hiking. Education, you know. For my daughter."

The man spat more tobacco juice. "I have my orders." He eyed us down the length of the gun. I closed my eyes and held my breath when it clicked, but nothing happened. His laugh was a low growl. "You two best come with me."

I pushed into Merry's leg, but he didn't move. Instead, he stared off into the field, hypnotized by the men marching in rectangle formations. His jaw was tight, and his eyes were really wide, like the field was full of ghosts. I cleared my throat. "What is it, Merry?"

"I—" He blinked and shook his head, and his eyes were normal when he looked down at me. "It's nothing, Em. This whole scene is......familiar."

The end of the gun tapped Merry's shoulder. "Let's make it even more familiar, shall we? Now, move."

Merry brushed off the seat of his pants and started walking, and I slipped my hand in his and clung tight, while the soldier pointed the way with the end of his gun. We passed rows of cannons. Troops in old-timey uniforms. Most of them stopped when we passed.

"Prisoners." It was all the soldier ever called us as we marched across the field. Smoke tore at my eyes and made them water. At least, that's what I told myself it was. I clutched Merry's hand and tried to copy his walk: clipped steps and straight back. He looked more like a soldier than anyone else.

Over a rise, a lanky man stood beside a dirty tent, his head shriveled under a shock of bright red hair. Merry stopped, and I almost bumped into him.

The soldier pushed us up the hill with his gun. When we reached the top, he spat a stream of tobacco juice on Merry's boots and saluted the red-haired man. "I found these two spying in the woods yonder. Other side of the field."

Merry broke in. "Don't you think you're taking your ancient war games a little too seriously?"

The man with the carrot hair and horsey face walked up to Merry and stood, nose-to-nose, in front of him. For a few seconds, he just breathed, in and out, and glared at Merry without blinking. Merry stood at attention and never broke his stare. If I weren't so scared, it might've been funny. I'd seen boys act that way on the playground, right before they started to fight, but I didn't think grown-ups did it, too.

The soldier spoke through clenched teeth. "War is serious, and you, my friend, are in serious trouble." He cut his eyes. "Put them in the tent. Tie him up, but you can leave her free. I'll keep watch."

I heard a crack, and Merry fell forward on his face. The back of his head was bleeding. I dropped to my knees and pressed my hands to his head. "Why did you have to shoot him? What did he do to you?" I felt my eyes tearing up, but really I was just mad.

The red-haired soldier picked Merry up under his arms and dragged him into the tent. A hand tugged at my arm and made me follow the grooves his boots made in the dirt. The soldier's gun was bloody at the butt, and he slung it over his shoulder. "He'll be all right. Might have a headache later. Though, with what he's got coming, he'll likely wish I'd shot him."

MERRY

My eyes wouldn't focus. I blinked, but every movement was like a knife through my skull. I'd endured that brand of pain. Once. The last night of my life.

I bit into my leather sleeve to keep from crying out. Sweat ran into my eyes. I could see exactly what happened the night I died.

I was traveling the Natchez Trace with a small party, on my way to Washington DC. Originally, I intended to go through the port at New Orleans, but physical maladies pulled me off the river at Memphis. I languished for almost two weeks before the commanding officer decided I should take my servant and follow a Chickasaw Indian agent along the Trace as far as Nashville.

He was a quiet fellow, the agent. Kept to himself, like me. Silence always made for faster travels. I preferred it. Thus, I had come to like the man by the time we pulled up in front of Grinder's Stand, a day's ride south of Nashville.

That last night, I ate dinner early. Didn't feel well. I decided to retire to my room and gave my servant leave for the evening. My room was small but serviceable, a sleeping pallet and one wooden chair. I left a small candle burning next to my bed in case I awoke during the night.

A scratching sound startled me. Insistent. Rhythmic. From the other side of my room.

I peeled open my eyes and saw the Indian agent. He leaned back in that wood chair and let it fall to the ground. A crude rocker. My mouth was muddy when I spoke. "Did I oversleep? I can be ready in—"

He leaned forward, and light caught a line of metal splayed across his lap. "Ssh. I think you're ready. Wilkinson, he thinks you're ready, too." He lurched from the chair, and it crashed against the wall as the muzzle of the gun found my head. The world between my ears exploded, and I sunk into blackness.

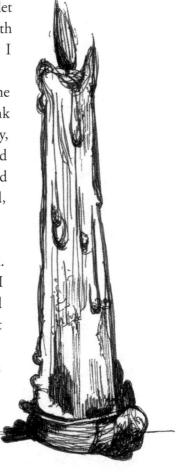

Did I imagine him there?

I don't know how long I was suspended. It could've been minutes or hours. When I awoke, the room was dark, the candle snuffed out. My breaths were shallow, and when I felt my head, part of it was gone.

I tasted blood and realized I'd bitten through my tongue to staunch the pain, but it still felled me in waves. My throat vibrated, like I cried out, but I was deaf to my own voice. If anyone heard me, no one came.

When I shot an animal, there was always that fine moment, the one where it accepted death. Not the same thing as dying, but the hush, the silence, that descended ahead of the end.

My body convulsed, and that peace entered me. I didn't want more agony. I'd read about men who were shot and lingered for days, screaming and wailing in torment. I was in control, and I knew what to do. With a quaking hand, I reached under my pallet and found my gun. I could only lift it as far as my gut, but I was always the master of the mortal shot.

It didn't matter how I finished it.

A head bobbed in my sight lines, hair a corkscrewed mess. I sat up and grabbed around its neck. Pressed my fingers into flesh. *I won't let you kill me again. I won't. I—*

"Merry!"

Emmaline. Her face was flushed, her eyes buggy. How did she wind up at my deathbed?

I released her, and my world righted. My last assignment. Nowhere. Mississippi. A little girl looking for her father. I reached out and pulled her, coughing, to me. "I'm sorry, Em. I thought you were someone else. I—"

In that instant, I understood why people had kids. Why I should've tried harder to find love and settle down while I lived. Her face beamed straight into my heart. I wanted to teach her everything I knew. Take her everywhere I'd been. Protect her from every threat.

Emmaline coughed again. "You s-s-scared me, M-m-merry. I th-th-ought—"

I brushed her hair away from her face. "Ssh. Delusions from this crack on the head. I'll be all right. Did I hurt you?"

She wiggled in my lap and nuzzled into my chest. "A little bit, but I'm okay now. I can shake it off. Like Daddy." She looked up at me. "Like you."

I wiggled my wrists and saw indentions where rope had been. Emmaline's eyes followed mine. "I untied you. After the red-headed soldier left. Nobody's been outside in a while."

"How long?"

"I don't know. It's dark now. Everybody's down the hill, around a big bonfire."

I slipped my head out of the tent and sniffed wood smoke. In the darkness, a lone fiddle accompanied a female voice. A haunting tune I remembered, it called down the tunnel of time.

Why did I e'er leave this fair cot,
Where once I was happy and free;

Doom'd now to roam, without friend or home,
Oh! dear father, take pity on me.

Tears hounded the edges of my eyes, and I brushed them away before Em could see. When my sight adjusted to the dark, I scanned the area around the tent. A crude table and chair. A cluster of trees.

And a horse. Tied to a thick pine.

I scooted back into the tent and crawled to Emmaline. "Em, we have to hurry. There's—"

Before I could finish, a rustling interrupted me. Emmaline screamed and scrabbled behind my body.

As I looked over my shoulder, Wilkinson stepped through the tent flap. I got up on my knees and shielded Em. A pathetic defense. She buried her face into my back, and I could feel her breath burn through my jacket.

Skin creased around Wilkinson's Nowhere eyes when he smiled. "Meriwether Lewis. It's good of you to deliver my little beauty to me."

EMMALINE

I could hear the Judge's voice, even when I plugged my ears with my fingers.

The Judge. His creepy smile swallowed me.

I took a step back. How did the Judge know where to find me? I saw what he did to me with his eyes, and I wanted to run away as fast as I could. If I hid in the woods in the dark, could the Judge find me there?

Would he find me anywhere?

The Judge pulled out a gun with a silencer and pointed it at Merry, but he couldn't tear his eyes away from me. He snaked his tongue over his lips. "Well, little beauty. Your Merry here is as resourceful as ever. I was beginning to think I'd lost you for good." He rubbed sweat from his forehead with his free hand and held it out to me. Palm open, like he wanted me to take it. His fingers shook. "Why don't you come over here? Stand by me? That way, you won't get bloody when I shoot Merry."

I grabbed Merry's waist and clamped my hands together. "Don't you shoot him. I'll scream and scream. I won't go anywhere with you. I won't. I—"

The Judge lurched over to us. He lodged his shaky fingers under my arms and pulled me free of Merry. I kicked along the ground as he dragged me to the other side of the tent. The gun clicked in his hand. He flung me to one side and took aim.

It was my only chance.

I balled my body up like a ball and bowled myself into the Judge's legs. Stars twinkled behind my eyes when I hit him, but it worked. He staggered to one side, and his shot fired wide.

Or, I thought he missed. When Merry backed into a folding table and started to fall, I thought maybe I was wrong. I looked up at the Judge and, in that moment, I hated him enough to kill him, to take his gun and point it at him and pull the trigger. If Merry died, I couldn't be left all alone. With the Judge.

Merry rolled sideways, and when he popped to his feet, he held another gun. He pointed it at the Judge's head and never once looked in my direction. "Give Emmaline to me, Wilkinson."

The Judge kept his gun trained on Merry. Another adult staring match, only with weapons. I bit my lip and waited for a way to do something—anything—to help Merry.

The Judge chuckled. "You know what will happen if you shoot me."

"You'll be sent back to the beginning. Have to start Nowhere all over. How many times will that make for you?"

"I've only started once that I recall." The Judge's belly rippled when he laughed. "That's right. I ditched my last assignment when I figured out I could make the rules work for me here. And they have. Spectacularly. An eternity to build an empire, to savor my Ann here. My little beauty. If I'm smart. If I don't get caught."

"How do you make your own rules in this place? Tell me."

The Judge took a step toward Merry. "You always were a good soldier, weren't you, Lewis?"

"I—"

"Every time I saw you, you were kissing ass. Doing the right thing. Upstanding. Ethical." He spat. "Me? I only did that when it moved me ahead. Advanced my agenda."

The Judge stopped. He panted like a dog when his eye fell on me, and I shrunk against the side of the tent.

"The only thing I've plotted is how to find my Ann again. That's what happens, you know. At the end of all this, this Nowhere. Our spirits are gobbled up by living souls."

"And you think—"

"My Ann's soul is in that little beauty. Yes. You can shoot me now. Send me back. But I'll find her again. It will only be a matter of time. Because, we both know in Nowhere, we've got nothing but time."

Merry cocked his gun. "You won't remember her if you go back, Wilkinson. That's the deal I got. Everything about your tour in Nowhere is erased. The only thing you'll recall is your miserable life."

"The best thing about my life was my Ann. Her spirit will call to me. From Nashville. Isn't that where you father is, little beauty?"

Instead of answering, I reared back and spit as far as I could. It landed like bird droppings on the toe of the Judge's shoe. He kept the gun trained on Merry and smiled at me.

"I thought so."

"Leave Em alone. Let's have our little duel according to Nowhere's rules. Loser goes back to the start."

I twisted my head between the Judge and Merry. What were they talking about? Where was Nowhere? Even though I knew it was a bad time, I opened my mouth to ask, but Merry stopped me.

"You were the most self-interested son of a bitch I ever met."

"I had to survive. I had a family. A wife. God, I miss my wife."

Merry spoke through gritted teeth. "I missed my life, you bastard. Here I've been wandering through this hell all these years, worried about the taint suicide would lend my legacy. I had to spend all this time here to know who killed me."

The Judge pulled a lever at the top of his gun and tensed. "You gave up on your life. You were a manic depressive drunk who committed suicide in the middle of nowhere, one dark October night."

I watched the end of the Judge's gun shake, his finger hovering over the trigger. I went to the Judge and took his hand. When I talked, my voice was different. Flirtatious, my mother called it. The voice I used for her men. "Judge. Put down that gun and come to me." His head jerked sideways, and I could see hope in his eyes. I stoked it. "Please. I want you, like you said. I want to be with you."

The Judge's whole body jiggled before he turned and fell on his knees in front of me. His fat fingers stroked my face, and his eyes were glassy with tears. I held my breath to keep from smelling his cigar stink and forced myself to smile as he ran his lips all over my face. "Oh, little beauty. I knew you'd know me when the time was right."

Shouts sounded in the camp, and a commotion worked its way toward our tent. Merry caught my eye a second before a popping sound ripped the air behind the Judge, and as he turned, the sides of the tent melted together and parachuted to the ground. While the Judge watched it flutter around us, I clasped his hand and raised it to my mouth.

And bit him until I tasted blood.

He shrieked and teetered backwards into a big fold in the falling tent. His blood was salty on my lips. I wiped it away and dove under another ripple before he could grab me again.

My heart beat so fast, I thought it would explode. "Merry! Where are you?" I swam through the sea of muddy canvas. It scratched my face and tugged my legs. When I tried to breathe, it was like I was drowning in cloth. I kicked my legs as hard as I could. "Merry! Answer me!"

The Judge's voice seeped through the gloom. "He can't give you what I can, little beauty. Come back to me."

Hoofbeats pounded the ground a few feet from the tent and echoed in my chest. I clawed in their direction through the dirt. When the tent parted, a cool breeze hit my face. I crawled through an opening into the night air.

Merry.

He galloped toward me astride a black horse. He swooped down an arm and picked me up, and the whole sky tilted when I landed between him and the horse's streaky mane. With one arm, he held me close in front of him. "Hang on, Em. I won't let you fall."

I looked back to try to see him, but instead, I saw the Judge pop out of the tent. He raised his fist, and when he yelled, my heart flip-flopped in my chest.

"I'll always find you. Wherever you are. You'll always be my little beauty."

THE JUDGE

Decades. They rolled into a century. And more. The whole time, I stalked the spirit of my departed Ann, knowing she would land somewhere eventually. Her light was too ebullient to be kept from another life. I knew her essence would be lessened when absorbed into another person, but she would still be there.

I believed she could be coaxed to the surface. Somehow, she would remember me. The love we shared. It would bring her spirit to the fore and consume the outside person.

She was so much like the child. Sumptuous curls for my hands to get lost in. The first time I saw her, she tossed her powdered head. It was Philadelphia, her hometown. She was astounding, in her Parisian silks, set against skin of alabaster. Her eyes caressed every man in the room.

But, they rested on me.

Lingered.

I was a moth to her light. Lost at her side. Me, a pauper. From pitiful Maryland stock.

She overlooked my failings. Her eyes bored into me, and I saw the man I could be. A man of importance. Property. Even fame. With a tilt of her head, she mapped the cartography of my life. And, I followed her directives, until the moment she died.

Find me, she said, as the air seeped out of her. I gazed into her unseeing eyes, and I was obsessed.

I could still taste her, underneath the hoofbeats that reverberated in the still air of autumn.

The child didn't recognize me, but that didn't matter. My Ann was there. When the time was right for the child to know me, she would be mine. Underneath every protest, she called to me.

I'm here, Jimmy.

You've found me.

At last.

Go after them, I said.

MERRY

Sunday. October 9, 1977. Somewhere along the Natchez Trace, Missis-sippi.

Hoofbeats flayed the ground behind us. At least two horses, if my instincts were right.

I wrapped one arm around Emmaline to hold her in front of me in the saddle and tugged the reins with the other. Another set of hoofbeats ripped through the darkness. Our horse reared. Bolted in a dead run through pitch blackness. The sharp thwack and flay of the branches switched our flesh. Spanish moss clawed at my eyes. The horse swerved and ducked, picking up blind speed in the wake of more shouting. I clung to Em, fighting to keep the horse on the blinding trail.

Each fresh sound was a searing reminder that no wound could kill me. Not really. Wilkinson could shoot me. Banish me to a bar at the backend of Nowhere. A form of Hell.

Em was the one who was truly in danger. I couldn't see her harmed on my watch.

I ran the horse as fast as I dared. Maybe fifteen minutes. Maybe an hour. Fear always distorted the perception of time. Everything happened in slow motion and all at once.

The slice of night sky shone brighter through the gap in the trees. I pivoted in the saddle and pulled one arm toward me to jerk the bit. The horse tossed his head but didn't break his thunderous stride.

"Whoa!" I rasped.

The black devil ran for another hundred yards before he gave out and slowed to a trot. He halted and stood in a deep gouge, and I shifted my head and listened. Over the shocked cacophony of night noise, I strained to hear the gallop of pursuit, the splinter of bullets on tree bark, and the shouts of muddled men, but the air was as void as our surroundings, without form in the blackness.

I slid to the ground. Eroded dirt piled up on both sides of us. Either we were on the Old Trace or in a ditch, for while I pointed the horse in a northerly direction, I didn't know where we were, nor were there enough visible stars to divine coordinates. If I pulled us off the trail and into the trees, maybe we could hide out until morning, figure out what to do.

When I turned back to Em, she still clung to the horse's neck, her eyes wide as saucers. Her whole body spasmed at my touch. I gathered her into my sore arms and hugged her fiery body to me. Her arms and legs twitched like rattles, and when I waved my hand in front of her eyes, she didn't respond. I shook her, gentle. "Em. Emmaline. Can you hear me?"

Her breath came shallow, and she stared, unseeing. Still holding her, I tied the horse's lead to a tree and lowered her to the ground. She roiled in the dirt, her body out of control. A dusting of earth clung to the sheen of sweat on her cheeks, her hands. I tugged at the saddle bag, frantic for anything that might help her. Inside the leather flap, I found a tiny flashlight.

When I flipped the switch, Em's dirt spattered face filled my vision. Her pupils took up most of the cornflower hue of her eyes. I tried to rub her hands, but they were white-knuckled. Next to her, I mounded up some leaves and twigs

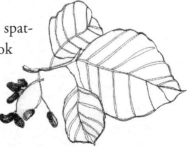

and balanced the light on them to free up both hands.

Sweat matted her hair. When I peeled back her jacket, her top was ringed with more perspiration, and her skin sizzled to the touch. I picked up each leg and ran my hands along them under the light, checking for gashes. A dislocation. Swelling. Anything out of place. When I finished, I exhaled a deep sigh of relief.

She was whole. On the outside, at least.

I rubbed her hot forehead and searched the fringes of my medical knowledge for the cause of her sudden malady. When severely frightened, could a person go into shock? For an inexperienced girl, she'd shouldered a lot on our trek: swimming the Mississippi, hiking long distances, sleeping outdoors. An interview with Wilkinson followed by a first frantic horse ride in the dark could be enough to drive the heartiest people over the edge. Had I pushed her too hard?

Helpless, I ripped off my jacket and wrapped it around her. Held her close. By the opaque quality of the atmosphere, it had to be near five o'clock in the morning. The darkest moments before sunrise. A twig snapped, and I strained to make out any unseen threat. When I held my breath, I heard nothing. No bird song. No breath of breeze.

Em shivered, and I rocked her in my arms. Tried to think of a song to sing, bad as I was at crooning. Her eyes raced back and forth underneath her eyelids, delirious. No matter how much I tried, I could not heal the sick little girl in my arms. Not in the dark. Without proper supplies. I couldn't work a miracle on my own.

The lonesome blackness brought that other thing. Its dark teeth gnawed at my insides from time to time. I told myself it was just a feeling. Being trapped in the shroud of night need not summon the real monster.

Failure. It destroyed my every accomplishment with the Corps of Discovery. Ate away at the last years of my life. When I stood in my office, alone, I studied myself in the mirror and wondered how my fame evaporated. How I went from 'Meriwether Lewis: Celebrated Explorer and Scientist' to 'Meriwether Lewis: Failed Politician.' I didn't even understand how it happened. One day, men worshipped me. The next, they shunned me.

And, the more I tried to regain their favor, the deeper I sank into the morass.

Birds. Leaves. Even bodies of water and the sky. I was comfortable with them. But, I never understood people.

This time will be different. I'll finish the job. I have to do it for Emmaline. I'm not the same man.

I'm not.

"Merry." Em's voice came in a breath so soft it was as though I hadn't heard it.

I shifted her, brushing the hair from her face. "I've got you, Em. Stay with me, okay?"

"I...hurt. Everything...hurts. I'm so...scared."

"I know, I know. It's almost light, all right?"

"Mmmm." Her head lolled to one side, and I lost her again. I adjusted her on my legs to massage her scalp with one hand.

Out of the corner of one eye, a figure darted across the path, as low to the ground as we were. It tore through the trees on the other side of the trail. Round and black, with stubby legs, it was a monster I'd encountered too often in my time.

Footsteps pummeled the dirt in pursuit of the animal. Still holding Emmaline, I grabbed the reins of the horse with one hand to steady it.

A gunshot streaked through the beginning of sunrise. The horse reared against its tether, and Emmaline screamed awake. Her hands scrabbled along the sides of my neck, nearly cutting off my flow of air while I fought to keep the horse from breaking the lead. Fireworks went off in my sight lines, and I pried her fingers off with one hand and laid her well away from the horse at the same time it broke its tether and bolted. The metallic gleam of a pistol caught the light as a lone man raised his weapon.

I rolled on top of Em. "Don't shoot! We're not armed, and she's hurt."

The only response I got was a guttural snort. Grunts. A wild boar crashed through the trees at the top of the rise and bored into us with its manic eyes.

MERRY

The massive boar wheezed the remnants of its last meal in my face. Bile rose in the back of my throat. A monster. Five feet long with sharp tusks jutting from the sides of its mouth. I'd seen men flayed open and trampled

189

to death by smaller beasts.

The boar dug its front hoof into the ground and grunted, preparing to charge through us into the trail. I kept Emmaline close to me and rolled. Muddy ground came up and hit me in the face, and I tasted rot. It hurt to breathe, but I shouted at that ogre. Obscenities. A sewer of them, to no effect. It narrowed its eyes and lowered its head in preparation to career our way.

A shot crackled through the mist, and the boar pivoted sideways, its eyes wide and its mouth slack, before it tumbled down the hill, stopping on its back mere inches from my feet. Its legs twitched, and its belly rose and fell in panicked breathing.

I turned to find a wiry hunter with a black goatee holding my horse's reins. A pistol smoked in his other hand. He wore an orange hunting cap over a messy black ponytail, and his dark eyes were trained on me.

"Unbelievable. Almost lost. To a wild pig." He took a step toward us. "Not how I planned to kill one, in front of a child."

I hugged Em close and scrambled to my feet. I watched him as he retied my horse's lead to a tree. "My daughter here needs help. Our crazy horse got spooked. Took us on quite a ride. I think Em—my daughter—I think she's in shock from it. Is there anywhere close that maybe I can take her? Get her checked out?"

The hunter strutted over to us. With tender fingers, he felt along the sides of her face, her neck. "She is in shock. It is clear, yes? With some rest, she'll recover."

"Still, I'd like to make sure for myself."

He stepped back. "The closest clinic is Tupelo, about an hour's drive from here." He squatted next to the boar and listened to blood gurgle in the back of its throat.

"I don't want a clinic. I know what's wrong with her. Surely there's a farmhouse? Something? Any place where we can use an extra room?"

"Only my house. For miles." With cold calculation, he stood up. A single shot pierced the morning air and hit the writhing boar between the eyes. Its legs stopped, and it rolled on its side and was still. Blood seeped into the bed of decaying leaves.

"I don't want to cause offense. I mean, you probably saved our lives. But I'm not sure I want to go to your house."

He raised his shaggy brows. "I am not sure I invited you."

As we stared each other down, faint hoofbeats sounded from the direction we traveled overnight. I fumbled with the horse's lead, hobbled by fear of discovery and the unconscious girl in my arms. Before the anonymous rider breached the bend in the trail, I shouted, "You could at least help me free this horse."

A brown gelding trotted up beside the stranger. He cut his eyes to the new man, one of his Latin kinsman, and muttered something in Spanish. I stopped struggling with the tether and followed their gestures in a vain attempt to decipher the exchange. I knew a bit of French, but Spanish had always eluded me. Nowhere gave me little opportunity to practice, with its constant game of starting over. Forgetting.

When they finished, the second man dismounted, tied his horse to a tree and unsheathed a jagged knife from a leather scabbard. I jumped back and stood between Em and the knife, a flashlight my only weapon.

I braced myself for a struggle, but the man ignored us and tore into the dead beast, slitting it open from chin to gut. Even though I knew what to expect, I almost vomited when I sniffed the foul juices. The Spaniard smiled at my discomfort. "Meet my foreman. Luis, he will stay and prepare the meat while I take you and your daughter home."

"I thought we weren't invited."

"My friend, you are in no position to quibble."

I looked down at Em's ashen face and traced the outline of her cheek with my finger. Nodded my assent.

"Good. *Vale.* Can you manage your daughter on your mount, or do you need me to take her?"

I pulled us into my saddle with one hand and held Em's limp body in front of me. "I've ridden plenty of horses in my time."

His eyes crinkled at the corners. "I toy with you. I like to tease my friends. My name is Hector de Silva. And you are?"

I watched him and his foreman for a beat. Teasing peeved me. Always had, especially in dire circumstances. It did nothing to diffuse a stressful situation. While the foreman cut out the boar's heart, De Silva's smile faded under the weight of my stare until I was satisfied he got the message. "I'm Merry."

"Merry. Well. It is a good thing I maintained my schedule this morning, yes?" He gestured to the carcass. "I try to be out with the rising of the sun. I like to be alone sometimes. I suspect you are the same, no?"

"Yes. I'm alone. Most of the time."

With one athletic leap, De Silva was in his saddle. He clicked his heels against the horse's side, guiding it through the tunnel of trees. I nudged my horse forward. We rode abreast in silence for a while. Every so often, I sneaked glances his way. A Spaniard, in the middle of Mississippi. How did he get here? Why did he choose this place? I remembered Wilkinson's storied connection with the Spanish, and my veins ran cold. I looked at the top of Em's head, and I said the first thing I could think to protect her. "Hector, if we wanted to hire a car to get to Tupelo, how far would we have to go?"

"Tupelo is the closest town, but here, close is a relative term."

"So? How far?"

He shifted in his saddle. Smiled. "She will be fine at my estate. It is large. When here, I like seclusion."

"I see."

"Do you have a place to stay in Tupelo? A motel, perhaps?" Our horses plodded a symphony into the ground. I could see bits of blue through the canopy of fall color.

"No. Look. I don't like the idea of staying with you. I'd rather be on our own."

"From the looks of her, you may be on your own soon enough. She needs rest."

Her head lolled against my left arm. I studied her face, shrunken and pale. "All right. One night. If she's not stronger in the morning, we need to get to a doctor. She's not burning up like she was before, but she's still pretty out of it."

He shifted sideways in his saddle and studied her. "*Muy hermosa.* She'll be fine."

"I hope so."

"Where are you and your daughter headed?"

How many lies was I going to have cobble together before my job was done? My voice was even when I went on. "Memphis. We live there. I thought it'd be educational to take Em on a trip through history for a few days. Not to mention fun. Better than sitting in a stuffy classroom, you know?"

"Outdoors. Always better. For everything." He looked at the clear sky through the shudder of wind in the leaves. "Perhaps you will join me for dinner this evening. Fresh boar with all the trimmings. We can let the girl rest and get better acquainted. A new experience, yes?"

"I appreciate the offer, but I think I should stay with Em. Do everything I can to get her ready to move on."

He pulled his horse to a halt. Twisted in the saddle to face me. "My house sits well off the Trace, on a road that leads to Tupelo. I can take you there in the morning and drop you wherever you like." Without waiting for me to agree, he flashed his white teeth and continued. "Good. It is settled. We will leave your horse in my barn." He winked. "My staff will take excellent care of your daughter, and for you, what can I say? I will be a charming host."

Before I could argue, he nudged his horse and trotted through the ruts ahead of me.

I had no choice but to follow.

MERRY

Several miles west of the Trace, the trees gave way to thick pine along an undulating horse path. The earth was darker, like the Spaniard. Would following De Silva off course be our refuge? Or a trap? In my lengthy experience with people, Spaniards were impossible to read.

We rode through early morning, the only sounds the occasional bird call, the hooves of our horses on the packed dirt of the trail, and the whistle of the wind. At last, we pulled up behind him at an entrance camouflaged by a thicket of heavy scrub. Designed to move like a living gate, it warned a visitor to go away.

If one noticed it at all.

Em stirred in front of me, and I patted her shoulder. She leaned her head against my chest and looked up at me. A lovely face, even upside down. Her cheeks were pink, but her eyes were glassed-over. "You look funny, Merry."

My chest was light enough to float. Was this what it felt like to lose one's heart to a child?

De Silva dismounted in one graceful move, spreading his arms in an expansive greeting. "The edge of my estate. I will open the gate, yes? Wait here."

I nudged my horse through the gap before De Silva bolted the lock and mounted his horse behind us. His smile was inscrutable, his face a mask. He gave the horse its head and beckoned us into his paradise.

In my experience, paradise did not exist. I'd encountered variants in my lifetime. My disappointment in the Corps of Discovery's failure to find a Northwest passage was counterbalanced by the highs. The West was a wonderland for a loner like me. A slow-moving stream at dawn, its waters cold and sweet. The springing flight of a prong horned critter along the floor of a slot canyon. Round birdhouses strung along the White Cliffs of the Missouri. Fish that jumped through the rainbow made by a misty waterfall.

Perhaps I wasn't being fair, but in my experience, Spaniards were shifty. Throughout my entire career, they were the enemy, herds of people waiting across a waterway or an imaginary line. Life experience was hard to shake in Nowhere, especially when I couldn't remember whether anyone there could rise above a stereotype.

And, what about Wilkinson? I heard the rumors of his Spanish duplicity while I was alive. If he was a Spanish spy, would he seek out his Spanish friends in Nowhere? Recruit them to carry out his misdeeds? I pulled Emmaline closer and wished I'd remembered to bring Wilkinson's gun.

We galloped along a wide avenue lined with cypress trees, into a clearing ringed by orange and yellow and wide open sky. Four bays of a stone mansion sprawled there. Leaded glass windows winked in the morning sunlight.

On the great lawn that stretched before the house, the towering statue of a man on horseback stood watch, his metal clothing molded like armor, a bronze gun in one hand. De Silva eased his mount to a stop, and I halted alongside him. "If you couldn't tell from my accent, I'm Spanish. Old country."

I eyed the statue, its clothing that of a conquistador. A conqueror. I swallowed my mounting fear. "Is this a fancy, Welcome-Wagon version of you?"

He did not smile. "We have no welcome wagon here."

De Silva turned his horse's head toward a barn of russet wood. Inside, fresh sawdust and leather soap tickled my nostrils. Horses leaned from their stalls to nuzzle a greeting to their master. I watched as De Silva made the rounds, patting wet noses and whispering sweet Spanish words in frisky ears. At the end of the walkway, he picked up a phone and pushed a lit button before he directed me to an open stall. In murmured Spanish, he conversed with someone on the other end of the line.

I led my horse into his quarters. It smelled of hay and cedar. De Silva stuck his head around the corner. "It is settled. Your room is ready."

"That was fast."

"I keep a small staff here. They take care of things. Please, follow me."

De Silva's boots clomped along the wide floorboards. I squinted with the shift from dim to bright and followed the Spaniard in silence, still holding Emmaline close to my chest. Her legs dangled, knocking gently against my side.

We walked along a stone path through a formal garden of boxwoods pruned into odd shapes. Fantastical, as Emmaline would point out if she were awake. I missed her running narrative, her enraptured view of the world. I stared at her closed eyes and imagined what she would say. Her fascination with mermaids. Fish. Flowers. Childish things that smacked of magic.

Through her eyes, the world was magical again.

Dear Emmaline, you have to be all right.

De Silva led us to a door of sliding glass, recessed under a canopy of copper. At the clap of his hands, the glass slid aside. Heat from inside mingled with the crisp cool of the fall morning. He trooped along a vaulted corridor streaked with light that fell on a thick wooden door. It was padlocked. De Silva pulled out a fat ring of keys and inserted one into the lock. The door yawned into a cavernous circular room where glass-and-steel stairs wound upward and disappeared.

Was De Silva our jailer? Or our savior?

He swept his arms through the opening. "Welcome, my friend. Your suite of rooms awaits you, two floors above."

Emmaline rustled in my arms as we ascended the turret. "Is this Rapunzel's house?" She yawned, and her head lolled against my chest, unconscious once again. I tried to recall the Rapunzel story. A princess trapped in a tower. Her only escape a wily prince and her torrent of golden hair.

I was no royal. And, I had already cut the princess's shiny locks. I twisted a clipped curl around one finger and hoped we'd be all right. De Silva was taking us to a respite.

Or to our mutual end.

When a ringing telephone ricocheted through the corridor and up the stairs, De Silva stopped, and I nearly collided with him. He looked back before making a slight bow and slipping past us. "Last door on the left. *Uno momento.*" His boots clipped along glass and marble as he hurried back the way we came.

I dithered. Eavesdrop on De Silva or continue alone? His voice wafted up the stairs, and it made up my mind to wait.

Holding my breath, I weighed De Silva's words.

"It is just as likely one of your toy soldiers shot him, no?" De Silva's voice dripped with disdain. He listened for a few beats and cut in again. "I am certain you do not, but in any case, I have seen no one fitting that description." De Silva was a practiced liar. "I will be in and out today. If I come across anyone, I will consider your request, *Señor.*"

I'd heard enough. The Judge was looking for us. That much was clear.

De Silva joined us a few moments later. He studied me, and I fought the urge to squirm. Emmaline lifted her head and smiled at the Spaniard. "You're a nice man."

His face melted. "Ah, beautiful girl. Good to see you awake."

I cleared my throat. "I know I should explain—"

"Not now. Her health is more important, yes?" De Silva's black eyes sparkled. He continued down the hallway and stopped in front of a door of carved wood. When I looked closer, each panel depicted an intricate hunting scene. He grasped a lever. "The entrance to your rooms."

I turned and almost stumbled as De Silva pushed us through a doorway into a white room bathed in light. Floor-to-ceiling windows lined one wall, their panes criss-crossed with jail-like ironwork. When he followed us inside and closed the door, I didn't miss the click of the lock.

THE JUDGE

I always detested enclosed spaces. A stifling office or the front berth in a keelboat. Perhaps that's why I was the kind of leader who always chose the field. People usually found me patrolling the streets of New Orleans or galloping over the countryside. The front lines were the best place to demonstrate my mettle, to avoid situations that boxed me in.

In Nowhere, I retained my sense of self-preserving claustrophobia. Surprise was the best way to keep an underling in line. I used it often, but not too often. People reveal their basest selves when they're allowed to relax. To believe themselves invincible. Security makes a man slipshod. Slow.

I never had the luxury of feeling secure. Not while I lived.

Not now, in this grimy motel room in a town more forgotten than it was when it was settled. I rode through it once, on my way to Richmond on a mission to clear my name. Pioneers buzzed around my horse, awed by my uniform bedecked with gold braid and my cougar skin saddle blanket. I walked my mount down the street just outside this window, and people followed me. Transfixed.

Of course, my journey was a success.

But, I never imagined I'd be back here, holed up in pitiful room that reeked of moth balls and mold, dueling a pen against the tremor in my hand. The hand that touched my Ann. For a brief gift of seconds, I held her again. I could still feel her skin burn into mine.

God, how I missed her.

Water smeared paper. I wadded another effort into a ball and cast it aside. No subordinate could receive a letter from James Wilkinson and suspect him of crying.

I took out a clean piece of parchment, and I steadied my hand.

And, I started again.

Dear Sir, I wrote. Herewith you will find my instructions on a pressing matter.........

EMMALINE

He was the handsomest man I'd ever seen. Handsomer than Daddy, even. He ran his hand along my forehead, and I didn't feel all better right then, but I knew I would.

"I've never had a handsome man doctor." I tried to make my voice sound stronger than I felt.

"I am no doctor, but I am here to take care of you." His eyes moved from mine to Merry's, and when he talked, his voice was musical, like Daddy's, but with a funny accent.

Merry carried me into a ginormous bedroom, all white, with a frilly canopy bed. When he set me down, the mattress came up to his waist, and it was firm with silky covers. I always wanted a canopy bed in my room, but my mother wouldn't allow it. I sunk into softness and thought about the other things I wanted before I ran: to wear Levi's instead of frilly dresses (good); to see the world outside of New Orleans (mostly good); to find Daddy (excellent).

Anyway.

I knew it would be, when we found him.

Merry stroked hair out of my face with his rough fingers. "I've been worried about you, Em. Good to see you're feeling more yourself."

"What happened? I only remember little bits. Loud voices. The whole tent fell down and—and the Judge was there, wasn't he?"

"Ssh. Let's not relive it just now. It'll get you all worked up again."

The man—Mister De Silva—he came in and stood next to Merry. He cleared his throat, and Merry moved aside and let him get closer to me. I almost squealed when took my arm and pressed my wrist with his fingers. They were strong and cool. He looked at his watch and counted with his lips, but he didn't make any sound. When he finished, he smiled, and I felt my face turn red. "I will help you sit up, yes?"

He put his hands under me, and when he helped me up, I got a little dizzy. He steadied me and listened to my heart from the back, and even though it was beating really fast, I took the biggest breaths I could. I tried not to bite down on the thermometer he stuck in my mouth, because Aunt Bertie told me it had something poisonous in it that would be bad for me to swallow. Instead, I watched the shapes the sun made through the filmy curtains. Like clouds on the floor and up the walls. After he peered down my throat with a popsicle stick, he smiled. "All done."

"It's shock, right? Just as I thought." Merry watched from the end of the bed, twisting his hat in his hands.

"Her temperature is a bit high, but it is nothing serious. How long were you outside?"

Merry looked at the ceiling, counting the time in his mind or trying to decide what to tell him. I didn't know which. He finally looked at Mister De Silva again. "Several days."

"This child is badly sunburned and mildly dehydrated. Exposure, aggravated by the shock of a sudden fright. The boar, or something just before, yes? She needs rest—several days' worth—and she must recuperate indoors."

I sat up. "But—"

"Unbelievable. Just what sort of parent are you—"

I tugged at Mister De Silva's sleeve. "But—"

"I do not understand why you would drag this child through the woods for days, without proper hydration, adequate food, ample clothing or even a first aid kit. On a single horse. Could you not even take time to put together some supplies?"

Merry opened his mouth to talk, but Mister De Silva held up his hand. "I do not want to hear it. I ordered some juice from the kitchen, and my cook will prepare her a decent meal. She must stay quiet tonight. You will remain with us for several days, until she is fully—"

"No!" I jumped to my knees, and even though my legs were stiff and sore and the room wobbled a little, I crawled toward Merry. "We have to leave tomorrow, at the latest. We *have* to. Merry, tell him we have to."

Merry's eyes were glassy when he looked at me. "De Silva's right, Em. I've put you through a lot these past few days, more than most adults would have the mettle for. You need to rest."

"No. *No.* Daddy will be waiting for me. On Wednesday, he'll be there." I knew it was a mistake as soon as I said it. Merry rubbed his face with one hand, and Mister De Silva put his hands on his hips. His voice was tight when he spoke, and his nostrils flared.

"You said you were the girl's father."

I looked from Mister De Silva to Merry and back, and I knew I had to do something, something really big, to save us, to keep Mister De Silva from telling anybody where we were, to get me to my daddy. I opened my mouth.

And I spoke the truth.

His eyes got big when I stood on the bed and told them about Daddy, about how much I missed him, about how I hadn't seen him in forever. I told him about my mother and her men and the Judge, and how she made me serve tea and show off my chest and talk to them. When I got to the part about how I got away from the Judge, Mister De Silva's mouth dropped open. I hugged Merry and told Mister De Silva how he found me in the rain, and we ran away from the Judge and his men, all the way to the river. I told him about the Mardi Gras floats and Mister Jim's boat and about how I wanted powder blue Levi corduroy pants and pink rubber bands, and Merry bought them for me with a two dollar bill I wrote a message to Daddy on. I told him about Mister Jack's birds and doughnuts with cinnamon and the man in the doorway of the bus, about the swamp and the alligator, and all the muster, and how the Judge showed up and kept calling me 'Ann.' I didn't remember much after that. Their voices were all a bunch of noise in my mind. I told him my mother was dead because Merry saw it in the paper, and I didn't know where Aunt Bertie was.

"So, you see. I have to be in Nashville on Wednesday. I know Daddy will be there, waiting for me."

When I finished, I was standing in the middle of the bed on wobbly legs. I got so worked up telling our story that I didn't know I'd been jumping, and covers and pillows were strewn every which way. I tried to calm down by crossing my legs and plopping to the mattress while I waited for Mister De Silva to say something.

He rubbed his temples and squinted. "Unbelievable. You will write novels someday."

I couldn't read Merry's face, but I hoped he was proud of me. Mister De Silva took a couple of steps toward Merry. "This story is true?"

"I sure couldn't make it up."

"Did you shoot a man at the muster? The person on the telephone earlier said you did."

Merry turned away and walked to the window. "I don't know how I could have, but the whole thing got kind of jumbled at the end. When I saw Wilkinson—the Judge—and his weapon, I knew I had to get us out of there. I grabbed a gun and shot out the support for the tent, and I think there might have been some other gunplay as it fell. I know I didn't fire again. I was too afraid I'd hit Em, but I don't think I hit anyone else, either. At least, I hope I didn't."

I scrambled to the edge of the bed, next to Mister De Silva. He scratched his beard. I could almost see the wheels and levers turning in his brain. Some people thought really loud. He jerked his head and stepped over to the window, next to Merry, and put his hand on Merry's back. "I will help you, my friend. Between us, we will decide the best way to get you to Nashville by Wednesday."

He slapped Merry on the back and strutted to the door. When he closed it, Merry sat on the bed beside me, and I snuggled next to him.

"Merry. While I was asleep, I had the best dream."

"I'm surprised you can remember your dreams, as out of it as you were."

"Well, I remember it all. I dreamed that Daddy was waiting for us in Nashville, right where I thought he would be, and I was wearing a Wonder Twin costume, and you got to live with us in Nashville, because you became his very best friend ever, because he was so glad you brought me to him he didn't want you to leave." I tugged on Merry's jacket and pulled my face closer to his, until our foreheads and noses touched, and my eyes almost crossed. "I don't want you to leave me, Merry. Not ever."

I hoped Merry didn't want to leave me, either. My brain screamed the words for him. *I'll be with you forever, Emmaline Cagney. Forever and always.*

His voice sounded clogged. "When you see your father, you'll forget all about me, Em."

"No! I won't ever ever ever forget you! I won't!"

He ran his fingers along my cheek, and I relaxed and snuggled into him. His chin moved on top of my head when he talked. "When I was nine, I thought I'd remember everything forever, too, Em. But, time robs us of a lot of the things we thought we'd miss for life, things that seemed important at the time. Critical, even. Life compresses our circumstances into highlights."

I fought the tears that pressed against the backs of my eyes. My voice quivered, but I didn't cry. "Well, you will always be a highlight in my life, Merry. I know it."

"I hope so, Em. Just like you will always be a highlight in mine."

I thought back over everything that had happened since I ran, and I remembered almost all of it. But when I tried to recall my room in New Orleans, I could only see things that mattered: toys on the floor; the fan in the window; my Marie Osmond comb. Merry was right about the highlights. I couldn't even see the details of my mother's face anymore.

I pulled my head from under his and looked up at him. The skin under his eyes was dark, like somebody hit him. "Do you think my mother knows where I am? If she's dead, can she see me?"

"Do you want her to be able to see you?"

I sat up taller and burrowed between his arm and his chest to hide my face and think. Did I want her to see me? She wouldn't like anything I'd done. My dirty fingernails and my shorter hair were the person I'd become. More the girl I wanted to be. "Do you think she is nicer now that she's gone?"

"Who knows, Em? Maybe dying improves some people."

"I want to think she's nicer. That she would protect me and love me and watch over me. That she would want me to find Daddy." My voice broke at the end, and I scratched at my eyes while Merry stroked my hair. I tried to memorize what it felt like to be that close to him.

"If that's the way you want things to be, Em, then believe that's the way they are."

"I don't think my mother was good to me, Merry, but I didn't want her to die."

"I know you didn't."

"I want to talk to her one more time, to tell her I'm going to be okay, that Daddy will take care of me."

He guided my face up to see his. His eyes were sparkly blue. "What's your favorite memory of your mother, Em?"

"I used to watch her brush her hair. She had a hairbrush with pearls on the back, and she tugged it through her long black hair. It was so shiny and pretty when she finished. Sometimes, she would pull me to her and wrap me in her soft wall of hair. She looked at us in her vanity mirror and called me her beautiful girl. I want to hear her call me her beautiful girl again. Just once."

I cried for real, then. Not like a baby or a spoiled brat. My tears came from somewhere older. More mature. It was the first time I really understood that my mother was gone, that death stopped everything. The only way I could change her was in my mind, my memories. I wanted to remember something happy, to wash her clean and make her good. She could live forever, or at least, as long as me.

If I thought about it hard enough, maybe I could convince myself it was true.

To Live Forever

MERRY

Monday. October 10, 1977. South of Tupelo, Mississippi.

I didn't know why I scratched at the pages of my journal. Was it a tick, held over from life? A constant reminder of my failure to publish my expedition journals? Delusional hope that I would get to keep a scrap of memory from failure to Nowhere failure?

I rubbed my eyes and looked around me. Started to write what I saw.

I couldn't help myself.

Hector De Silva's truck was a rusty red farm model, and a behemoth at that. Through the vents, I breathed in a mingling of engine oil and rubber. Emmaline slept with her head in my lap. I put my arm around her to keep her from bumping too much.

Hector's battered leather suitcase shifted in the bed of the truck, next to our duffel bag of new supplies. It was kind of him to put together enough to see us the rest of the way.

"Sorry I cannot take you all the way to Nashville, my friend. I am due in Jackson this evening to make my flight to Spain."

"I'm sorry as well. It's hard to find people to trust, especially after what happened at the muster camp."

"In that case, I have helped you. I made a phone call before we left. I have some friends in Tupelo. People I trust. You two will be safe with them."

I bit my lip and watched the landscape scroll through a cracked window. De Silva went out of his way to help us: new supplies, a bed for the night, the ride to Tupelo. But, I couldn't stop thinking his charity could be a delay. While he pretended to help us, Wilkinson could be anywhere.

De Silva's thumb tapped the wheel. "Do you think she will be well enough to finish? To find her father?"

I rubbed my face and looked at blurred trees and cloudless sky. Stalling. "Whether she is or not, I think you know she won't stand for additional delay. Her daddy matters to her more than anything. I have to help her. There's nothing more to it. You're sure we won't be putting your friends out?"

"They are eager to help." He braked at a rusty stop sign. I followed his gaze to a plume of smoke rising from the tree line ahead of us. Hector scratched at his beard and flicked his eyes back and forth from the road to the rear view mirror.

"What is it?"

"A car seems to be following us. Coincidence perhaps, but it has been on our tail through three consecutive turns."

"Can you lose it?"

"*Si*. Please brace yourselves."

Em's head popped up when Hector cut the wheel a hard right and bumped through a field. "What's going on?" Her voice was drunk with sleep.

I turned around and saw the car. It slowed down but kept to the roadway.

Hector pushed a button on his visor, and the woods in front of us parted. We shot through the gate, and it locked shut before the car could follow. Limbs scraped along the sides of the truck, and my head brushed against the ceiling. Emmaline dug into me and held on, white-knuckled.

Hector pulled to a stop at smooth tarmac, devoid of traffic. He hung a left and we puttered away from the setting sun. "Still my property. Unless they have more than one vehicle, they will have difficulty finding us."

I leaned my head against the cool window glass. "Thanks, Hector. That was the break we needed."

"I wish I only had good news, my friend."

I shot forward. "What do you mean?"

"You know they ruled the death of the girl's mother a homicide. They released a description of the prime suspect, along with a pencil sketch." He reached under the seat and flung a page from the Tupelo newspaper toward me. I studied a dog-eared article in the upper-right hand corner. My own eyes stared back at me. First time I'd greeted my face in a while, but I was captured down to the fine lines around my eyes. I tossed the paper on the nearby seat.

"I only have to get Em to her father. To Nashville. Then, I'll disappear. They can't follow me where I'm going."

"Someone will surely finger you as a murderer from this drawing, my friend. Not to mention the shooting at the re-enactor camp."

Emmaline's head swiveled from Hector to me. "But Merry didn't kill my mother, and he didn't shoot anybody. This paper is a lie."

"Em, calm down. We know it's a lie, but that doesn't mean they can't print it." I turned to Hector. "Look. I'm not exactly worried about my reputation at this point. Getting Emmaline to Nashville is my job, and I am the best person to take her there. I know how to evade these guys. Our biggest problem will be transportation. I was reticent to hitch before, but it's out of the question now."

De Silva rubbed his hairy chin, and his eyes followed a cardinal as it flew across the road. "My friends in Tupelo will figure something out. I promise you, they will not leave you stranded."

A vein twinged above my left eye. An impending headache. Did they always hit when I was running out of time? I blinked it away and tried to lean back but rest was impossible. Every time a car passed going the opposite direction, I imagined it turning around. Following us. Wilkinson taking Em away from me.

His portly face crowded the edges of my mind. If Em reminded Wilkinson of his dead wife, he would never stop until he found her, particularly since he blamed me for her demise. If I lost Emmaline to him, I was sure my failure would be my lake of fire. It would torture me throughout eternity.

Would I feel as empty when Em rejoined her father at the end? Or, would success be the same as failure?

Success was an unknown. I thumbed through the back of my journal. Blank pages with scattered remnants. Words that no longer made sense. Would success wipe my journal clean again? Give me a new identity? A new purpose? Or, would I fade into the soul of someone else?

I stuck the nib of my pen into a blank page and ground it into the paper. Her name. *Emmaline.* Whatever waited for me on the other side of success, it couldn't compare to my days with Emmaline Cagney.

Hector's foot pounded the brake, and he steered the truck onto a washboard dirt road. His olive hands shuddered on the wheel.

"Are we almost there?" Emmaline laughed at the rhythm the road made in her voice, and she kept saying it. "Are we almost there are we almost there are we almost there?"

Hector touched her cheek. "Not long now, beautiful girl, before I leave you. My heart, it is sad."

"But once we find Daddy, we can all come back and visit. I know he'll want to thank you for helping me."

Hector's dark eyes met mine over her curly head. In that moment, a distant ghost whispered to me. From somewhere beyond the Nowhere I was.

I studied a Spanish conquistador's epic journey in preparation for my own trip to the Pacific. His exploration of what became the Southeastern United States—including the land around the Trace—was legendary to men like me. His was an example of what not to do: abuse the natives; introduce diseases; force the place to acclimate to foreign demands. His were brutal footprints that shredded the veil of mystery.

In some ways, I was just as bad as he was. My journey of discovery robbed people of their lands. Their homes. Their identities. A few of them cursed me to my face.

Maybe that was why I was still a Nowhere Man.

EMMALINE

On the bumpy dirt road, the tires of Mister De Silva's truck sounded like the old machine Aunt Bertie sometimes used to wash out her underwear. Behind us, a long trail of dust tornadoed up from the road. We shot around a curve and hit some potholes. On one, I bounced almost all the way to the ceiling. When I landed, Merry pulled me to him and held me in his lap. The world spun a little outside the window.

After what felt like forever, Mister De Silva stopped the truck in front of a falling-down house. The boards of the front porch looked like crooked teeth. In every direction, I saw nothing but thick trees.

Mister De Silva turned off the engine and waved his arm toward the place. "My friends' hunting cabin. They should be here soon. Most secluded place we could think of. I'll wait with you."

Merry stared at the peeling paint. "Why can't we stay here? If it's out of the way, it might be safer."

"You can decide when they get here. Trust them. They will know the best way to keep you safe. Perhaps, you can go to their diner in town for a hot meal, yes? It is closed. Completely secure." He turned to me and winked. "Would you like that, Emmaline? To sit at the counter and eat an

217

ice cream sundae with dark chocolate sauce and a cherry on top?"

"Could I have more than one cherry? I really like them. I like how they turn my tongue all red." I tugged at Merry's sleeve. "Can we go into town, Merry? I've made us waste enough time."

He ignored me, and when he did that, it usually meant no. Merry wasn't very good at saying no to me, but grown-ups didn't always have to say no to mean no. Instead, he climbed out of the cab and stretched, looking at the house. "How old is this thing?"

Mister De Silva pulled me along the seat and carried me around the front of the truck. I dangled my legs and hugged him.

"Two hundred years or thereabouts, but the Hinkle twins have carried on the family tradition of maintaining it."

"You call that maintenance?"

"A rare stand along the Trace. The old road runs just there." He pointed through the trees. A ditch plowed through the wet ground.

I put my mouth close to Mister De Silva's ear, because talking made me tired. "What's a stand?"

"An old hotel of sorts. People who traveled the Trace used to stay in them."

Merry's forehead was creased when he turned to face us, and his smile wasn't real like usual. "If we end up having to spend a night here, this will be perfect. Thanks for all you've done for us."

Mister De Silva smiled and walked around to his side of the truck. When he came back, he held a box in his hands. He offered it to me. "A parting gift for you."

I ripped through the brown paper and found a Halloween costume box with a clear plastic window on top. The white fabric glowed through the film. "The Wonder Twins?" I tore the top off the box and waved the outfit all around me. "Oh, Mister De Silva. How did you know I love the Wonder Twins?"

He looked at Merry. "Someone told me. I picked it up for you last night, along with your other supplies. I hope it fits."

I started pulling the legs on over my jeans. "It doesn't matter. I'll wear it anyway."

"Em, you can go inside and change if you want."

"You mean, I can wear it right now? As my clothes and everything?"

"Sure, if that will make you happy. Let me check out the house before we take our stuff inside. Make sure everything's okay in there."

Merry clomped up the steps and opened the squeaky door. When he went inside, the door slapped shut.

I waited with Mister De Silva and closed my eyes to imagine what it would be like inside. Would there even be a bed? I was still sleepy. Could I warm up some canned ravioli on a stove and eat it from a real plate? Would it have a bathtub and a shower? After Mister De Silva's house, it was hard to imagine not being clean and warm and cozy comfortable.

Merry's head appeared behind the screen. It made him look like a ghost. "Come on in. I'll bring our stuff. Just leave it."

I jumped up the steps and ran into the tiny house, and Mister De Silva followed me into the big room with a light bulb hanging from the ceiling. Two beds were shoved in the back corner, covered with faded quilts, the sewn flowers curling up like soft petals. Just like the quilts Daddy used to wrap me in when he rocked me to sleep. Too bad the whole place smelled like a stinky shoe. It made me sneeze.

Merry rubbed his face and cleared his throat. "With any luck, it should be tolerable in an hour or so. I've opened most of the windows to air out the place for us, Em. We'll wait outside while you change."

Their voices hummed through the windows while I peeled out of my shirt and pants. The white fabric itched, but the Wonder Twin suit fit just like it was made for me.

Because it was.

I walked outside and twisted my hips in front of them.

"It's perfect. See? I love it so much. Thank you thank you thank you." I hugged Mister De Silva as hard as I could and stuck my nose in his hair. I wanted to remember what he smelled like. A mix of wild animal and shaving lotion. After everything I'd been through, it was harder to let people go. It was a rip in the cloth of my life, and the missing people left holes. I never understood that before I met Merry.

I never understood a lot of things.

Mister De Silva's eyes sparkled. "Ah, you are welcome. Now, let me help Merry move your things inside. Perhaps I can convince you to rest before my friends arrive."

Merry chuckled. "I don't think 'rest' and 'Wonder Twins' go together very well."

While Merry and Mister De Silva carried our bags into the house, I stood on one bed and looked out the windows. We only had two light duffel bags, one for me and one for Merry. They made a little pile in the middle of the floor. I unzipped mine and started spreading things around the room.

"Em. Don't get all that stuff out." Merry stood watching me from the doorway, leaning on the opening.

"But—"

I stopped arguing before I started, because the wind carried another noise. An engine. It reminded me of Daddy's upright bass, and it chugged closer. I stumbled to the open door and slid under Merry's arm to watch the road.

An old black convertible with a round front and long fishy fins in back putted into the clearing. I blinked when two men came out of the drivers' side. They walked side by side, like they were joined at the hip. Their faces were the same, and they wore matching white clothes and white paper hats. We followed Mister De Silva outside to meet them.

It was only when they stopped in front of us that I realized the truth: they *were* joined at the hip. I read about Siamese twins in school, but I never thought I'd see any. I blurted, "You're stuck together?" Before I could stop myself.

"Em—" Merry had his *stop-talking-right-now* voice on. I was getting better at noticing it. Mister De Silva just laughed.

"It's okay. We been getting that question since we can remember." The twin closest to me did the talking.

"So, where are you stuck together?" I wondered.

I could tell he wasn't mad because he smiled at me. "Without getting all birds-and-bees-ish, we share a liver. These days, it's pretty common to separate twins like us, but in our case, our parents would've had to pick which one of us got to live. Which one'd get the liver."

Could I decide something like that? Who lived and who died? I spoke my truth. "I wouldn't want to have to pick."

"Well, they had some time to get to know us both by then, and thankfully, they liked us both, so it wasn't a hard decision. My brother don't talk, so he needs me around to take care of him. Be the loquacious one. Know what I mean?"

"No. I don't know what lo-qua, lo-lo, whatever you said means." When I looked over at Merry, he had a real smile on his face, not that worried look he'd worn for the past couple of days.

"Well. I suspect you're loquacious like me."

"I am not loquacious. I'm not stuck to anybody. Clearly." I rolled my eyes. Grown-ups could be so dumb sometimes.

"Loquacious means I talk a lot."

"Oh."

"That's definitely you, Em." Merry laughed.

"Oh, Merry. You're happy again. Look, he's happy again. I always love it when you're happy, Merry."

"Glad to give you a bit of what you love, Em."

I fluttered around the porch to show off my Wonder Twin suit. It was cool that we were going off with real twins, and I was dressed up like a Wonder Twin. "I'm Emmaline, and you know Mister De Silva, and he's Merry, and we've been hiking for days and days and days, and Mister De Silva saved us from bad people, and what are your names?"

Their hands sort of spun in front of me, probably because of all my twirling around, or maybe it was a hangover from my sick time. I heard Aunt Bertie say hangover once after she spent a lot of time in bed during the day, so I decided that's what it meant.

I blinked to steady myself and watched the twin on the right. "We're the Hinkle twins. And this is our hunting shack. That's Crit. And, I'm

Pudge. We're going to take care of you."

"We really appreciate your help." Merry shook Pudge's outstretched hand and then turned to Hector, squinting at the sun. "Well, Hector, if you're going to make it to Jackson tonight, you should probably get going."

Mister De Silva clasped Merry's hand. "I only wish I could see you to the end." Mister De Silva turned to me and swung me into his arms. His triangle beard was rough against my cheek when he gave me a kiss. "I will miss you, my friend. If I'm ever in Nashville, I will look for you." I slid down his leg to stand beside Merry. When I squinted through the sunlight, it made a halo around Mister De Silva's black hair.

"And Merry. You have to promise to look for Merry, too."

"Ah, Merry and I. We are kindred souls. Friends always know where to find one another, yes?"

Merry hugged Mister De Silva to him with one arm. "I'm sorry I doubted you, Hector."

Mister De Silva gave him a long look and turned, his boots kicking up dirt on the way to his truck. He started the engine and waved before backing along the road. We stood outside and waited until we couldn't hear the truck anymore. Side-by-side with the twins and our pile of supplies.

Pudge turned to us. "Want to try the best food you'll ever have in your life?"

Merry looked at me. "Are you sure it'll be safe?"

But I wasn't paying attention to Merry's worries. My mouth started watering just *thinking* about an ice cream sundae with extra cherries.

"Yes, please!" I nodded.

Mister Pudge stepped the twins toward the car. "I secured the place myself before we came out here. You'll be fine."

"Only if you're sure." Merry's fingers laced with mine, while Mister Pudge maneuvered them into the car.

"Grab your bags. It'll be dark by the time we get into town. Let's get a move on."

MERRY

Monday evening in downtown Tupelo saw the storefronts locked up tight, warm lights glowing from the few houses that greeted us on the outskirts of town. Even Main Street felt abandoned. Bereft.

Emmaline's curls bounced around her wan face. Her stomach growled into my side. "I'm hungry, Merry."

"There's the restaurant up ahead."

I pointed toward the checkered awning on Main Street that read "The SkyView," twinkle lights chasing around its perimeter. I reminded Pudge that we couldn't park on the street. I'd spent much of the ride watching the blur of forest with one eye and studying the twins with the other. They were easy together.

Hector trusted them, but could I? Now that we were beyond the swagger of Hector's personality, I had my doubts.

Emmaline amused herself with requests for the radio, giggling every time Crit—the quiet one—pushed a different plastic button, ushering in another flood of 1970's musical sound. Snatches of *Love Will Keep Us Together. When Will I Be Loved.* A sad female voice *Making Believe.*

I was still partial to the fiddle. The sweet, vibrating strain of a horse hair bow on string took me back to the happiest times of my life. To the shimmer of moonlight on muddy water at the base of a chalk-white cliff, and the rush of cataloguing my daily specimens in my journal while our lone fiddler played under falling stars.

Pudge's flinty eyes caught mine in the rearview mirror. Locked away, those eyes. He wheeled the car down a side street and into a parking space next to a dumpster and pointed to a rusty door with faded letters that read "SkyView."

"Our diner's breakfast and lunch only. We never open for supper time, so we should be able to get you all filled up in peace." He winked at Em. "Crit here makes a mean peanut butter and banana sandwich. Toasted. White bread. That sound good to you?"

Emmaline scooted across the seat with a little more life. "I've never had it before, but I'll try it."

Pudge opened the door, and he and Crit slid along the front seat in an awkward choreography. Before my eyes could adjust to the evening light, they were guiding us down a fluorescent lit hallway and into the cracked vinyl and stained formica of an old-style diner.

Crit turned on the cook surface, its metal caked with the grease from decades of fried food, while Pudge chopped bananas next to him, his big hands and knife a blur.

Em crossed her arms and put her head on the counter. "I wonder if I'll like peanut butter with banana." Her eyes drooped.

"It'll perk you up."

She sighed when I patted her head and swiveled my stool to the windows, only to notice a car passing outside. Slow. Familiar. Afraid to be recognized, I turned my face away from the street and watched the car's reflection in the chrome cladding over the counter. Window down. A silhouette inside, gaze directed toward the building where we sat. It stopped for a few seconds, idling. I held my breath and willed myself not to grab Emmaline and run.

When I looked up again, the car was gone. I hurried to the window and watched it disappear down the ribbon of Main Street, before flicking the blinds closed.

Was it the car that had been following us earlier that day? I rubbed my face and blinked, trying to recall its shape. It was more foreboding in my mind's eye.

This job is making me paranoid. I muttered it under my breath and rejoined Em, just as the phone jangled along the back wall. "Don't answer it." Did I say it out loud?

Pudge dragged Crit along with him to pick up the dingy white receiver. "SkyView...Uh-huh, we got 'em...Naw, don't you worry about that. We'll figure something out and see you tomorrow...Right. You take care of yourself."

He replaced the receiver, and they see-sawed back down the counter to us. I held my breath and waited for the lights of the black car to pull up outside, for the bad guys to storm the building and take us away. Instead, Pudge scratched his arm, and Crit mirrored him. "Change of plan."

"What do you mean?"

"The lady that's supposed to be picking you up in a little while got delayed on a delivery. She can't get here 'til morning."

"Can we go back to your hunting place for the night?"

"You could, but it's in the wrong direction for her. She's a truck driver. Keeps to a schedule." Pudge looked around. "I reckon it'd be best for you to stay here. We got a couple of cots pushed together in back, for days when we're too beat to go home."

"Will that be okay with you, Em? Staying here?"

She drummed her fingers on the counter. "If it means I can get to Daddy faster."

I mussed her hair and fought the urge to promise the outcome she wanted.

My mouth watered as the twins worked in tandem, frying up good smells. The aroma of expert cooking always got me going, especially when I could watch someone do it special, just for me. Crit flipped things around while Pudge set out plates and looked at me. "You're having a Coke, right?"

"If it's not too sweet."

"Two Coca-Colas, coming right up." Crit bent down with him, keeping time, while Pudge grabbed two frosty bottles from the under-the-counter chiller. He popped the red caps and handed them across the counter.

Emmaline brightened when she saw the misted bottle. "Coke adds life, Merry! It's my favorite drink ever. Do you have a straw, Mister Pudge?"

He reached under the counter and gave her one. When she unwrapped it, she stuck its swivel-neck into the bottle and blew bubbles and laughed.

I looked at Pudge and groaned. "Sugar is like rocket fuel for children."

She talked into the straw, foam spilling onto the counter with her underwater words. "What does that mean?"

"Nothing." I put the cold bottle to my lips and took a sip and winced. It tasted like I'd licked a cold cube of sugar. I pushed it a little to one side.

Emmaline tipped her head and guzzled her drink until it was gone. When she set the bottle on the counter, she wiped her mouth with the back of her hand and burped. The most personality she'd shown all day. She blushed, but that didn't stop her laughing, and I had to smile a little. It vanished when the reflection of lights made another slow pass beyond the closed blinds. I watched its distorted shape move along the chrome and kept my voice light. "Em, doesn't that hurt your throat? Or give you a cold headache?"

"Nope. I love Coke. I'll drink yours, if you don't want it. I spilled most of mine." She ran her hand along the counter, but I batted it away.

"None of us need to be privy to that, Em. You're hyper enough without sugar and caffeine."

Pudge laughed. "She is a spit-fire."

"Yeah. She keeps me on edge most of the time."

"What does that mean, Merry? A spit-fire?"

Pudge turned his head to the side and smiled at her. "It's a compliment, trust me. Our mama is a spit-fire, and we adore our mama."

Something about the whole scene felt off to me, but I couldn't finger what it was. I needed to move. Action always cleared my head. "Why don't we go over and inspect that thing in the back corner, Em."

She followed my eyes to the behemoth jukebox. All red and blue lights and chrome. She hopped from her seat and skipped barefoot along the tile floor to press her nose against the glass. Coca-Cola worked miracles, apparently. "Merry, do you have any change?"

Pudge piled steaming fries on the counter. He swiveled his head around Crit's back and winked. "Just bump the thing real hard when you see a song you like, and it'll play it for free."

Emmaline studied the scrolling dial, while I moved two slats in the blind and watched the same car creep along the street outside. Black, with a dent in the passenger door.

"Pudge, you seen that car before?"

He walked over to the window to peer through the crack, bringing Crit with him. "Don't look familiar. Why?"

"I think that's the third time it's gone by in the past fifteen minutes."

Pudge scratched his head, and Crit just looked at me blankly.

"Do you think we should get out of here? Go back to the place in the woods? I don't like the sight of that car."

The blind smacked together when I let it go, but I was still unsettled.

He worked them to the telephone and dialed some numbers. "You'll be fine. Tell you what. I'll get the sheriff out here to scare them off."

"Don't mention us to the sheriff."

"You don't have to worry. I gotcha."

I shifted the blind and studied the backend of the car, bouncing once again over the railroad track.

Emmaline cackled behind me as the strains of a song started up from the jukebox. With more spring than I'd seen in two days, she shook a leg across the floor to me.

"*The Streak*, Merry. It's my favorite song ever. About a man who—"

"I know what a streaker is, Em." I had to shout above Emmaline's high-pitched singing. *Oh yes they call him The Streak...boogity boogity.*

Pudge and Crit slapped oozing peanut butter sandwiches on the counter. They watched, grinning, while Emmaline pogoed over the square floor tiles, her shrill little-girl voice belting out the chorus. I plugged my ears with my fingers and went to the window again.

Nothing. The street was empty.

The twins slipped to the end of the counter, and one of them pulled the jukebox plug out of the wall. The music slowed to a stop.

Emmaline whirled on them. "What? I love that song. Why did you unplug it?"

Pudge wielded a battered guitar of midnight blue. His skinny fingers strummed a chord, and he winked at her. "Let those fries cool a spell, little girl." He turned back to the guitar, his digits coaxing out a lazy tune. Countrified.

Crit closed his eyes and swayed back and forth, trance-like. Rich and layered tones filled the room. A song I knew I'd heard before, perhaps on another assignment. *Are You Lonesome Tonight?*

I lifted Emmaline into my arms and swayed slightly, hoping she couldn't feel the jolt of my nerves. She sighed and put one arm around my neck. Rested her head on my shoulder. I tried to forget about circling cars and evil men, about how lonesome I'd always been.

"Do you think Daddy misses me, Merry?" She whispered.

"I'm sure he does, Em. I'm sure he does."

When I brushed my lips against her hair, the remnant of a chord was shattered by a knock on the back door.

MERRY

Pudge dragged Crit along with him as he pushed us around the end of the counter. Through a doorway. I had scant recognition of mops and a bucket before Em and I were plunged into dark.

I held my breath and listened to the clatter of steps headed to the back door. Emmaline wrapped her legs around my waist, burying her head on my chest. I strained to hear over her frantic breathing.

Pudge's voice was muffled. "Who's there?" The back door scratched across the floor tiles and hit the wall with a thud.

An effeminate male voice echoed through footsteps down the back hall. Something about the Sheriff. A man and a little girl. Kidnapping and murder.

That voice. It had a New Orleans cadence, like the one who chased us through the alley the night we fled.

Pudge's aw-shucks tone filtered through the space. "Them's serious charges. Deputy, what's all this mean?" Behind his casual reply, I heard the rumblings of fear.

A different voice. I assumed it was the Deputy. "Pudge, I don't know how to say this, given we're sorta friends and all, but these fellas got me to bring them over here. Said it looked like you had a couple of customers in here. A man. And a little girl."

"Nobody here but us."

New Orleans again. "You sure? He looked like this man. Right here."

Pudge paused. I held my breath and waited for his answer.

"Hadn't seen him."

The Deputy's saccharine voice morphed into steel. "I sure am sorry, Pudge, but I got a responsibility to these fellow officers. Got to let them look around. You know, help them out."

"Have you run this by the Sheriff? You and I both know how he feels about other law-folk cluttering up his patch."

A shoe squeaked along tile. "Sometimes, I am beholden to people bigger than our Sheriff." Paper snapped the air. "I got a warrant for these boys to search this place."

Pudge's outrage permeated through the flimsy door and into the closet. "Hey—"

Emmaline's heart pounded against my ribcage, and I squeezed her closer, a silent warning. Curses mixed with the thud of the door against the wall. Leather slapped on leather, and New Orleans took over the interview. "We saw this man, this one right here, through your window not fifteen minutes ago."

"I'm telling you, I hadn't seen any man looked like him."

"Then it won't trouble you if we poke around your place, right?"

Pudge cleared his throat. "Suit yourself. Hope you don't mind if we set to cleaning up our mess."

"Go ahead."

Chairs rattled. One cabinet opened, followed by another. A knife pinged against the cutting board, and a door slammed somewhere in back. Shoes drummed the floor.

"Bathroom's clear."

Pudge snorted. "Glad to hear we left it decent for once."

A shadow hovered in the wedge of light under the door. Our door. The handle rattled against wood. New Orleans leaned on the door, his bulk hitting the jamb like a muffled punch in the gut. It took the wind out of me. I put my finger to Em's lips.

"Open this door."

Outside, pots clanged, and dishes clattered as the twins made a show of looking for the key that I knew was in Pudge's pocket. The sizzle of meat burned through the cracks in the door, but the shadow stayed put.

"Can't seem to find the key. Maybe—"

Metal ground on metal. "Look harder." I wasn't well versed in modern firearms, but I guessed New Orleans held some sort of handgun.

Pudge's voice wavered between outrage and terror. "Hey! No need for threats. If I can't find the key, I can't find it."

Shadows clogged up the crack at the bottom of the door. New Orleans leaned back again. "Go over there and check their pockets." Steps advanced, slow, followed by a familiar jangle. New Orleans shifted his weight against the door. "Bring them over here and hold the gun."

When the first key slid into the lock, the handle rattled and held. Rattled again. Wrong one. New Orleans pulled it out and replaced it with a second key. It tripped the mechanism, and the knob squeaked in a turn.

I scrambled through my recollection of the space, trying to recall any place to hide Emmaline before light flooded in.

Before she was trapped, and I vanished into the bowels of some bar forever.

"Stop." A deep male voice split the air. Someone new. The knob quit moving. "You. Put that weapon on the floor and slide it toward me."

Steel skittered across floor tile while I fought to keep still. To stay as we were long enough to let the scene play out. Emmaline's hands dug into my upper arm, and her breath puffed on my cheek.

"Walk toward me. Single file. Hands out wide."

"You can't arrest us. We're the law, too. From—"

"I don't give a good goddamn if you're from New York-fucking-City, and my deputy here knows it. Deputy, I don't know what you've been up to, but I certainly aim to find out."

"But, Sheriff. I—"

"You heard me. March."

Footsteps herded across the floor. A door slammed. After a long moment, Pudge's voice filled the void. "Damn, Sheriff. Didn't think you'd ever get here."

"Got held up by the train. Other end of Main Street."

"What's the Deputy up to?"

"Don't know. He intercepted your call on the scanner. Been suspicious of him for a while now."

"Me and Crit was almost dead."

"Almost but not quite. Remember that. I'll call you later."

"Thanks, Sheriff. Me and Crit are much obliged."

Their voices dissolved behind another smack of the door. Emmaline squirmed in my arms.

"Wait for the twins. They'll know when it's all clear."

Her head nodded against my chest as the twin's syncopated drum approached the door and sprung it open. Blinded, I stumbled into the fluorescent glow of the room. Pudge's voice issued from the joined bodies silhouetted against the light.

"Sheriff says he'll come up with a way to hold them 'til tomorrow morning."

I shifted Emmaline to the floor and took her hand. "That means we've got to get out of here tonight. Can you take us further up the Trace? Somewhere we can spend the night that's out of the way? I don't care if we have to camp."

Emmaline shook my hand. "Merry, I—"

"Not now, Em. Well? Can you?"

Pudge adjusted his paper hat on his soot-colored hair while Crit stared over my head. "Sure you don't want to stay here?"

"No. After that scare, we need to move on. Now."

Em wagged my hand. "But Merry, I really—"

"Em, shush." I studied Pudge and Crit. They proved they weren't the enemy, but Em and I needed full-blown friends. People who knew when to do the right thing, even if the right thing didn't make sense. Pudge shifted the pair of them. When he nodded, Crit mirrored him.

"All right. We'll get everything cleaned up here and take you on. I'll try to let our friend know where to pick you up in the morning. If she calls. She may just show up here."

Before I could answer, Emmaline exhaled beside me. "Merry! I really, really have to pee."

Crit's eyes almost creased with a smile to join the nervous laughter from Pudge and me. I tried to embrace the momentary release while Emmaline waddled to the toilet, holding her legs together.

How many more times would Em make me laugh before I was through? Time with her was already bittersweet.

Just like I told her time could be.

To Live Forever

MERRY

I bumped along in the back seat, Emmaline still clinging to my hand. My fingers tingled, nerves and adrenaline fueled by near discovery and another brush with the evil we faced. Em could not end up with Wilkinson, a slave to his demented cravings. Besides, I couldn't imagine spending all this time in Nowhere, only to wind up with my essence imprisoned in the life of another. Wilkinson was wrong.

He had to be.

I breathed deep and focused on the flash of autumn colors caught in the headlights as we sped by. The land rolled, lazy-like, and I remembered the occasional mounds of grass, set back in open fields. They were ancient, those mounds. More than a thousand years old. America before America was. Earth and ashes. Broken pottery. The ghosts of damaged souls. I felt them when I passed that way before. They called out in the rustle of knee-high grass, the clap of leaves.

I flexed my fingers and felt the throb of blood coursing through my arm. Ground my mind back to the plan. Visualizing. That's how I got my men up the Missouri. Across the Bitterroots. Through the gorge of the Columbia. All the way to the Pacific. I saw it all. Mapped it in my mind before we set out. I envisioned a different outcome, a Northwest Passage we could navigate to the sea. My imagination wasn't powerful enough to overcome the whimsies of geology.

Maybe seeing the end would work this time.

"Where did Mister Crit learn to sing that way?" Emmaline's breathless words tumbled into the front seat.

Pudge chewed the nub of a toothpick in the corner of his lip. "Don't know."

"My daddy sings pretty like you, Mister Crit. And he can play the guitar, too, like you, Mister Pudge."

"Can he, now? I've always just been a picker. Nothing serious."

I shook myself out of the fog. "It seems like something of a miracle, Crit not speaking, and yet he can sing."

"We were pretty taken aback too. Happened kind of sudden."

"Recently?"

"Yep. Couple months ago. August. He started singing along when I played. Faint, at first. Almost like a ghost, you know? But his voice grew into something powerful."

I thought back through my medical training. On the expedition, I treated stab wounds and blisters, frozen toes and sprains. My specialty was venereal disease, as the men couldn't stop themselves from doing the business with the natives. But, I never saw a patient go from mute to singing. Unusual, Crit's ability.

Pudge caught my eye in the rearview mirror. "Say, not to change the subject, but you sure you're going to be all right out here overnight?"

I rubbed my eyes and forced a smile. "Yeah. We'll be fine."

"You look wore out."

"Traveling with Em is a big responsibility. The weight of it gets to me sometimes."

Emmaline's face colored when she looked at me. Crestfallen woe was etched around her eyes. Her disappointment yanked at my heart.

"Getting Em to her daddy is very important to me. I want to follow through, you know? Do it right."

"Kind of the same way it works with me and Crit."

Emmaline relaxed and snuggled up to my side, her blonde curls falling forward.

"Thank you, Merry." Her voice was drowned with sleep, and her head lolled against me. In less than a minute, she was unconscious, her breath warming a spot on my hand. How did kids go from frenetic to still in the span of two seconds?

I wrapped my arm around her, thinking about Nashville. What would Lee Cagney be like? Childish idealism informed her whole idea of him, a man who, in the end, had abandoned her. She was so proud of her ruined stack of letters from him. Sporadic postmarks and shifting addresses. The last one from Nashville nearly two months ago. She believed her father wrote her every day because her Aunt Bertie fed her that story, but I had my doubts. Did he really deserve a girl like Emmaline? My heart tore a little at the thought of finishing my assignment. Of giving her up, especially to a man who might not want her.

What would happen if we never found him at all? It was a scenario I'd never considered, the mechanics of technical success without the actual hand-off. If I got Em to Nashville but we couldn't find this Lee Cagney, was I still doomed to go back to the dumpy hell-hole of a bar? And, if I disappeared, what would happen to Emmaline?

I leaned my head back on the seat and watched shadows scroll by. Somehow, Wilkinson had managed to evade capture in Nowhere for more than a century. Even built his own empire, a thing he craved in life. If he could wrangle his Nowhere experience to suit his evil purposes, why couldn't I use my own to give Em a real father? To give her me?

I ran my hands over my face to dispel the thought. We had to find Cagney. It was my mission. Even when it was impossible, I always finished a job.

Pudge turned the T-bird onto a dirt road and rattled to a stop in a dusty parking lot. Along the edge, the ground dropped off and disappeared into nighttime behind a lone wooden sign. Bear Creek Mound. I had heard of this place, one of the oldest Native American mounds along the Trace. Restless spirits shimmered just under the surface of the air. Pudge's lights illuminated the ghost of a jagged rock face. "There's a cave down there."

"Good. We'll make that our camp."

"You two ought to be safe this time of day. Nobody much stops in this forgotten corner of northeastern Mississippi."

"As long as the right person stops, that's all that matters to me."

"Leslie said she'd be along tomorrow, late morning."

"No problem."

"If it gets chilly, the trees ought to hide your campfire, but I'd be careful all the same."

"I'm good at hiding. We won't need a fire." I jostled Emmaline to rouse her and opened the back door. She crawled into my lap and lay her head on my chest. Still asleep.

I hoisted Em with one arm and walked around to grab our things from the trunk, piling them on the ground. Two packs plus a sack of diner delicacies for our breakfast.

Back at the driver's window, I grasped Pudge's hand and shook it firm. "Don't get out. It's too much trouble for you and Crit."

"Wish you'd reconsider."

"Can't do it. We'll be harder to find if we're away from town. Your diner'll be the first place they come looking."

His eyes failed to meet mine. "All right."

"I'm mighty thankful for everything you've done for us. Hector was right about you."

"The Spaniard. Good man. Likes peanut butter and banana sandwiches."

Emmaline's groggy voice rang out against my jacket. "Will we see you again, Mister Pudge?"

"I hope so. You always remember our song, young lady. If you're lonesome, think of us, and we'll be with you." He looked at me. "Good luck, Merry."

"Never had much, but I'll take it." I watched the lights of a truck lumber up the highway. Into Alabama. I shifted Em and memorized Pudge's soulful eyes, the flip of his black hair. "Thank you. For everything."

Pudge gave us a nod and backed out of the parking lot. I watched until the tail lights were lost behind a knot of trees. I gave Em a gentle shake and clicked on a flashlight. Muted shadows dodged along the ground, as light skittered through my fingers. Em picked up the strap of her pack and dragged it down some hewn stairs into the ravine while I slid my way along the wet rocks toward the open mouth of a cave. Somewhere, water dripped. I skirted an entrance littered with boulders to stand under the cave's solid roof. A cool draft blew from under the earth, but the ground was level.

From there, I couldn't see the parking area or hear the traffic on the road. Emmaline dropped her pack on the ground beside me.

"Where will we put my tent, Merry?"

"If we stay right here, we ought to be covered enough not to have to deal with the tent. All right? Just our sleeping bags and what we can see of the night sky? Maybe the rhythm of falling water?"

Emmaline nodded, her mechanical arms tugging at her sleeping bag. "I'll eat when I wake up. Okay?"

I glanced up at the shard of moon in the darkening sky. Sleep called to me louder than my stomach, too.

In minutes, I had her tucked into her bag. I zipped it closed and crawled into my own. Up above, the dusty arm of the Milky Way draped across the black sky. My breath misted next to the stars when I whispered my lone desire.

Just get through tomorrow, Merry. Tomorrow, this will all be over, and then you'll be a new man.

To Live Forever

EMMALINE

I couldn't remember how I got to the foot of the mound. I thought I followed a tanned girl with high cheekbones, not much older than me, with shiny black hair like my mother's. Her dress was the color of her skin, but I kept my eyes on her sparkly hair all the way.

When I got to the bottom of a grassy pile of dirt, she was gone. The sides of the mound were higher than my head, so I couldn't see the whole thing. I scratched my eyelids and blinked, tired, but not sleepy any more.

Wildflowers grew up the side of the mound, and the night wind blew cold on my skin. I rubbed my hands together to warm my fingers. Merry taught me that trick. I blinked again and looked for the girl.

The sky was really black, and it showed lots of stars. I kept looking up at it as I walked all the way around the mound. It was like a humongous mud pie, blurred around the sides and fallen in the middle. It was more square than round. Did somebody build up the dirt that way? I couldn't understand why anybody would make a big dirt pile in the middle of nowhere.

I found hollowed-out steps and climbed to the top. The stars lit up a dark bowl at the top of the mound, fuzzy weeds growing along the slope.

I used my feet to feel my way, just like Merry taught me to do when I couldn't see in the woods. If he saw me, he would be really proud.

Finally, I got to the middle, and I could lie down and stare at the night sky. The crickets were really loud, but the raised sides blocked out a lot of the spooky night noises. The trees that knocked together and the low blurps of the frogs. They scared me.

I turned my head sideways and tried to see the sky from the corners of my eyes. Sister Mary Caroline told us our eyes saw light better from the sides at night, but it was hard to see if she was right in New Orleans, because we had lights everywhere. I never knew there were so many stars until I found Merry. He even told me some of their names. From the mound, the stars were even brighter.

When I shifted my head to the other side, the girl was there. She lay on the ground beside me.

Hello. Her voice was whispery in the back of her throat.

When I jumped to my feet, weeds tangled up in my legs and tripped me. I bit my lips together to keep from crying out for Merry. Briers pulled at the skin on my knees when I fell.

Don't be afraid.

I spat dirt out of my mouth and looked back. Her eyes were like coal, but I could see a pretty row of teeth inside her smile.

"Where did you come from? You weren't here a second ago."

The girl sat up and hugged her knees to her chest. *I'm always where people want to find me. I'm glad you found me.*

"What's your name?" I scooted closer. She was relaxing to me. Like Merry, but different.

Talisa. It means 'beautiful water.'

"That's pretty. My name is Emmaline, but I don't know what it means."

Maybe names are a bigger deal to my people. She looked at me funny, as if she was trying to figure me out.

"Where are they? Your people?" I asked.

Around. Everywhere.

The slice of moon went behind a cloud and came back, brighter. I looked around the top of the mound and didn't see any of her people, but I decided not to point that out. With a sigh, I stretched out on the ground. "Do you like to look at the sky at night?"

Oh, yes. She eased her hands under her head and smiled. *I love the hunter that twinkles for his supper and the seated lady with the flowing dress and the cup that could hold an ocean. When they preen across the edge of the atmosphere, they're like old friends, coming to greet me after being away for the day.*

I rolled on my side and perched my head in my hand. "How old are you? I'm nine."

Her eyes squinted. *We think we'll live forever when we're young. Maybe we will.*

Talisa kept her eyes on the sky. Starlight twinkled in the whites of her eyes. I laid back on the grass and reached for Talisa's hand. It was slight, almost like air. I thought about what she said, about living forever.

"I hope I don't have to live forever to find my daddy. I've been without him for six months, and that feels like forever to me."

Talisa pumped my fingers. *You'll find him, Emmaline. Your souls are intermingled, magnetic, like the sliver of moon you see orbiting our circle of earth.*

"Do you feel that way about your daddy?"

I couldn't tell if Talisa made a sigh or a sob, but her voice was steady when she talked again. *My relationship with my father was very different from yours. Although, like you, I was young when I stopped living with him.*

"Why did you stop living with your daddy? Did your parents divorce, like mine?"

Nothing like that. I went to live with my husband, as was our custom.

I bolted up and looked down at her unlined face. "You mean, you're married? But you're not much older than me."

People haven't always waited until they were older to marry. Besides, my father was preoccupied. He never paid much attention to me. Not cruel, exactly, but vacant of love.

"That sounds sort of like my mother was. She's dead. Is your daddy dead?"

Dead? Yes. Her stare scorched me. When my face burned, she shifted her eyes back to the sky. The anger swirling there made me want to run away again. *I thought his love would surface in the end, but it didn't. And now, I'm here.*

Talisa pressed my sweaty hand for a few seconds before she stood. She had dried grass in her black hair, like it grew there. *I belong here. Beside this beautiful water. Staking a claim to this mound of my people, this mystical place where we split the seams between worlds and blurred the lines between illusion and reality.*

I rubbed my eyes. Was she saying she wasn't real?

"What are you talking about, Talisa?"

I experienced it all, Emmaline. It's the only way to live. Knowing you could die any minute makes you wring the life out of every day you get. When you consider the night sky, listen for me singing among the stars.

Talisa floated above me, her face turned to the twinkly sky. Her eyes rolled back, and when she screamed, I tried to reach out to her. To protect her. To keep her with me.

"Emmaline! Em! It's okay." Merry was shaking me, but the echoes of Talisa's scream still pounded in my ears. Only, it was my voice. My scream. Merry's face was scrunched up with worry, and he took me in his arms. He ran his fingers through my hair and kept asking me if I had a bad dream.

I just clung to him. It was all I had the energy to do.

MERRY

Tuesday, October 11, 1977. Bear Creek, Mississippi.

"And then she just walked away. I think I heard a scream, Merry, but really, it was like a hole opened up in a painting, and she walked right through it. Do you think it was a dream?"

Emmaline fluttered around me. Her feet barely hit the ground.

"What do you think, Em?"

"I think she was real. Her name was Talisa. She was my friend."

"Friends are good things to have, however we meet them."

At the base of the mound, she bent to pick a faded wildflower, a ball of dusty pink petals. She waved it around in one hand while grasping my palm with the other. Our arms swung, linked together in the space between us. Connected, yet free.

I'd barely had a drink since we floated up the Mississippi, but my head was mushy with a sleepless hangover. Every car that passed on the road overnight was a possible danger. I crept to the rim of the cave to keep watch, every light and shadow threatening to undo us.

I always tried to be sensible, because I was the leader on our team. A burgeoning father figure. But with one snap of a branch in the dark, I reverted to what I was. Afraid. Bewildered. A failure.

I failed to find the Northwest Passage. Bungled my appointment as territorial governor. I couldn't even make my expedition journals ready for publication. Clark probably finished that task for me. My light reached a pinnacle and fizzled. I never could reignite it.

Emmaline's hyperactivity ran counter to my desolate exhaustion. I relished watching her renewed energy, but I shook my head, hoping to banish my familiar monsters that had lingered so long they were almost friends.

The ribbon of road snaked off to the northeast. To Tennessee.

My heart twisted. It was a haunted place. A desperate place. The last place I walked in life. Breathed my last breath. A neighborhood I never thought I'd be forced to walk again. What would happen if I stepped across my own grave? The exact spot where I expired? The shallow trench where they threw me? Hasty, like they wanted to blot out the evidence of what they did. What they made me do.

Emmaline cartwheeled across the field. Her Wonder Twin costume was hiked above her grass-stained knees, and it already sported a small rip in the seat. "Watch me, Merry! Can you do a cartwheel? I bet you can't!"

"I'm hopeless with that stuff, Em. Always have been."

"Well, I'm real good at it. See?" She took another tumble and landed on her bottom in a patch of tall grass.

"Look, you need to change out of that outfit. You're going to ruin it."

She stopped tumbling and stood still, her face pensive. While I watched, a layer of her childhood peeled away. Danced in the air and evaporated. Her carriage bent a little with the added burden. "You're right, Merry. I need to wear something more mature for Daddy. Show him how grown-up I've become. He will be so proud of me."

Sunlight sparkled in her hair, and as I watched her, another twinge hammered my chest. I realized my misgivings with a pristine clarity. I wasn't afraid of running the gauntlet of Tennessee. It couldn't do me any worse than it had already done. No, my ache arose from the thought of losing Em in the end. Without my noticing, she'd become my reason for being. I had many more things to show her, to teach her, a lifetime of hugs to give her. And less than a day's worth of time.

I sighed and tried to memorize the feel of her miniature hand in mine as I reached to help her up from the grass. "All right, Em. We need to get back to the cave. I'm going to pack everything up, and we can wait for our ride, okay?"

"Okay." Bounce-bounce. "I'll help."

We descended into the ravine and sorted our gear in the shade at the mouth of the cave. A car slowed down on the highway, approaching the entrance to Bear Creek Mound. My eyes followed the flash of morning light on window glass and dark paint as it sped up and disappeared over the rise into Alabama. I rubbed my face and noted the position of the sun. Around eight o'clock.

"Let's hurry with this stuff, Em. We can leave it behind those rocks over there until Leslie arrives. Pretend like we came to see the sights along the Trace if anybody comes along. Don't tell anyone we camped."

"How long will we be here?" She stuffed wads of corduroy and cotton into her bag. Set out a clean outfit to change. I knelt beside her and helped her fold them neat.

"Pudge promised me he'd try to get our ride here early, but who knows? She might have been delayed again. We might have a while to wait. It's about eight o'clock now."

"How do you know that?"

"How do I know what?"

"How do you know what time it is by looking at the sun? Most people just wear a watch, but you don't. You always know where we are and what time it is."

I clutched her sleeping bag and rolled it up like a snail shell. "I guess my step-father taught me."

"I don't know any daddies who teach stuff like that."

"Well, I am a lot older than you, remember? Anyway, it was a long time ago."

She pulled herself up on the rocks at the cave's entrance and balanced on both hands before sliding back to the ground. I kept one eye on her and started to fold the other sleeping bag as she climbed the rock again. "How old are you? I mean, I don't think you're really old, like fifty, are you?"

She hovered at the top, waiting.

"Fifty isn't really that old, Em. But, no. I'm not fifty."

"Well?"

Slip-slide down.

"Well, what?"

"How old are you, then?" She stopped in the midst of climbing to watch me. I avoided her nosy eyes and strapped the sleeping bags to the packs. Zips and snaps and the distant caw of a crow.

"I was, *am* thirty-five. Thirty-five years old."

Her lips moved as she counted on her mud-caked fingers. "That's my daddy's age, Merry! You and him are the same exact age! Isn't that amazing?"

I threw the packs up over the lip of ground. They landed with a puff in the dirt next to the trail from the parking lot. "Yeah."

"Maybe you will be best friends because you're the same age."

"Em, come here a minute. Sit next to me, okay?"

I sat on a cool, flat rock and waited for her to come and stand in front of me. Almost eye to eye. She smelled like mouldering leaves and Tinkerbell.

My hands hovered over hers, but I pulled them back and looked away, into the nothingness of the cave. "You have got to understand something about me, Em. Promise me you'll try."

"What?"

"I won't be staying with you in Nashville."

"But—"

"It's my job to take you to your father. If I complete that job, I'll get another one. I think."

"But you can get a job in Nashville. Daddy'll help you."

"My job's kind of unique, Em. It takes me all over. You won't see me anymore."

Her lower lip trembled. "Don't you love me, Merry? Because I sure do love you. Almost as much as my daddy."

"Aw, Em. Come on. You're tearing my guts out here. Of course, I love you."

My heart lurched like I'd been shot. I took her in my arms and pulled her to me. While she cried, I spoke into her frizz of hair. "I'll always love you, Em. No matter where I am. No matter what I'm doing. A part of me will always, always be with you. Even if you can't see me."

"But how will I know you're there if I can't see you?"

"You've loved your daddy all this time, Em, and you haven't been able to see him, right?"

Her hair tickled my nose when she nodded.

"You'll know I'm there. Somehow, you'll know."

"Do you promise?"

I turned watery eyes to the sky and uttered empty words to form what I hoped would not be a lie. "Yes. I promise."

MERRY

An eighteen wheeler. I gauged the retreating sun as it pulled into the parking area. Almost sunset.

Em and I spent most of the day at Bear Creek Mound, running up and down its dirt sides and wading in the creek, looking for a ghost. We even explored beyond where we slept at the entrance to the cave. She didn't squirm when I hugged her more than my share of times. In my heart, I counted them all. One less time, and one less time.

Another day almost gone.

The truck pulled to a stop, and I studied our ride. A black hulker with a chrome grille pulling a refrigerated tank. A white-haired woman drove that monster. And yet, she was agile when she hopped down from the cab. Hands in the back pockets of her jeans, she walked over to us. Her gait was unguarded. Casual.

"You Merry?" Her voice boomed like a man.

I stood to greet her, pulling Emmaline up beside me.

"Yes. Nice of you to pick us up." I stuck out my hand, and she shook it hard.

"Leslie Lynn, and it was no trouble a'tall. Sorry I'm so blasted late. Ain't always easy to find enough fuel for that rig to drink these days."

"It's a problem everywhere, I hear."

"Yep. Managed enough to get us to Nashville. I got another delivery up there tomorrow, so I can take you then. These beasts ain't allowed on the Trace, but I make up my own rules and mostly, nobody cares in this back end of nowhere. That plan suit you? Going on in the morning?"

My throat dried up. I covered my mouth and coughed, trying to expel my growing dread. "I guess it will be fine."

Leslie eyed me for a beat. Seer's eyes. The kind that could read minds. She jabbed her thumb over her shoulder. "Throw your stuff in the back of the cab." Turning to Emmaline, she knelt, and her gruff edges dissolved into grandmother-hood personified. "You ever ridden in one of these big trucks...what's your name?"

"Emmaline. And I've never even seen a truck like yours up close."

"Well. Are you in for a treat."

"Can I ride in the front? Do you have a CB? What funny name do people call you on it? Can I talk on it? Will anybody answer me? Does—"

"Whoawhoawhoa. Slow down, girl. It ain't wise to throw your skirt up in front of strangers."

Emmaline's brow crinkled. "Huh?"

With a hand on Em's shoulder, Leslie led her to the truck. I picked up our gear and followed their tracks, a few steps behind, fighting to get my gnawing funk under control.

"Always best for a girl to maintain some mystery."

"My mother always said that, but she never explained what it meant."

Leslie took her hand. "So, she wanted to keep things a mystery to you."

"Oh. I get it. It means holding some things back, right? But how can I have mystery, Miss Leslie?"

"Watch folks before you ask a bunch of questions. Sometimes, they'll tell you what you want to know without you ever having to say you wanted to know it in the first place."

I studied Leslie's close-cropped grey hair and tried to imagine her younger, charming the britches off men. Her lean figure and ready smile made that vision no stretch.

She lifted Emmaline into the cab. I went around the other side and climbed the chrome steps into the passenger seat. Emmaline twitched beside me, but she didn't touch anything. I could almost see her thinking that she had to act grown-up.

I rubbed my temple to block out the tell-tale starburst that flashed at the corner of my left eye.

I tossed our things behind me, into an alcove with a narrow bed. The proportions, the sheer size of the cab, made me dizzy. I slumped against the glass of the window, cooling my forehead against it. A solitary crow circled, up high.

Leslie pulled herself into the driver's seat and started the engine. It sputtered deep music, a mechanical rumble. I watched her feet work the pedals as she shifted gears. Almost like synchronized rowing. I leaned my head back and closed my eyes. Tried to breathe through the panic that was overtaking me.

When we took a left turn along the main highway, a wave of nausea assaulted me. Foreboding. I swallowed and squeezed my lids together. A stab at sleep. I shut my eyes against the familiar things that flashed outside. The flat, swampy stretch of Alabama. The Tennessee River. That wandering ridge line that rose and fell all the way to Nashville, broken by one hideous spot. My spot. A roadside attraction for the few who remembered it.

"Where did you say your place is again, Leslie?"

"Near old Grinder's Stand. Ever heard of it?"

My eyes fluttered open. I swallowed and flicked a trickle of cold sweat from my forehead. "Yeah. I have."

"You can walk there if you want. Along the Old Trace. They keep it maintained pretty well."

Emmaline reached out and held my hand, but I could barely feel it in mine. The fireworks were coming faster behind the whites of my eyes. I shielded them with one hand and sighed into the pain.

"Grinder's is famous. Or infamous." Leslie's hands were steady on the huge wheel.

"Why?" Emmaline leaned her head on my arm and kept her eyes on the road scrolling through the glass.

I forced myself to answer, to talk about the damned place. Maybe describing it in advance would dull its edge, mute its power.

"Lots of people were robbed there. Stands were big places for thieves. Some travelers were killed, and others...well, they just died."

"The stand burned to the ground a while ago. All that's left is the old stone doorstep." Leslie downshifted and motored the rig uphill. "Pretty quiet there, most of the time."

"Will we see it, Merry? On the way to Daddy?"

"No. We won't have time to stop, Em."

Leslie ruffled Em's hair with one hand. "I'll take you over there. Merry don't look like he feels too good. We can let him rest while we go exploring. How does that sound?"

I slumped further in my seat, my pounding head against the headrest, facing out the window. Mountain trees whizzed by in the light of dusk. Faded reds and yellows and oranges, a hardwood kaleidoscope of autumn. The air was crisper, the chill of higher elevation.

Or, perhaps the cold emanated from inside me. My breath froze on the back of my hand, and my toes were numb. Whatever would be, my end was close. I concentrated to keep my teeth from chattering.

"You can stretch out in back if you want, Merry. You look like you could use some rest."

"You wouldn't mind?"

"Nah. I got to clean up back there before I go on another run, but it'll serve for a nap."

I nodded and flung a shaky leg over the seat, dragging the other one behind me. The bed was too short, leaving me to curl up like an unborn babe, face to the trembling back wall.

Starbursts pulsed behind my eyelids, regular. Maybe Leslie would forget about me when we got there, leave me in the truck the whole time. Wake me after breakfast, when it was time to leave for Nashville. Maybe I would sleep through the whole thing.

I hovered above the road. Feverish. The ghost-like imprint of my surroundings invaded my dreams. Everywhere, they breathed their chilly, shimmering breath. I saw the winding wagon ruts. The leaning boughs of trees. The play of sunlight and shadow on the worn ground beneath my horse's feet. A crude fence and a grazing cow. The inside of a rustic room.

Two bursts of gunfire on a lonesome autumn night.

EMMALINE

"Can we play this game, Miss Leslie?"

I pulled out the big white piece of plastic with bright colored circles on it and spread it out on the floor. Miss Leslie came in from the kitchen, a cup in her wrinkly hands.

Hot chocolate. For me.

I took it from her and let the steam wet my face. It smelled like warm cake. I stuck my tongue in to test it, coating it with creamy liquid as far as it would go, before I put it on the floor. "I'll wait for it to get cooler. Will you play this game with me?"

Miss Leslie rubbed her back and cocked her head to one side. "You like Twister?"

"Yes. I love it. I'm real good at it. See?"

I bent over and reached my arms through my legs and put my hands flat on the floor. My face was hot when I stood up straight, but I still did a back bend. When I came up, I saw stars and stumbled a little. "Whoa. Maybe I should rest and drink my chocolate before we play."

"Sounds good to me."

Miss Leslie sat on her orange sofa and put a pillow behind her back.

She patted the seat, and I crawled up beside her. I held my hot chocolate in both hands, careful not to spill any. My mother never let me eat or drink on the furniture, but when Daddy was around, we ate whole meals together, always in front of the big stereo, listening to all kinds of music. I liked it when we danced with sticky food fingers, because it felt like we could never let each other go.

Kind of like Merry. He made me do so many new things, stuff I always wanted to do, even if I didn't know it. I thought back over the things he taught me: how to set up a tent and where to step in a rocky stream and how to read the map of the night sky. He never got scared, always tackled everything like he knew he could do it.

He was the kind of grown-up—the kind of person—I wanted to be.

Miss Leslie sipped from her cup. "Should we go check on Merry?"

"Maybe he should sleep for a little while longer. He's got to be tired, because I'm quite a handful."

Miss Leslie threw her head back when she laughed. "Yeah. I can see how you could be."

"Merry always seems sad. Sometimes, I do things just to try to make him laugh."

"Well, men like Merry, they need to laugh now and again."

"When we get to Nashville, Merry and Daddy will be best friends. Daddy makes everybody happy. That's what I told Merry. I said it to make him feel better, but it seemed to make him sadder. Do you think Merry won't like Daddy?"

Miss Leslie put down her cup. "Aw shoot, honey. I don't got no way of knowing the mysteries of man things. Men are a funny bunch."

"But I'm sure Daddy will love Merry, because he worked so hard to get me to Nashville. We've been chased and shot at and thrown from horses and hid in closets and everything."

"Yeah. You've been through the ringer, all right. Wicked folks have always been attracted to this patch of country."

"Do you know Mister De Silva, too?" I ran my tongue around the lip of my mug. Remnants of chocolate melted in my mouth.

Miss Leslie shifted on her pillow and stared out the window. Moths beat against the glass, just under the porch light. She sighed. "Yeah. I know him."

"How?"

"Well. See, that's a complicated story. Might be too much for you, at your age and all."

"Oh, Miss Leslie, you can tell me. My life is pretty complicated, you know."

Miss Leslie cleared her throat and looked at me. "Um. Well. My daughter. She used to have quite a thing for Hector. Still does, truth be told. In fact, they were married for a little while.

"They aren't now?"

"Nope. Men like him jump when a better offer comes along."

"What does that mean? A better offer?"

"Well, some people, they have what's called a wandering eye. They don't ever see what they got, because they're always pining for what they don't. Hector's one of them people. Good heart. Just gets bored with women."

I looked at the pattern on the Twister board. Green and yellow. Blue and red. Is that why my mother had all her men? Because her eye wandered? She accused Daddy of cheating on her, but she had men around her as long as I remembered. Maybe she got tired of Daddy. Not the other way around.

Miss Leslie stood up and stretched. She stepped on a red plastic circle. "Let's fun things up a bit, shall we?"

I slid my foot to a green circle. But I couldn't make my mind stop thinking. Would Daddy go to hell because my mother divorced him? My stomach turned a somersault, and yuck came up in my throat. I never thought to ask the nuns at school. Thinking about it made my eyes burn. How could anybody sort through everything and decide who went to hell? It was all so tricky.

I jumped a little when Miss Leslie touched my back. "Hey. You there. What's going on in that head?"

"Do you think people who get divorced automatically have to go to hell?"

Miss Leslie blinked. "Whoa. Deep thoughts, and here we are supposed to be playing a game." She chewed the inside of her cheek and looked at me. I could see her brain trying to come up with the right answer for a child, but I wanted her to treat me like an adult. I put my hands on my hips and waited, while she walked over to the window. She didn't look at me when she went on. "Emmaline, I don't think divorce sends people to hell. Who taught you a thing like that?"

"Nobody, exactly. I just—"

She whirled around to face me, and her eyes were shiny. "Look. I'm no expert on the hereafter. Nobody is, 'til they've been there. But, I don't believe people go to hell for making mistakes. If that's the case, heaven'll be a pretty lonesome place." She took a step toward me, the lines on her face softer. "Now, I don't know about you, but I need music to play some Twister."

I stood on the side of the plastic square while she walked over to the stereo. A country music record scratched through the speakers. It turned out Miss Leslie was just pretending to be old, because she could touch her hands to the floor and bend in funny ways. Before I knew it, our arms and legs got all pretzeled together, and we laughed until my stomach hurt.

When we were finished with the game, Miss Leslie played the same record over again from the beginning. I liked the man's whiney sound, and I swayed around the room, opening drawers and looking for something else to do.

Miss Leslie picked up my jacket. "Want to walk over to Grinder's? It's only a short way."

"Okay. What's there?"

"It's the old hotel and historic site, one of the most notable ones on the Trace. It'll be educational. Plus, we might be able to see the Milky Way. It's a new moon tonight."

I pushed my arms into the sleeves of my jacket and followed her out the front door. Her big truck sat quiet down the driveway. "Do you think we should wake up Merry?"

She locked the door and clicked on a flashlight. "Let him rest. We won't be gone long."

MERRY

I woke to the chanting of tree frogs, still in the cab of the truck, curled against the cold back wall. I rolled over and glimpsed faint constellations through the windshield. Both dippers and the hunter twinkled bright. No moon.

With stiff legs, I vaulted to the front and climbed from the passenger side of the truck. My eyes lit on a cozy log cabin. New cedar construction, but built to look like it had been there a couple hundred years. Around the corner of the house, light spilled from a window onto a broad front porch, and a wooden swing creaked in the chilly autumn breeze.

I stepped to the edge of the porch and peered in the window. The abandoned room was homey, with some sort of game spread out on the floor. Two mugs sat on the table under one window. *Maybe Leslie is putting Em to bed.*

I moved to the door, ready to lock myself inside for the night. Faint music swam through the cracks. A ghostly tune I knew from someplace I couldn't remember.

Blue eyes crying in the rain....

It was how I existed most of the time. Damn my watering eyes. I couldn't let Em see me cry.

Turning from the door, I spotted a clear path through the trees. A leafy tunnel paved with prehistoric dirt. Applause feathered through leaves and brushed my face. Beckoned me to retrace my own footsteps through the shadow of my undoing.

A dry stick cracked underfoot, but my heart was quiet. At peace. No scrim of cold sweat formed on my brow, and my headache fled. I held up one gnarled hand and waited for the tremor, but all was still. The only sound was my footsteps, advancing along the Old Trace in the dark, merging with the echo of the path I had traveled so long ago.

I saw it all again, outlined in the dewy grass. Ghosts shimmered everywhere.

Hoofbeats pummeled through my chest, and a tired horse whinnied close by. The air carried the stink of back flow from a chimney, and through the clearing, a boot scraped on stone. When I closed my eyes, candlelight flickered in a dimly lit room. In my mind, the place was the same as when I left it.

Except for one thing.

It jutted from the ground at the far end of the meadow as though lit by an unseen spotlight. Its glittering mineral deposits hypnotized me. Without control of my steps, my feet trudged toward the substantial marker with its stacked squares of graduated stone and a broken pillar at the top. It loomed larger with every step.

Unbidden, a cold chill hacked through me. I knew I should run, but my feet wouldn't cooperate with the demands of my brain. Another few steps. I strained to read the letters etched in the rock, willed them to be something other than words that knit together my name.

MERIWETHER LEWIS.
HIS COURAGE WAS UNDAUNTED.
HIS FIRMNESS AND PERSEVERANCE YIELDED
TO NOTHING BUT IMPOSSIBILITIES.
A RIGID DISCIPLINARIAN YET TENDER AS A
FATHER OF THOSE COMMITTED TO HIS CHARGE.
HONEST, DISINTERESTED, LIBERAL, WITH
A SOUND UNDERSTANDING AND A
SCRUPULOUS FIDELITY TO TRUTH.

Why would someone inscribe those words about me?

I scratched my eyes. In the center of the rock, I saw it all again. The unfurling of my life.

I had always loved the outdoors, but in my life, it became my glory. The dream of America gave me access to powerful people. Responsibility. Its whispering trees and rushing waters erased my penchant for dark thoughts. Nature made me whole, an exploration of sheer joy.

Or so I thought.

The success of my trip to the Pacific was some kind of powerful drug. Everyone knew me. I was envied for my skills. In my dreams, I heard their whoops, their breathless expressions of admiration and awe.

Until success abandoned me.

It evaporated while I pushed papers, trapped inside a jail of an office in a position I deplored. A job I took from a monster. Wilkinson. He knew the art of the smear against his fellowman, and he wielded it like a master. Everywhere I turned, he laid snares to trap me. To thwart me. To make me a mockery. Letting him best me was my biggest mistake.

Dying does funny things to a man. Death seethes in the bowels of memory. I didn't know the truth until I breached the divide. Eternity wasn't golden streets or a lake of fire. It was Nowhere.

I rubbed my face and turned my back on my own grave. It was a sad thing that lost souls never died. We couldn't be buried in the ground. It was my lot to hack my way through my insufferable existence. To reclaim the promise, the glory, that slipped through the hourglass of my life.

A cloud of breath issued from the trees. I blinked. Once. A single blink, and a hulking image materialized on the other side of my grave. The Judge. Wilkinson.

And, caught between his hands was my darling Emmaline.

She struggled to break free and run to me, but the Judge's fingers dug into her arms. A vice that would crush the life out of her.

When I breathed, I realized the stink of his cigar had been there all along. An extravagant foulness. Like burning money. He smiled through a cloud of smoke. "Meriwether Lewis. Will you ever be rid of me?"

MERRY

Emmaline's face was streaked with tears. When she spoke, her voice was a croak.

"He killed Miss Leslie, Merry. He shot her. I saw everything."

I pivoted to face that monster, but when I opened my mouth, Wilkinson bested me.

Always, he bested me.

I could imagine him, minutes after my death. Feet propped on a remote desk. Mouth curled around a cigar. A smile to celebrate the demise of his nemesis.

My story couldn't end that way.

"Give the girl to me, Wilkinson. She belongs with her father, not with the likes of you. I don't care who she reminds you of."

I held out my hand and prepared to take her from him, but he stepped them out of range. Blew another plume of smoke and let his knowing eyes roam over me.

The cigar burned between his lips. Ash fluttered down on Em, into her hair and across her face when he spoke. "I think intelligent people will see this differently, Lewis. And, if I can convince them, well.........you already know winners write history." He clenched Emmaline in his arms. "Here's how I see it. You're the one that's led us on a chase through four states, killing innocent folks all along the way. Emmaline's mother and now this trucker woman. You shot at men down in Mississippi. If we get technical, you even tried to kill me."

Em kicked back at the Judge and screamed. "He didn't have anything to do with my mother's death. You—"

He twisted her arm behind her, lifting her from the ground until I heard a sickening pop. Her face contorted, and she bit down on her lip to keep from crying out.

Wilkinson put his cheek close to hers. "You may not know me now, little beauty, but that's all right. I'm patient. My wife lives within you. Given enough time—years, even—I'll draw her out."

"No part of me will ever love you. Not ever." She thrashed against the prison of his grip.

God damn him. I took one step in his direction before he stopped me with the grinding click of a pistol. Pointed at my head. My skull lurched at the memory of shattering at the wrong end of a gun.

Would a head shot feel the same in Nowhere?

I sucked in air. "You know you can't kill me, Wilkinson. I'm already dead. Just like you."

Em lifted her gaze to me, questioning.

"There are worse things than death." He wrapped Em's slender body in the crook of his arm and brought her head close to his. "Watching your only love expire right in front of you: that's worse. Being forced to live without her: that's worse, too. No, I've toiled here for too long to fail now. Not when I've found her." He stroked her cheek, but Emmaline's eyes were vacant, like she'd retreated to some inner place.

"Emmaline is an innocent child. She's not your dead wife. Don't sentence her to hell before she has a chance to live. Stop raving, Wilkinson, and give her to me."

Wilkinson exhaled smoke from a fresh cigar, and his belly shook with a guttural laugh. "Raving? Me? Didn't they say you were unstable?"

People said all manner of things in the wake of my death. How many times did people connect the wrong historical dots?

I refused to let him bait me. "I am not leaving here without Em. You hear me, Em? I won't let the Judge have you."

Emmaline's voice was a feather in the air. "Why did you take my daddy away from me?"

Wilkinson's eyes twinkled. "Your own mother orchestrated the removal of Lee Cagney. When she discovered my interest, she was happy to stoke it, perverse as it seemed. Her only concern was the money."

She sagged against his leg, defeated.

I clenched my teeth. Her own mother. It took one monster to kill another.

He fingered Em's hair. "Your mother deserved to die for what she put us through. Half a million was what we settled on, to be exchanged when the little beauty here turned ten. I'd have her before anyone else did, and I'd wait until she was ready. Until she knew me. She bewitched me the moment I saw her."

"When was that?"

"A year ago. She was playing in the courtyard at her mother's house. My Ann's voice whispered through the heavy air, right before I turned the corner and saw her there."

Could it be? Sweat trickled down a deep ridge in his forehead, his face transported through time.

"Can you imagine it? What I felt? When my wife died, I was lost. It was only in Nowhere that she spoke to me, that I realized I could find her again."

"You always played every situation to your advantage."

"Everything I did was for my wife. To bring her back to me."

His hand slipped on Emmaline's arm. The opening I needed. I leaped across the space between us. Stars exploded inside my eyes when I hit his hard body and dragged him and Em to the ground. When I twisted his hand, Em bit the fleshy sag of his cheek. His hefty form writhed in pain, and he released the gun. It hit the dirt with a thud. Clattered over my grave and into the darkness.

My teeth crunched when Wilkinson's fist knocked across my jaw. For a moment, everything went numb. I waited for the sensation of my body dissolving into the bar. The final time. Instead, dirt and blood mingled in my mouth. Wilkinson pushed me off him. Ground my face into the earth.

Against the weight of his body, I hoisted myself to my elbows. Scanned the clearing. "Emmaline!"

Her footsteps pummeled into the packed earth. She sprinted through the clearing. Back toward Leslie's house. Wilkinson heaved himself to his feet and hobbled after her. I struggled to stand. Staggered in their wake.

I put myself in Wilkinson's back flow. Could hear him panting as he ran. When I reached through the air, he stopped, sudden. Threw out his arm like a clothes line. My rib cage crunched, and I shot backwards and landed on the ground. Unable to take on air. Fuzzy stars faded in and out, blocked by the bulk of his head.

He loomed over me, the weight of his boot on my throat. My tongue. Thick in my mouth. I struggled. Crushing boot. Pain. Needled my skull. Body jerked. Almost gone.

In a last desperate convulsion, one leg knifed into his open stance. Plowed him into the dirt. I rolled away, the rush of new air twisting my lungs in pain. I moved just in time to miss the force of another kick, but Wilkinson was invincible. With a graceful pirouette, his other leg blasted into my ribs. Agony sizzled along my spine. Squeamish from the pain, I stretched along the ground, grabbed a handful of dirt. Threw it at Wilkinson's eyes.

His electric roar lit up the night. He toppled to the ground and scratched at his eyes to clear them of debris. I rolled behind my own gravestone.

His temporary blindness was my chance. Somehow, I had to finish him. My fight with him was Emmaline's fight to find her father. I was fighting for her life, for what history would be recorded about her.

"I know you're behind that ugly monument, you son of a bitch." His words came out jagged. Disjointed against the racing pulse of his breathing.

I clawed my hands up the cold stone and waited. My breath misted in the crisp air, giving me away. I sucked it in and held it. Wrapped one arm around my chest when I slid my feet underneath me. I closed my eyes and waited for Wilkinson to breach the side of my tombstone, for the final blow that would propel me to what was next.

When I opened my eyes, he hurtled through the air and landed on top of me. His hands crabbed around my throat, squeezing the air from me as we rolled across the grass. Fireworks exploded in my vision, along with the ghostly image of his face. His dirt-ringed eyes and clenched teeth. The mass of his body slicing my back into cold metal.

Wilkinson's gun.

With a last burst of strength, I clawed my fingers into his wounded eyes. He yelped, and that single sound relaxed his hold. I dug my hand underneath me and grasped the sleek pistol.

Some people believe our whole lives flash before our eyes in the moments before we die. I knew that wasn't true. But, between the time I wrenched that pistol from behind me and the flash of gunfire, I lived the best parts. Every glory of my life coalesced in that clearing when Wilkinson teetered toward the ground.

MERRY

Emmaline's feet pounded the ground. Before I could turn to face her, she flung her arms around my waist and squeezed hard. I pulled at her arms and tried to shield her behind me.

"Em, I told you to run back to the house. This place isn't safe. What the hell were you and Leslie doing out here at this time of night?"

I smothered Em in an embrace, oblivious to my aching side. "Em, I'm so glad to see you, to see you safe."

"Merry, you're crying, just like me." She ran her fingers along the worn creases in my face. "Are you crying for Miss Leslie?"

"Leslie. Where is she?"

Emmaline pointed to a patch of trail beyond my marker. "Over there."

My sore legs loped behind Em's as we hurried across the clearing to the mouth of the old road. To Leslie, sprawled on her back, one arm at an unnatural angle and blood gurgling from her mouth. I knelt down and met the reflection of Death in her eyes.

Emmaline cradled Leslie's head in her lap and brushed her fingers along the side of her agonized face. I ripped her shirt away and found her chest chewed open by a bullet, right at the heart.

"That sonofabitch...needed...to be shot." Blood ringed Leslie's teeth.

"Don't talk." My fingers probed the wound and found the point of entry, along her side. When the bullet crashed through her ribcage and exited out front, it gnawed every vital thing. I wiped at the blood and tried to make her comfortable. It was the only thing I could do.

Leslie's glassy eyes fought to latch onto mine. She spoke through clenched teeth. "Who...are you...really?"

I put my mouth close to her ear and whispered my name. "Meriwether Lewis."

Her body convulsed beneath my hands. One long exhale. Her dying breath merged with the remnant of all others. She hovered in the air around us. I could feel her. Would she slip into Nowhere, too?

"Godspeed, Leslie Lynn. May your beautiful spirit brighten the next thing." I hoped she heard me.

Emmaline's hands shook Leslie's head. "Do something to help her, Merry."

I scanned the cold air for the mist that was left of her, hanging in the atmosphere. Of all the places to die...

Emmaline's teary face glowed in the light of the fire. "Why'd she have to die? Why?"

"Come here, Em. Let me hold you."

She collapsed into my arms, and I let her cry. In the force of her sobs, I found a few more tears of my own. Pent-up grief for my own wandering soul. Sadness, because in facing my grave, that outpost of my original destruction, an innocent woman died. I concentrated on Em's eyes, hoping to see Leslie there. Cloudy blue stared back at me.

I couldn't finger the moment when my desire shifted. When staying with a little girl became all that mattered. When reclaiming my name—being remembered—wasn't important anymore.

I spoke into Em's hair. "Thank you, Emmaline Cagney. You saved me."

"How did I save you, Merry? You shot the Judge. When your gun went off, I saw him fall."

"You saw him fall? All the way to the ground?" I blinked. By the time he hit the ground, he should have been gone. That was how Nowhere worked: Death erased our previous experiences. Took us back to a no-count bar to begin again.

My eyes wandered across the grass, next to the broken shaft of tombstone. I rocked to my feet, taking Em with me. My eyes raked the clearing. Starlight played tricks on me. Faint shadows. Shifting shapes. The lingering stink of tobacco.

"Run, Em! Now!"

I set her down and grabbed her hand to make her keep pace with me. We sprinted back toward Leslie's cabin, our feet drums on the moldering soil in the blind night. My side throbbed with the effort to stay upright, to keep Emmaline with me.

When we jumped over a log, Em's fingers slipped from mine. A dull thump hit the dirt, and she cried out in pain.

I turned and picked my way through the blackness. Even the crickets were silent, watching for what might happen when Wilkinson burst from the woods, gun blazing. I gave an involuntary shudder and followed the sound of her breathing. A rhythm mixed with something else.

The rattle of branches. The crunch of leaves. The haunting stench of cigar.

My toe collided with a log. I groped along the other side and found Em. I picked her up and latched her to my side. "Wrap your legs around me, and hang on."

I darted through the forest with her burrowed into me. We followed the scent of the trail left by untold others. In less than a minute, we stumbled into another clearing. Light burned in the window of Leslie's cabin.

A flimsy lock on a door would not stop Wilkinson. He could blast through it with the gun I left behind. Burn us into the open. I had one choice: to get us away from Leslie's. Fast. With a drowning heart, I knew the only way.

Leslie's rig.

I ran to it and hauled open the driver-side door. Emmaline slipped inside ahead of me, scrambling along the seat. "I thought you couldn't drive."

"I can't."

I slammed the door and ran my hands over every foreign thing. Knobs. Wheels. Buttons. Levers. The cold sliver of key. I turned it in the ignition, and the truck rumbled to life.

"Hold on, Em."

I ground the truck into gear. The window cracked on my side, and we jerked to a stop. A single hairline fracture spider webbed over the surface of the glass.

Did I slam the door too hard and break the window?

Distracted, I turned my attention back to the dashboard. The engine growled, low and powerful, and I settled my foot on the gas. Eased the clutch. I'd watched other people drive. I knew I could do it if I tried.

Em gripped the dashboard. "You have to turn on the lights, Merry."

I nodded and flicked the switch for the headlights. Emmaline screamed. The front of the truck lit up with the bloody face of Wilkinson. One hand clutched his ribs. In the other, a gun pointed at my side of the windshield.

I tugged at the gear shaft and floored it.

We braced ourselves as the truck darted forward. Wilkinson rolled out of the range of my headlights. I battled the gears and fought to keep the truck in the middle of the driveway, away from the trees. A crack breached Emmaline's window, and she jumped in the back before it shattered in toothy pieces, raining all over her seat.

I pushed the pedal all the way to the floor, and the rig shot forward, its force jarring my teeth. White-knuckled, I gripped the wobbly steering wheel and squinted into the distance.

A sign. The brakes squealed, and I used both feet to muscle the behemoth to a stop.

Nashville, it read, with an arrow pointing left.

MERRY

Wednesday, October 12, 1977. Somewhere south of Nashville, Tennessee.

"The whole goddamn thing is out of control! Hang on, Em!" I grappled with a grinding wheel while Em crashed around the space behind me. The truck slid off the road and down the bank. I quit steering and braced my arms in front of Emmaline to soften the impact. We whiplashed forward, into the heft of the dashboard. Em's body crunched into mine, but I held us inside the rig. We plowed to a stop in a ditch as the sun rose noon high.

Dust swirled in the mirrors, down the sides of the truck. My journal fluttered open to a page with one salvaged word: hope. The creamy paper winked at me. A tease? Or a promise? I didn't know.

I turned my attention to Emmaline. She ground her teeth and gripped her arm, but her eyes were dry. Determined. "You okay? Tell me what hurts, Em. Let me see."

"Just my elbow, but I'm all right."

"Let me take a look at it anyway."

"Really, Merry. It's got to be all right. Daddy is waiting for me in Nashville today. Nothing is going to stop me from getting there, if I have to walk from here all by myself."

275

I took her arm and felt along the curve of bone, pressing in different spots. "Does that hurt?"

"Ow! Stop it." She yanked her arm away and dove for the key. "How do we restart the truck?"

"Em, I don't know if we can restart it. And, even if I can get it cranked, I know enough about trucks to realize I shouldn't drive this rig."

"You haven't even checked to see what's wrong, Merry." Her liquid eyes pleaded with me, her voice almost a prayer. "Daddy could be waiting for me right now. Please, you have to get me there."

I threw open the door and took in the lone stretch of highway. We couldn't be more exposed if we were buck-naked. After wandering lost in the labyrinth of Tennessee back roads for most of the night, I finally found a straight shot to Nashville around mid-morning. And, I thought navigating this place on horseback was bewildering....

A white car came up over the rise from the direction of Mississippi, and I froze. Every policeman in the state of Tennessee was likely looking for me. When the car got closer, it slowed to check our situation, but I waved it on and gave them a thumbs-up sign. Hitching a ride was not something I was ready to do.

Not yet.

I took a slow turn around the truck, checking one wheel at a time, hoping I'd be able to figure out what went wrong, but every inch of that blasted machine baffled me. I knew how to take a bunch of animal skins and craft a boat that would float, but Nowhere did not allow me the time to master the mysteries of the mechanical. Whatever I learned on other assignments, experience was no aid without memory.

Helpless, I examined the truck, every rod and bolt and seam that ran along its skin. I heaved open the hood to check the engine, but all the hoses and wires and containers undid me. If the problem lurked there, I would never resolve it.

When I looked in the cab, Em was passed out, her arms flung up over her head and her hair haloing her face. I watched her breathe and marveled at her faith in me. Would she ever forgive me for my uselessness, for keeping her from finding her father?

Under the seat, I found a smashed candy bar. Its wrapper fell apart in my hands, and I chewed on chocolate and caramel. If I couldn't get us to Nashville today, I would vanish. I was sure of it. Em would be left to find her way alone. It was the only possible outcome. With renewed energy, I jumped out of the cab and pressed on.

It was close to two in the afternoon by the time I crawled under the truck, shirtless and sweating. And swearing. The front passenger tire wasn't buried in the mud. It was flat.

I beat the ground with my fist, causing a storm of bugs that flew up my nostrils and made me cough. I shimmied out into the sunshine, rubbed my dirty face and strategized. It was too dangerous to rustle up some help on the CB. Besides, I didn't know the proper lingo.

I stuck my head back in the cab and whistled to rouse Em. Her sleepy head popped around the corner of the driver's seat. "We blew out a tire. We can't make it to Nashville on a blown tire."

"You have to change it, Merry. That's what happens when a tire goes flat. You put on a new one and go on with your trip." She pulled herself through the opening between the seats, her face comprehending the possible extent of my impending failure. "Do you know how to change a tire?"

Heroes. They outshine others in the firmament of heaven, but they sizzle brightest when they fall.

I stood straighter, trying to muster a posture of confidence. "How hard can it be?" I rooted around behind the seat and found a slender kit labeled "Tires," lettered in a strong, feminine hand. "I've figured out tougher things."

"I thought all men knew how to change tires. You're really weird, Merry."

"I'm just different, Em. Always have been."

"But it's more than that. I don't understand what the Judge meant. Why did he keep talking about Nowhere last night? And he said you were dead."

"Goes to show what he knows. I'm not dead. Clearly."

I ignored her deflated kicks against the dash and heaved the box into the sunshine. It rattled when I threw it on the ground. I opened the lid and set to sorting long steel bars and a thing that fit around something that was supposed to do with tires.

Em's voice distracted me. "But he kept calling you Meriwether Lewis. That was the name on the big statue, too. I know all about who he was in history. His trip to the Pacific with Clark was one of my very favorite parts. He's one of my heroes."

I swallowed a *Really?* Americans learned about me? In school? I was painted as a hero?

For so long, I wanted to be remembered. Celebrated for my scientific discoveries through exploration. Recognized widely for the contributions I made. I chose Nowhere to make that happen. I guess I never thought it could happen on its own.

I tried to let the knowledge of my fame seep into my cracks. Make me whole. Complete. But when I stood at the other end of Emmaline's gaze, all that mattered was her.

I sighed. Kept the conversation on course. "People have the same names, Em. Happens all the time."

"I bet nobody is named Meriwether today. Nobody."

"I told you. My name is Merry."

"Well, I still don't get it."

"That's life, Em. A parade of events we don't understand. It's how we deal with our bewilderment that separates us from everyone else."

Before she could ask another question, I shifted my back to her. Checked the container again. Where was the contraption that lifted the truck off the ground? There had to be one, because even I knew a tire couldn't be removed with the weight of the truck bearing down on it. I rummaged around in the cab, a sheen of desperation building underneath my armpits, crawling up my back.

I knew how to motivate a team of men to push a boat upriver. I understood how to read the pattern of the sky. Hell, I could even identify most critters by sound alone. Yet, in my current conundrum, I was lost. Was it possible for one man to change a tire on a big rig? The way it handled, I was surprised a lone man could drive one. I thought of Leslie, even more agog that our wheels had belonged to a woman.

When I peeled my hands away from my face, another vehicle broke the southern horizon. It moved like a race car, low to the ground. A driver with a purpose.

I stuck my head inside the cab. Told Em to hide.

She scrambled over the seat while I took a defensive position behind the open door, watching the silver sports car screech to a stop. Tinted windows blocked out prying eyes. I gripped a metal rod from the tool kit and waited.

The passenger window scrolled down, and I met a pair of black sunglasses molded into the incredulous face of a man. When he moved a lever between the seats and leaned over the leather armrest, I was run over by a sense of the familiar.

Had I met the man before?

Before I could place him, he frowned. "What the hell happened to you?"

"Got a flat tire." I was proud of myself for waving the rod in my hand, showing him I knew something about tires. "Thanks for stopping, but we've got things under control. I'm working to change the tire, see?"

He left the car running and stormed into the open air. "Control? Seriously, Son. I don't even think the messiah himself could change a tire on this rig. Have you tried to lift one of these fuckers?"

My mouth was open, but I couldn't find my voice. A detail that didn't matter, as it turned out.

"Didn't think so. You got to get one of them services out here. You know, one of them trucker tire-changing outfits. They come and do the whole mess for you, while you sit over there, sipping booze in broad daylight, if you planned for contingencies. From the looks of your sorry ass, I'd say you reserve planning for your encounters with other girly-men."

One of the most famous explorers of the early nineteenth century? Effeminate? I balled up my empty fist and prepared to educate him on that score, but he strutted around the front of the truck and bent over the desecrated tire. "Goddamn. Do you even know how to drive, Son? I never seen such carnage to rubber and steel in all my life."

Emmaline stuck her head out of the passenger door. The man's avian face softened at the sight of her. With a flounce, she tossed her head. "He can't drive. He told me."

"And, who might you be, young lady?" He took a step toward her, his face colored with interest.

"She's none of your business." I stepped around the cab and put myself between them. I couldn't shake the feeling that I needed to keep him away from her. With one arm, I shoved Emmaline back into the truck and shut the door with my elbow before turning to face the stranger. "I need to change the tire."

"I already told you that, Son. What are you? Slow?"

"Actually, I thought you might help me."

The man eyed his suit of black wool. His indigo silk tie. His spit-shined shoes. He unleashed his small man fury on me. "You are a goddamn idiot. That's what you are." His busy hands windmilled everywhere. "You see this suit? Custom. Couture, they call it. I had it made in Italy. I bet you're so stupid you don't even know where that is. But, I'll tell you one thing right now: I'm not crawling around on the goddamn ground in this get-up."

Another vehicle approached from the south, drowning his spirited soliloquy. A rattletrap of a red ruck. I pulled the man behind the door with me and watched the clunker chug by. Its windows were too grimy to see inside, but it did not slow as it passed. It motored across the opposite horizon, out of sight. When it was gone, I was still holding the man's tie. "If you can't help me change the tire, you have to get us out of here. Now."

His expression didn't flinch. "Where are you and the girl headed?"

Emmaline jumped out of the cab and landed two-footed on the ground beside him. "We're going to Nashville, to—"

I pulled her to my side. "Yes. We're going to Nashville."

"Well, goddamn. What's your business there, Son?"

"We're meeting some family. Reunion."

"Huh. Nashville. That's where I'm going. Where I live, as a matter of fact. Been there the whole of my life. I'd say if you're going to a family reunion, we might be related, but I couldn't possibly share bloodlines with the likes of you. Her maybe, but definitely not you."

I ran one hand over my face to keep from hitting him. "So you'll take us?"

The man's head scoped between us. "What's the address?"

I swallowed. "Address?"

"Goddamn, Son. You really are stupid, aren't you? The a-d-d-r-e-s-s. You know, the street number assigned to the place where you're going to your no-count, inbred family reunion."

"Look, I'm not sure of the address. Just take us to wherever the Natchez Trace ends in Nashville, and we'll find our way from there."

"The end of the goddamn Trace? Why do you want to go there for?"

"It's as good a place as any."

"I reckon so, if you like a lot of nothing, and you sure as hell won't find another ride. Not much there these days, except industrial wasteland and the Cumberland River."

I shot Em a warning look. "Just take us somewhere in that general vicinity."

Before I could stop her, she bowed in front of the stranger. "Thank you for giving us a ride, Mister. I'll never, ever forget it."

His skepticism evaporated, and his cheeks flushed underneath the dark lenses. "Well, now. I, uh...it'll be a tight fit. Car's a two-seater. I got a crawl space behind the front seats, if you can wedge back there. Let me go and clean it out."

He walked around the front of the truck while I put my face close to Em's and whispered. "You cannot tell that man about Nashville, Em. About what we're doing. You especially can't tell him about your daddy."

"Merry, trust me. Sometimes, it takes a woman to get a job done. Plus, he seems nice."

"Nice? Don't you hear the names he calls me with that sewer of a mouth?"

"You said 'goddamn' when you were wrecking the truck."

"Most people swear when they're stressed, Em, but they don't make it a syllable-by-syllable part of normal conversation."

"What does that mean?"

"Never mind. Just don't say anything, and I mean *anything*, else. No matter what he says to you. You sit in the back of that car, and you keep your mouth shut."

"But, Daddy—"

"We'll find your daddy. You just let him get us to Nashville, and leave finding your daddy to me."

The man stood at the nose of the rig, watching. I didn't know how long he'd been there, whether he heard our conversation. He cleared his throat and smiled. "If I'm gonna take you to town, you can at least tell me your names."

I stood tall and kept one hand on Em's shoulder. "I'm Merry. This here's Em."

"Uh-huh. A girly name for you, and a boy name for her. It fits."

Emmaline curtsied in front of him, and I clenched my jaw. A curtsey? In 1977? She kept her head low. "And what might your name be, Mister?"

He stepped up with his hand outstretched and waited for her to take it, like some kind of damn king. "My name is Garren. Garren Teed. Country music promoter extraordinaire. Mighty pleased to meet you, young lady."

EMMALINE

I leaned forward from the back of Mister Teed's sports car to stretch my legs. Because of the angle of the back window, I had to scrunch up so that I couldn't feel my feet. He looked in the rearview mirror and winked at me, and I winked back. Mommy was right. It was easy to get men to give a girl what she wanted. She just had to know how to work them.

Country music twanged through Mister Teed's speakers, and it reminded me of Miss Leslie. I had a nightmare about her in the truck. She came back to life and met us in Nashville instead of Daddy, and she wouldn't tell me where he was because we ran away and left her like we did. When I woke up, I told myself we had to leave her there to get away from the Judge.

Would anybody find her?

Merry didn't talk much to Mister Teed. Instead, he stared out the window. Pouting. Every time I opened my mouth, he twisted his head back and glared at me long enough to remind me to keep quiet. At first, I felt bad about letting Mister Teed talk without answering him, because it was rude, but I guess it didn't matter to him. He talked enough for all of us, and he asked all kinds of questions.

"Where are you from? You couldn't have been born in Nashville."

I bit my lips together to keep from telling him, and Merry stared straight ahead.

"What do you think of the music city, then?"

I looked at the heavy gold ring on his third finger, the one with the green stone. It made pretty light when it caught the sun. I wondered whether it had special powers of some kind, like my Wonder Twins. Merry still looked out the window and tapped his finger on the armrest.

Mister Teed tried again. "Have you listened to much country music? It's the sound of the goddamn gods, you know."

"I love Willie Nelson," I blurted before Merry silenced me with one swift look.

Mister Teed reached under the seat and pulled out an 8-track tape. A white case with no label. He shoved it in the player, and Willie Nelson vibrated through the speakers all around me. He pulled down his glasses and caught my eye in the rearview mirror. "One of my favorites, too." When we came to a stop sign, he pushed his glasses up his nose and shifted his eyes to Merry, sort of puffed up in the chest. "Do you know who I am, Son?"

Merry cut his eyes sideways. "Something about you is familiar, Teed, but then, you are such a...colorful character. The problem with colorful characters is they tend to be gaudy. Too over the top."

Mister Teed was speechless as he revved the engine and plowed through the stop sign, while I stared at the knobs on the console and tried to memorize the phrase "colorful character." I'd never heard it before, but I was sure I'd known a lot of them.

I closed my eyes and imagined what the end of the Natchez Trace would look like. Maybe it would be like everything else Merry and I had seen on our long journey. Dirt and grass and weeds, dead leaves and trees and sometimes water. If we were in New Orleans, I knew where Daddy might go, but Nashville wasn't the same. How would I ever find him in such a place?

"Merry?"

"Ssshhh."

"Will we be able to find Daddy in Nashville?"

Mister Teed turned around and looked right at me from the driver's seat. "Who's your daddy, young lady?"

The car bumped over grass when he ran off the road, and Merry twisted his arm back to steady me. I put my fingers over my eyes and watched a telephone pole get bigger through the cracks, but Mister Teed swerved to miss it, cursing Merry the whole way. Words I was too young to remember, let alone repeat. When he had us back on the road, he smiled at me in the rearview mirror. "So, who is he? I might know him, because I know everybody who's anybody in Nashville."

I looked between him and Merry, trying to settle on an answer that wouldn't get me in trouble again. I let out a breath and said, "You must be really big, if you know that many people."

"I know everybody worth knowing, that's for goddamn sure. If you're going to be in Nashville a while, maybe I'll introduce you to some of them. I been on the hunt for a child star to represent, and you're pretty enough. Doesn't matter whether you can sing. We can always fix that in the studio."

"I can sing. I get my voice from my daddy."

Merry groaned. "Em, stop talking. Now."

I rolled over onto my back and put my feet up on the slanting window glass. The sun was setting, and the sky was pink and orange and yellow and purple.

Merry lowered his voice but I still heard him. "Look, Teed, stop filling her head full of nonsense and keep your eyes on the road."

"It ain't goddamn nonsense, Son. I am the most powerful country music producer in Nashville, which means the most powerful one in the world, to translate for stupid people like you. I hope I'm not going to be late for my appointment because of all this horse shit." I felt the car speed up underneath me, and my head bobbed this way and that as Mister Teed zipped through traffic. "I got a big singer on the hook at the moment. He's going to be a sensation. I'm meeting him after I drop you off." The more he talked about singers and bands and the famous people he knew, the more reckless he drove, until I hung onto Merry's seat with both hands to keep from rolling all over the back compartment. I bit my lips together so I wouldn't scream, but I think a little one came out anyway.

When Mister Teed turned around to look at me, the wheel jerked in his hands. Trees rotated outside the windows as the car merry-go-rounded across the road, and I smelled the sour stink of burning rubber, right before we bumped over the sidewalk into a star dusted slice of heaven.

EMMALINE

The trees stopped moving. No crunching sounds or jolts of impact like when Merry wrecked the truck. Mister Teed let out a ragged exhale and rested his head on the steering wheel. He muttered under his breath and kept sitting like that.

When I poked my head out of the back, we were in a parking lot at the end of an open space lit by Christmas lights.

Merry reached back and pulled me into his lap in the front seat.

"Are you okay, Em?"

I wiggled a little to test everything out, but I was determined to meet Daddy, even if I was dead. "It's getting dark. We need to go."

Mister Teed dragged his head away from the wheel and fixed his sunglasses. His voice sounded a lot less inflated when he spoke. "End of the Trace is just there. Beyond that building a couple of blocks."

I turned my head and gasped. I knew where we were, only it wasn't in the right place. Marching rows of columns and a ginormous roof and the whole thing lit by twinkling lights. Grass stretched in front of it, with paths that were constellations on the ground. It was the Parthenon, not a ruin in Greece like the picture in my World Book Encyclopedia, but the whole building.

"Kind of magical, isn't it, young lady? Be thankful I can drive. Unlike some people."

I clawed at the door handle and strained to get out of the car, but Merry pulled me back.

"Em, wait."

"Oh, horse shit, Son. Let her go. It looks like she's got a date to keep." He took my hand in his. "I'm Garren Teed. You remember that."

Crickets chirped somewhere close, and Merry opened the door. "Say thank you to Mister Teed here for bringing us all this way."

I tried to be still and breathed *thank you thank you thank you* into Mister Teed's sad face, and he handed me a white card. "If you're ever inclined, young lady, use this card to look me up."

Merry slammed the car door and leaned into the open window. "Thanks. In spite of yourself, you've already done more for her than you know."

When Merry took my hand, I pulled on it, trying to make him run with me through the parking lot, but he held me back. Until the end, he would tell me to be careful. He would always protect me.

A sidewalk ran in front of a green park sloping all the way to the Parthenon. "Isn't it beautiful, Merry?"

"I prefer the ruin myself. The one in Greece. This is a bit pretentious for my taste."

I could see the charge in the air. "Daddy is here. Right this very minute. Let's go find him."

I tried to tug Merry across the grass, but he wouldn't go any faster. Impatient, I let go of him and darted ahead, along the dirt path to the fairy-tale building. We were at the end of the Natchez Trace, and we were in Nashville, and Daddy was in Nashville. I had to get to him.

Two solid hands grabbed my shoulders. When I turned around, Merry was there. He kneeled in front of me, holding me still. The whites of his eyes were red, and his lips shook a little when he tried to smile.

"I want to make sure I get to say a proper goodbye, Em. Just in case—

ah—just in case you don't see me again."

"But we already talked about this, Merry. You said you wouldn't leave me until we found Daddy. And he's here. Well, somewhere. In Nashville. And you have to stay with me 'til we find him because you have to meet him. I know he'll want to thank you."

"Em, I don't think—"

But I couldn't wait for Merry anymore. Daddy was there. I could feel it. The two-dollar bill said Wednesday, and I knew he would find me. I left Merry on the grass. Through the starry paths. To the big steps. I was panting by the time I stood under the roof of the Parthenon.

Alone.

The columns were giant poles, and rough—they scratched my fingers when I touched them. From the bottom, they reached all the way to heaven. My voice was a scary echo when I called out, "Daddy?"

I looked down the avenue of columns and waited for him to step out from behind one of them and fling his arms open, a picture of me in one hand and tears streaming down his happy face. Instead of moving, I clamped my eyes together, as tight as I could, until I saw stars, and I wished for Daddy to be there when I opened them.

The stars went away and my eyes adjusted. Still, nobody.

I shivered and turned to walk the long side of the building. My steps sounded hollow, just like I felt inside. There were benches between the columns and each time I got close to one, I expected to see Daddy sitting there. I tried to imagine him. Did he buy a special outfit to meet me? What did he think when he got my message on the two-dollar bill? Would he look the way I remembered him? Grown-ups didn't change as fast as kids. I worried that he wouldn't recognize me, because I was a different person than when he last saw me. Outside and in.

Because of Merry. He inspired me to do things I'd never do on my own. Without him, I never would've gotten out of New Orleans. I certainly wouldn't have survived the Natchez Trace. He made me look hard at who I was, and he challenged me to explore who I wanted to be.

By the time I got to the end of the building, I was breathing hard.

I walked all that way, and still no Daddy. He wasn't anywhere. Around the corner I found a short walkway that led up to a gigantic door. Light streamed out of it. I never understood why artists painted God like rays of light.

With a quick prayer that these light beams were different, I walked up the steps and went inside. The ceiling was as tall as outside, and it reminded me of a spilled box of crayons. Everything was empty and quiet, except for a giant pair of eyes that stared back at me from the face of a frozen woman. I almost screamed, until I realized she was just a statue in the middle of the room.

"This room must be for you." I waved my arms around the space and whispered, but she didn't blink or nod her head or anything.

Her robes reminded me of the cypress trees in the swamp, and her crown was thick and spiky. For some reason, she had another face stuck in the center of her chest, its mouth open in a round O, like it was trying to say *O, how did I wind up here?* An angel fluttered in one of her hands. Everything about her was white. I tiptoed around the outside of the gate that kept people from getting too close, and her eyes followed me, even when I was behind her.

My legs shook a little. The air was empty of everything, and the world stopped while she looked at me. "Are you God?"

My whisper firecrackered through the empty space. When she didn't answer, I crept closer, until I had to tilt my head so far back that it hurt my neck just to see her face. "If you are God, can you please show me where Daddy is? And make him and Merry be friends? Let them both always be in my life, forever?"

I closed my eyes and bowed my head to seal my wish. When I turned to go back outside, a shadow blocked the doorway.

I only had time to scream.

EMMALINE

"Daddy!"

"Emmaline!"

He ran up to me and picked me up in his strong arms, and we spun around and around in front of the statue. I cried, and he cried with me, tears that feathered out into the fine lines around his blue eyes. I touched them, because they were new. "Oh, Daddy, I knew you'd come. I knew it."

Daddy held my chin in his shaking hand. "Nothing, and I mean nothing, would've kept me from being here."

"Did you get my message?"

"It really did come from you." His fingers brushed against my cheek. "My friends told me I was an idiot. Wishful thinking. Too much of a coincidence. Well, we showed them, didn't we?" He reached into the pocket of his black jeans and pulled out my crumpled two dollars. I spread it flat and read my message again. It wasn't faded or anything. It was like I just wrote it.

I hugged him again and squeezed him as hard as I could. "You have to tell me how you got it, Daddy. Don't leave anything out."

With a teary smile, he pushed a strand of hair out of my face. I watched his mouth move while he told the story, and I couldn't stop kissing his face. He had a break between sets at a country bar, and he always allowed himself one drink. When he took his change, my two dollars was right on top of the stack, message side up. He touched the purple ink and called off the rest of his set, because he knew it was from me.

People laughed at him when he told them the two dollars was a message from his little girl. A couple even called him crazy, because there had to be a lot of girls named Emmaline in the world.

But he was convinced. When he showed one of my letters to his friend Big Rosie and they compared the handwriting, she agreed with him.

"But if Big Rosie hadn't seen the likeness, I still would've come, you know. I knew. I just knew."

Daddy waited for me all day. He showed people my picture and asked them if they'd seen a little girl that looked like me. When he got hungry, Big Rosie brought him lunch, fried chicken. He ate sitting on one of the benches outside. He even missed an audition, forgot to let the man know he wasn't coming.

"I'll probably be ruined in this town because of it, but I don't care. When I heard your mother had died, I packed up to go back to New Orleans to look for you. I mean, I didn't know where you were or anything. Nadine made sure of that, but still, I didn't want her to end up the way she did. Anyway. That gig last night was my final one before I was set to leave town. But now you're here, and with Nadine gone, nobody can take you away from me."

"Except me."

When Daddy spun us around, the Judge filled the doorway, a bent cigar burning between his bloody lips and the pistol that killed Miss Leslie in his scratched hand. The door scraped along the floor and closed with a boom behind him. He raised an arm, slow like it hurt, and pointed the gun at us.

"Put her down now, and back away."

Daddy's arms tightened around me. "Emmaline is mine."

The Judge's eyes were glassy with tears, and the gun shook in his hand.

"I don't understand, little beauty. After all these years, these decades, I've spent looking. Longing. Everything I've done to be with my Ann. Don't you feel anything for me, deep down inside?"

My stomach flip-flopped. Nothing could ever make me leave Daddy's side. I opened my mouth to tell the Judge, but the door screeched open and Merry screamed into the room and tackled the Judge. They rolled around on the floor, and Merry yelled, "That person is gone, Wilkinson. Dead. Your wife is dead."

Merry swept the Judge's body along the floor, his arms locked under the Judge's armpits. The Judge's face was red, but he grunted really loud when he kicked at Merry's legs. Merry's hands went wide, and he toppled to the floor. When he rolled over on his side, the Judge's hand shook with the weight of the gun. It clicked, and Daddy's arms tensed around me. Merry scissored his legs in the air, and the gun flew out of the Judge's hands at the moment he fired.

Daddy groaned. When he fell to his knees, he took me with him. Along his side, a big red stain spread on his shirt. His blue eyes glistened and turned white. His head thunked on the stone floor.

"Merry! Daddy's hurt!" My throat hurt from shouting, but when I looked over at Merry, the Judge sat on top of him. His hands squeezed Merry's neck hard enough to snap it. Merry's face was almost as blue as his eyes.

Merry kicked his legs, and the Judge's spine crunched when he fell backwards. Merry rolled along the floor toward Daddy and me. He coughed air back into his lungs, and one of his hands was electric when it brushed my arm. The Judge lumbered to his feet and looked at me, almost like he could see all the way inside me, to the very middle of my soul. I couldn't look away. Instead, I held my breath and waited. The Judge's chin wagged when he opened his mouth, but he made no sound when he turned and limped to the door. He looked back at me one last time and was swallowed by night.

Merry moaned when he sat up and ripped the side of Daddy's shirt away. His eyes frowned at the blood, and he pressed on Daddy's skin. "It's just a flesh wound. Grazed him but didn't enter the body."

"Please, *please* tell me Daddy will be okay." Words sobbed out of me, and Merry ran his fingers though my hair.

"Don't you worry. I don't even think he'll need stitches."

His face twisted up when he pushed himself to stand. He staggered behind the statue and came back holding the Judge's gun. "Wait right here. I'm going to finish this thing with Wilkinson, once and for all."

I cradled Daddy's head in my lap while Merry stalked through the door and into the moonless night.

MERRY

Tentacles of menace slithered through the air outside the Parthenon. They crawled along my body. Sucked at my skin. I stood on the grass, not understanding why I was still there. It didn't make sense. Once Em found her father, I should be gone.

Wasn't that my assignment?

A flash of movement drew my eye. Hulking. Unfinished. Its shadow crept along the side of the building, taking its time. When I squinted, I understood.

Wilkinson was wounded.

I limped around low bushes and tripped through piles of fallen leaves. I dragged myself up the grass and stumbled into the space under the portico. Stopped steps in front of Wilkinson. He was doubled over, holding his bulge of stomach with one arm.

His breath was shallow, and he leaned against the wall. A sheen of sweat coated his face. "Tell me something, Lewis."

"What?"

"Did you ever think this was all that awaited you on the other side of life? This......place that isn't a place, because you're Nowhere without the person you love?"

My eyes burned with tears. Of realization. Of relief. "We're not stuck here to make sure people remember our life accomplishments, to secure our fame. We already had our chance. Immortality comes when we pour our skills, our talents—ourselves—into someone else, and let them go."

Even when we loved them enough to endure an eternity of Nowhere to keep them with us forever.

His form sagged on the concrete. "Just tell me you see my wife in that little girl. You knew her. Let me hear you say it, Lewis. Just once."

When I looked at Em, I saw a strong female spirit swirling around inside, but that was all Em. A ballsy little girl who ran into the unknown to save herself. An expedition of will that ended up saving me. I stepped closer. "Just because Em reminds you of your Ann, that doesn't mean she is. You can't make her replace your wife."

Wilkinson's words sputtered out. "I...just...want to...love...her."

His tears sprayed my face when he plowed his elbow into my chest. I dived into him, a lunging tackle. Bone crunched against bone as we rolled along the floor and clotheslined around a column. The impact jarred the gun to life in my hands and vaulted Wilkinson away from me.

He hovered above the floor, holding his stomach. His mouth moved, but no sound could breach the divide between us. His body shimmered. Insubstantial. Those eyes were the last thing to disappear. They lasered into me even after the rest of him was gone. Back to some Nowhere bar in some Nowhere place to start over.

Would he be able to find Emmaline again? Would he even remember her?

In the quiet, my thoughts raced back to my mission. To the little girl I loved like a daughter. I wandered into the grass and shouted her name.

And, as though I conjured her, I saw her there. Across the lawn. Through the trees. Lit by a streetlight, clinging to her daddy's hand.

MERRY

The cool draft of autumn streaked across my face. Mussed my hair as I watched them together from the wet grass. Lee sat up, and Emmaline flung herself into his arms. I finally had time to study him. Sandy blond hair with a curl to it. No doubt her hair came from him. A sturdy man, not unlike myself. Worn at the fringes. Battered by life, but not beaten.

I held my breath and waited for her to turn. To see me standing across the expanse. To call out for me to join them.

It didn't matter what was next. My world was a little girl named Emmaline. She lit up my existence like some kind of angel. The days I spent with her were the happiest ones I could remember. Since I stared at the ribbon of a mighty river all those years ago on the mission that would make me. If I could stay with Emmaline...the daughter I was meant to have. She would be enough for me.

I watched Emmaline's rapid-fire gestures. Taken by the sheen of Lee's tears and by the hunger with which he drank his little girl in.

Still I waited. For her to say it.

One word.

Because she made me into a man who was merry. An explorer who sacrificed his ambitions on the altar of who she might become. I closed my eyes and waited. I willed her to say it. Just once. A single word to flutter along the current of the wind. To my ears. Before it was too late.

I opened my eyes, and the whole world swirled while I was grounded, watching everything drain away. The Parthenon spun in front of me. Uprooted trees pulled from the fringes, sucked into a void.

When I tried to call her name, I had no voice. Nothing that reverberated back to me through the rippling landscape. I felt the tearing away of time in the numbing of my body.

Was this the end of Nowhere? I reached my arms toward the draining earth, and my hands clawed toward the concrete roof of the Parthenon and tried to hook an arm around the gnarled branch of a tree. I grasped at anything that could anchor me where I longed to be.

Far below, Emmaline's tiny form ran into the grass, followed by her father. Her head twisted and turned as she searched the park. Looking for me. Her mouth moved. She was calling my name. I strained to hear it though the thick and swirling silence. I willed my voice to slice through the space that separated us, but she receded, grew smaller and smaller even as I drained into an eternity without her.

I love you, Emmaline.

* * *

EMMALINE

When we heard the gunshot, Daddy followed me outside. He held my hand to keep me close as we tiptoed around the building. The sky was the darkest I'd ever seen, and stars glittered everywhere. "Merry!" Are you hurt? Please, *please* answer me!"

Daddy's arm slid around my shoulders. "Don't shout. We don't know where the Judge is. It may be that he shot Merry."

"No. NO. If Merry was dead, I would know it. I would *feel* it, right here in my heart. I know he wouldn't go without saying goodbye."

Daddy held me in his arms on his unhurt side, like he always did when

I was a little girl. He played with my hair and listened to me. I told him all about how Merry found me and never left me. Not once. Daddy nodded and hung on everything I said. That was the thing I loved most about Daddy. Whenever I needed him to hear something, he always did. Always.

I loved Merry so much because he reminded me of Daddy. When I talked, he always paid attention. He even ruffled my hair, just like Daddy did. And he took care of me, better than anybody, just like Daddy had when he lived with me. Now that I loved Merry, I couldn't live without him. I would fight to find him, just like I did with Daddy, because Merry always had to be in my life.

Daddy's fingers brushed my cheek. "What's the last thing Merry said to you? Before I found you?"

"He kept telling me he had to go, that he might not see me anymore, but I wouldn't listen. He even stopped me on the grass right over there— see —right before you found me."

Daddy pushed the hair out of my eyes, where they stuck to my tears. "Stay close to me, and let's keep looking, all right? If he's hurt, we need to help him. Get him to a hospital. Anything for the man who gave my little girl to me."

My eyes roamed across wet grass. I stumbled over a root, but when I looked down, it was Merry's journal. All dirty on the outside. I picked it up and rifled through the worn pages. For all the time he spent writing, it was mostly empty. A few letters here. Some lines there.

Except for the last page. One complete sentence, written in Merry's hand.

I love you, Emmaline.

I tried to swallow the knot in my throat. "I love Merry, Daddy. He's my hero. He fought and struggled and wouldn't let anything stop him. And he promised me— he promised—he'd never, ever leave me. He told me he'd *always* be with me."

Daddy wobbled a little on his feet. When he pulled my chin up to face him, his eyes were far away, and his lips were creased in a strange smile. His look was different but familiar, somehow.

"Daddy?"

I waved my hands in front of his eyes, trying to get him to look at me. A cool blow rippled across my face as he stroked my chin in his calloused hand. When he mussed my hair and spoke again, I knew where Merry was. Where he would be forever. Just like he promised.

"I'll always be with you, Em. Always."

ACKNOWLEDGEMENTS

Immortality is both a physical impossibility and a psychological imperative. In this world, the closest we come to living forever is being remembered.

I owe much to the people who, knowingly or not, helped make this book possible. Thanks and recognition go to each of you for the contribution you made to this story.

Historians work to understand and interpret the past, and I've always been fascinated by both their tenacity and their passion. Thanks to John D W Guice, Jay H Buckley, and James J Holmberg for their book *By His Own Hand? The Mysterious Death of Meriwether Lewis*; Gary E Moulton, editor of *The Journals of the Lewis and Clark Expedition*; the late Andro Linklater, author of *An Artist in Treason: The Extraordinary Double Life of General James Wilkinson*; and the late Stephen Ambrose, author of the acclaimed *Undaunted Courage: Meriwether Lewis, Thomas Jefferson and the Opening of the American West*.

Amber Deutsch, your observations on the earliest version of this book helped make it both readable and magical.

Helen Rice, you brought Meriwether Lewis back to life with your inspired drawings. You drew exactly what I imagined.

Robert Brewer at Writers Digest, you introduced me to the bad rabbit in *Watership Down* and changed the course of this story.

Signe Pike, your thoughtful edits made this book stronger.

Cheryl Smithem, you made key connections at the right moments.

Rowe Copeland, you had the stomach to take on an unknown writer with a genre-bending book. I'm proud to call you my publicist.

Alice Guess and family, and Lance Hiatt and Tim Parks, you gave me free places to write. That they had mountain views was a bonus.

Jessie Powell and Scott Merriman, you connected several dangling ends and tightened the manuscript.

Blog Subscribers, thank you for believing in me, for cheering me onward, for making me laugh, and for always telling me I could write books. You are among the best people on earth.

Roy and Linda Watkins, you are amazing parents. Thank you for supporting me and for putting up with my versions of you. Joyce Maher, thank you for having your son, and for believing in me as your daughter.

Michael T Maher, you are my love. My muse. My inspiration. You said hello and changed my life.

Readers, thank you for making time to read and for choosing to read my novel. You give words life when you breathe them into your imaginations and plant them in your souls.

You are the reason I write.

ABOUT THE AUTHOR

Andra Watkins lives in Charleston, South Carolina with her husband, Michael T Maher. She is the first living person to walk the 444-mile Natchez Trace as the pioneers did prior to the rise of steam power in the 1820's. From March 1, 2014 to April 3, 2014, she walked fifteen miles a day. Six days a week. One rest day per week. She spent each night in the modern-day equivalent of stands, places much like Grinder's Stand, where Meriwether Lewis died from two gunshot wounds on October 11, 1809. In addition to celebrating the release of *To Live Forever: An Afterlife Journey of Meriwether Lewis,* the walk also inspired her upcoming memoir on the adventure, *Not Without My Father,* to be published Fall 2014. andrawatkins.com

THE THREE R'S OF 21ST CENTURY READING

• **Read** the book - Authors love to sell books, but they really want buyers to read them. If you've come this far, thank you again for reading. Your investment of time matters to me.

• **Review** the book - Amazon and Goodreads don't tabulate book rankings based on sales alone. Reviews weigh heavily into the algorithms for book rankings. Your review matters. More reviews mean higher rankings, more impressions and ultimately, more readers. Please take five minutes and write a review of this book. If you write the review on Goodreads first, you can copy and paste it into Amazon.

• **Recommend** the book - The people in your life value your opinion. If you enjoyed this book, recommend it to five people. Over lunch or coffee. At the water cooler. On the sidelines. Let people see and hear your enthusiasm for this story. Some of them will thank you for showing them the way to a good book.